DISCOVERING GRACE

DISCOVERING GRACE

An Inglewood Romance

SALLY BRITTON

For My Friends.

To my husband, forever and always.

CHAPTER 1

MAY OF 1814

Somewhere in the house a door slammed. Grace winced but otherwise did not react to the evidence of her twin sister's displeasure. She kept her hands busy embroidering a blue silk shawl.

Soon enough, Hope would come barreling into the morning room to interrupt Grace's peaceful occupation. The Everly twins, known throughout the neighborhood for their opposing temperaments despite their identical appearance, had developed something of a pattern when it came to Hope's rather outrageous conduct.

Hope would come up with a scheme, tell Grace all about it, then enact her plan. Sometimes it would be something as simple as arranging a picnic or musical recital for their friends, at other times it would involve somewhat more scandalous behavior. Most recently, Hope had taken to racing her phaeton against others with similar carriages pulled by ponies, often with Grace clinging to her bonnet with one hand and her seat with the other. Inevitably, when Hope did something that the local matrons frowned upon, news of it soon came to their parents.

"I did warn her this time," she whispered into the quiet of the room, breaking the silence before her sister could.

The rumors of the races had evidently reached Papa, given the raised voices heard moments ago. The door slamming meant the conversation had ended, not in Hope's favor, and she would appear at any moment to bemoan whatever punishment she had been given, while Grace listened.

Grace found her scissors and snipped the pink thread, completing the rosebud. She put her needles back in their box and tucked everything into her sewing basket. Then she folded her hands in her lap and waited.

She did not have to wait long.

The door to the morning room slammed open as though propelled by an explosion. Hope stormed in directly and banged the door shut again, her blue eyes flashing. "I cannot understand why Papa must be so sensitive to Mrs. Keyes's opinions. I know perfectly well that other young ladies race their ponies. It is not as though I am stampeding about on a great big hunter."

As usual, it fell to Grace to placate her twin. "Yes, but it is a matter of propriety. Simply because other young ladies do such things does not mean Papa wants his daughters to do the same."

Upon first meeting the sisters, people often expected them to be as similar in personality as appearance. They both had the same black hair, even if Grace preferred more mature styles over the enormous curls her sister favored, and the same deep blue eyes. Yet Hope's eyes were more likely to flash with passion while Grace's remained as tranquil as forest pools. Even their figures had remained mostly the same as they matured.

If one looked carefully, one might note the slightest difference in height. Hope was a quarter of an inch taller, and three quarters of an hour older. Both facts she had used in the past to get her way when they entered into one of their rare disputes.

Hope snorted in a most unladylike manner. "It is astoundingly boring to limit myself to what Papa and Mama think are appropriate activities. It is all very well and good for you to sit here and practice domesticity, but I wish for something more stimulating. We are twenty-four years old this summer and nothing of interest has ever happened to us."

Domestic. That was an apt word for Grace, and one she would happily wear with pride. Not that it did her any good when it came to finding a gentleman who might appreciate such a quality. Hope's firm rejection of marrying "too early" had come to include Grace through association alone, and Grace worried they had waited until "too late." Given that her thoughts naturally turned to one man when she considered the subject of matrimony, and that man showed no romantic interest in her, Grace put it from her mind.

There was no use examining such thoughts at the moment. Not with Hope's state of agitation.

"What is it that would suit your desire for excitement?" Grace knew the answers, of course. "There are no highwaymen to stop your carriage, no pirates to come ashore and rob you, and no hidden treasure for you to stumble upon in the woods. You must learn, dearest sister, that most people have ordinary lives."

"I hardly wish for anything so drastic." Though Hope spoke with a wrinkled nose, her tone was more weary than scornful. "But why can we not go to London for the rest of the Season? Or Bath to take in the waters. Or to the Continent now that the war has ended."

Mama did not like to travel, and Papa had no desire to go anywhere without her. They had spent most of their lives in their village of Aldersy. As Mama and Papa were considered to be pillars of the community, and their friendships included such people as the Earl of Inglewood, the Barnes Family, Sir Isaac Fox, and every member of the gentry within fifteen miles, they were quite content that neither themselves nor their children go wandering.

Grace did not bother pointing all of this out to Hope, as her sister knew it all well enough. But she did offer a commiserating grimace. "You need not go too far afield for adventure. You have proven that time and again."

"And suffered rather severely for it," Hope muttered. She went to the window and stood there, chin jutting out and brows drawn down into a scowl. "I cannot understand why you are like them rather than like me. Why do you not want to experience something more grand? Or *different*."

Oddly, that was not a question Hope had ever tossed at her

before. They had always accepted their disparity in personality, without complaint or judgment. Perhaps in part because they tired of everyone else around them asking inane questions about their twinship.

Grace considered her answer before giving it.

"I do not think I am necessarily like them. I am only myself. I enjoy our village, though I know it to be small. I find no lack of entertainment in our life here in the country. I have never thought to want more than what I am presently grateful for."

Except for one thing. There was one single thing that Grace had wanted, and even wished for, but it was not something she could discuss with Hope.

"You are as good as your name." Hope flicked the gauzy white curtain away from the window, peering down the lane. "Someone is coming to visit. I cannot tell who…"

Grateful for the change in subject, Grace rose to peer out the window as well. Hope stepped aside, pulling the curtain open wider.

When they stood next to each other, as they did to study the approaching gig, people had an easier time telling them apart. Grace wore subdued blues and greens, sometimes lavenders. Hope put on brighter colors, in yellows, peach-like pinks, and occasionally a daring shade of red. When they were younger, their mother had dressed them alike until they were old enough to settle on their preferences. Even in their sense of fashion, they diverged most naturally.

"I think it is the Carlburys." Grace pointed at the distinctive dappled gray horse. "See, that is their horse."

"Oh, lovely! And two women in the gig. Mrs. Carlbury must have Irene with her." Hope bounced up and down, her earlier scowl no longer in evidence. "Come, let us go down and meet them."

Miss Irene Carlbury and her family had settled in the neighborhood half a dozen years before and had almost immediately found favor in the Everly household. Though three years younger than the Everly twins, they formed a fast friendship with the newcomer. Irene's family had lived in the Caribbean, on an island called St. Kitt's by those who knew it best, and that exotic previous residence immediately endeared Irene to Hope. Miss Carlbury had come to

England with the hopes of becoming refined and genteel, which endeared Grace to her just as quickly.

Several times a week, the three could be found together with their heads bent over ladies' magazines or else walking along the beach, speaking of the doings in the neighborhood.

Grace followed her sister down the steps and to the small hall near the main set of doors. While Grace enjoyed the quiet of the house, having her younger siblings away at school did leave things a little too peaceful at times. They were not too far, but at enough of a distance that they boarded and came home to visit once a month.

Garrett, their butler, was opening the door when Hope and Grace stepped off the stairway.

"Mrs. Carlbury, Irene, how good to see you both." Hope offered her curtsy and Grace followed with her own. "I am very glad you have come to call."

"Ah, but I think you shall be even gladder when you have learned the reason." Irene appeared barely able to keep her grin from bursting onto her cherubic face. She was built taller than the Everlys and had a bright exuberance for life that Grace admired. Where Hope was wild and passionate, Irene was much more measured in the ways she found entertainment.

"Hush now, my dear. We must share our news with Mr. and Mrs. Everly as well." Mrs. Carlbury had caught her daughter's infectious grin but worked harder to keep it at bay. "Where might we find your parents this afternoon?"

"Father is in his study," Grace answered, eyeing their guests with good-humored suspicion. "Mother might be in her garden, given the mild weather." The Carlbury ladies exchanged a meaningful glance.

"I will fetch Mama." Hope turned to go without a thought for properly seeing to the guests first.

"And I will show you both to Papa," Grace added, making up for her sister's forgetfulness. She did not mind. It had become something of a habit over the years for her to smooth over the ripples caused by her sister's propensity to hurry about.

She went before her guests, who were still exchanging their secretive smiles, and led them to her father's study. She knocked politely on his door and waited for permission to enter before stepping inside. "Papa, Mrs. Carlbury is here, and she would like to have a word with you and Mother."

Papa sat behind his desk, his spectacles perched precariously on the bridge of his nose. He held a book in one hand and a sheet of paper in the other. He laid both items down and stood.

"Please, show them in." His study doubled as the family library. Their collection was not large, but it consisted of volumes dear to the whole family. Because the room was used for reading as well as business, there was more than enough furniture to hold everyone.

Papa stepped forward to bow to their guests, then kindly led Mrs. Carlbury to the most comfortable of the chairs. He was always thoughtful; even in the smallest details, Grace saw evidence of his kindness. Once their guests were seated, Papa removed his spectacles and tucked them into his coat pocket. Grace made note of it, as her father often lost his reading glasses, even upon his very person.

"Hope has gone for your mother?" he asked, his graying eyebrows raised. Grace knew her father well enough that she saw the question he would ask if the two of them had been alone. *Is your sister still upset?*

Grace shook her head slightly to answer the silent inquiry, while aloud she said, "Yes, they will be with us momentarily. Shall I send for refreshment?"

"No need." Mama's rich alto filled the room, her beautiful voice bringing a smile to Papa's gentle face. He loved her voice. Loved when she sang. Grace had not inherited that ability from her parents. They were both quite musical. Hope, on the other hand, could sing the birds from the trees if she wished too. But she was contrary enough to dislike singing. Likely because she had been forced into any number of duets with Grace when they were younger.

Hope never liked being made to do anything.

"Oh, I am glad to see you, Mrs. Carlbury. It has been too long since we last visited. Has your husband's business in London concluded at last?" Mama asked, coming into the room to sit near her friend.

"Nearly. Mr. Carlbury is still in Town." Though near the same age as their mother, Mrs. Carlbury always seemed several years younger, given her excitable nature. She continued to stare at them all quite as if she had a secret ready to erupt from her at any moment. "He is finalizing our removal to Saint Christopher's Island."

Grace reached for her sister's hand, as they sat in chairs next to one another, her stomach tightening with disappointment. Most likely, Hope's disappointment at such an announcement would be the same.

"Oh my," their mother breathed.

Their father leaned forward in his chair, scrutinizing the women before him. "I did not think you wished to return to the West Indies. I thought your family had finished with the place."

"We do not go back to take up permanent residence," Mrs. Carlbury said. She continued beaming, as though she had announced plans for a party rather than a removal. "We escort one of Mr. Carlbury's friends, a member of Parliament, to look into the conditions of the plantations and the workers. He is a man with an eye for reform. An associate of Mr. Wilberforce, if you can believe it. Our trip is somewhat diplomatic in nature."

"How long will you be away?" Hope asked, her voice quavering. "We shall miss you so much."

"Perhaps a little under a year." Irene moved closer to the end of her chair. "But I hope you shall not all have cause to miss us, as I have asked Mama for permission to bring a friend for companionship."

Grace's discomfort increased. Irene meant to take one of the two sisters to visit the Caribbean with her. With her throat constricting, Grace did not see how that would be of benefit to anyone. No matter which sister was chosen, the other would be left behind, disappointed and alone.

Rarely did Hope and Grace part with one another for more than a few days. If Hope went away, Grace would not be nearby to smooth her sister's path. If the invitation was extended to Grace, she would have to decline. Her, set sail for such a faraway place? Never. The prospect made her heart shudder and her lungs close up.

"If your family is amenable to the idea," Mrs. Carlbury said in a hasty manner. "We have secured three berths. One for myself and Mr. Carlbury, another for our eldest son, and one for Irene. Albert will find amusement enough for himself, but we should like Irene to have a companion for the voyage as well as our time touring the islands. Our youngest, Richard, is busy with his studies and will not accompany us."

"Dear me. This is quite the adventure for your family." Mama tucked her hands in her lap and looked to Papa, tiny wrinkles at her brow giving away her concern. "And such a long way to travel, so soon after the war's end. Do you not fear privateers?"

"Not in the least." Mrs. Carlbury waved her hand before her as though she could brush the idea of sailing thieves away as one might a gnat. "Our navy has cleared the seas and, as you said, the war is over."

Hope moved to the edge of her chair and leaned forward, as though she could not get close enough to the conversation. "Which of us do you wish to accompany you on your journey?"

Grace's eyes darted to her sister's, and she barely stifled a gasp at the naked longing in her sister's eyes. Did Hope not understand what it would mean to go on such a journey? To be away for nearly a year, whatever the adventure might be, with the uncertainty of traveling over an entire ocean in a small boat—No. Even Hope could not be so reckless a spirit as that.

"I thought it best to let your family talk it over amongst your-selves," Mrs. Carlbury said, turning to look from Mama to Papa. "You know your daughters best, and surely Irene ought not be pressed to decide between her two closest friends."

"It would truly prove too difficult a task," Irene insisted, lowering her eyes momentarily. "You have both been so kind to me since we came to the neighborhood. I love you equally, as I must, and I would be grateful to have either of you on this adventure. I wish I could bring you both."

Her mother patted her daughter's hand in a soothing manner. "We did discuss the possibility of such, but the expense and strain of travel is not to be taken on lightly. I could not possibly deprive you of both your daughters, either."

"A wise thought." Papa met Grace's eyes and she saw his lips turn downward, then he looked to Hope, and the frown deepened. He saw the light of adventure in her sister's eyes too, it would seem. Given he had recently lectured Hope on improper conduct, the prospect of letting her out of his sight could not be a happy one. "We shall discuss it as a family. When do you need a decision?"

"The sooner, the better. We leave in a fortnight, after packing and securing the house. Then we shall go to London to buy up what we need for the journey. As I have made the voyage there and back before, you can be certain I know exactly what is needed." Mrs. Carlbury stood. "You must remember that I am happy to answer any questions you may have about the voyage. I assure you, whichever of the Miss Everlys makes the journey, I will look after her as if she is my very own."

Papa and Mama had risen, as had Hope and Grace. With the alarming nature of the visit shared, their guests had nothing further to discuss. Sinking her hands into her skirts at her side, Grace clutched at the cloth as though it were an anchor keeping her firmly at home and away from the sea.

Why did either of them need to go? Perhaps once she reasoned with Papa, Mama, and Hope, they could reject the idea altogether. As much as she enjoyed Irene's company, Grace had no desire to part with home and family for a foreign land.

"Thank you, Mrs. Carlbury. I do not doubt you on that account one whit." Mama, ever the gracious lady, did not betray what she felt to their neighbor. In fact, she sounded grateful for the extension of the invitation.

Grace followed as they all walked to the front door again, no longer paying attention to Mrs. Carlbury's words as she discussed plans for closing up her house. Instead she watched her sister, sensing the building happiness in her sister through the air between them. Her heart ached at the idea of parting from Hope for so long.

Neither of them would go. Surely Papa and Mama would make certain of that.

After their guests drove away, Papa closed the door. He turned toward Grace, Hope, and Mama, his intelligent eyes taking them in. Grace bit her bottom lip, waiting for him to pronounce the very idea of one of them going a ridiculous scheme. Instead, he sighed and offered them a chagrined expression.

"Do we even need to discuss who will go?"

Hope stood on her toes, her hands raising to cover her heart. "Oh, Papa, really? You will allow it?"

Mama stepped to his side, sliding her arm through his in an easy manner born from many years of practice. Grace's heart sunk when she saw no evidence of hesitation upon her mother's face. "We know our girls," she said. "Hope has always wanted an adventure."

Grace's stomach dropped all the way to her toes, and she took a step back from her family. "No, Mama. You cannot mean it—"

Hope's squeal of delight drowned out Grace's whispered plea. She covered her mouth, as shocked at her outburst as she was by Hope's clear delight in the decision. Had her sister not thought of what it would mean?

"Thank you," Hope sang out, her voice echoing through the hallway. Grace winced, wondering if the whole county might hear her sister's happiness "At last, something marvelous has finally happened." She leaped forward and embraced first Mama, then Papa, laughing all the while. At last she turned to Grace, her pleasure undimmed when she took up her hands. "Grace, I am so happy. I wish you could come too."

Was that to be her only regret expressed on the matter? Grace ought to point out all the dangers ahead, all the drawbacks of leaving a settled and civilized country for the wildness of an ocean voyage and a visit to untamed islands. Months aboard a ship, even longer in the tropical climate, with foreign people and no family nearby for support. What about privateers? What of hurricanes?

When she hesitated to answer, Hope's excited grin started to fade. All the elder twin had ever wanted, ever dreamed of, was to experience wild and exciting exploits.

The Carlburys had been and come back again from the West

Indies. They were experienced travelers. They had given Hope the very thing her heart most desired.

Grace affected a pleasant expression. "We both know I could not enjoy it half so much as you. Congratulations." Those simple words, which Grace had to force from her tongue, were enough to brighten Hope's mood again.

"Come, let us find our atlas. We must plot the voyage." Hope took up Grace's hand and tugged her along, as she had all through their childhood, determined to make Grace enjoy the very things that made her most uncomfortable.

Whatever would Grace do without her sister?

⁂

AS ALWAYS WHEN he visited the Everly family, Jacob Barnes knocked smartly at the front door and preemptively removed his hat and gloves. The Barnes and Everly families had been on intimate terms since before Jacob's birth, and the few formalities he adhered to when visiting were still bent from time to time.

Their butler, Mr. Garrett, answered with his usual stiff decorum. "Good afternoon, Mr. Barnes." He stepped aside for Jacob to enter, accepted the articles handed to him, and then bowed. "The ladies are upstairs in the west parlor, sir." Garrett's eyebrow twitched to one side and the servant frowned.

"Should I wait to be accepted up?" Jacob asked, adjusting his cuffs.

"Not at all, Mr. Barnes." The butler's eyebrow twitched again. "The ladies will be pleased for the distraction your visit will bring."

"Distraction? What am I walking into, Garrett?" Jacob did not bother hiding his amusement. Something had annoyed the butler and it obviously had to do with one particular miss in the house. Everyone knew that when there was an upset or uproar, Hope most likely sat at the center of it.

"Effusions of joy and a confusion of packing," the butler said, then snapped his mouth shut. His eyes widened as though he could not believe his own audacity to speak of any matter pertaining to the family with an outsider, no matter how well he knew Jacob.

Jacob chuckled and pushed his blond hair back away from his forehead. "Never fear, old fellow. I will not breathe a word of your clever quip to anyone." Garrett had been a butler in the household for ten years and was perhaps only fifteen years Jacob's senior. He had been an upper footman who had dared to take Jacob to task once for encouraging "the young misses' misbehavior."

"Thank you, Mr. Barnes." Garrett gestured to the stairway. "Allow me to show you upstairs." The stiff primness returned, and with it the eyebrow twitch. For something to rattle the butler, there must be an interesting state of affairs in that sitting room.

Jacob did not allow himself to worry, knowing that all would be revealed soon enough. Whatever new trick Hope had got herself up to, or misadventure she had dragged her poor sister into, could not be so terrible as the time she decided to dress the sheep in every bonnet and shawl her family possessed. Or the time Hope had sent anonymous letters to all of their neighbors pretending she had spied upon them and discovered their deepest secrets. That had been a true mischief and she had been sentenced to her room for an entire month when it was discovered.

With that memory still fresh in his mind, Jacob entered the sitting room and delivered his customary bow. "Good afternoon, Mrs. Everly, Hope, and Grace." No one even batted an eye at their using Christian names with one another. How could they? Jacob, Hope, and Grace had shared nursery games almost as soon as the girls knew how to walk. He was only two years their senior, and quite a fixture in their home.

Even as they had all aged, adding new friends to their acquaintances, the three of them had remained close.

He took in the attitudes of the women in the room, sensing some sort of anticipation in the atmosphere. Mrs. Everly rose from her favorite chair, but she held a scrap of paper in her hand rather than her customary sewing. "Dear Jacob, how good it is to see you today."

Hope stood in the middle of the room and offered her curtsy, which was abbreviated in order for her to quickly take up pacing, which must have been her activity of choice before he entered. She moved rapidly, her eyebrows drawn down, but a wide smile turned up her lips. She said nothing to him, though her lips moved silently as though rehearsing something to herself. Jacob followed her progress across the room with his gaze before turning to Grace's customary place.

But her chair was empty.

Where was Grace?

"Good afternoon, Jacob," she said at last, giving away her position at the window, nearly tucked behind a curtain. "How is your family?" That was always Grace's way. She did not stand upon ceremony, but she always looked after the social niceties.

"They are quite well, thank you. Anticipating a visit from my Aunt Barnes, actually. I am come to visit and to ask your family to a card party while my aunt is here."

"How thoughtful of you," Mrs. Everly said, somewhat distractedly. Returned to her chair, she now scrutinized the paper in her hands and barely glanced up at him. "But some of us may have to decline the invitation, depending upon the date. We are all rather distracted at the moment, you see."

"Ah, are you?" Jacob came further into the room, standing nearly directly in Hope's way when she turned and retraced her steps. They must have been out of sorts, given that no one had even asked him to sit down yet.

Hope nearly ran into him but stopped muttering to herself long enough to realize he stood directly in the middle of her path. "Jacob," she said, nearly gasping out his name. "You do not know." She looked from him to her mother, then to where Grace stood.

Jacob, though he would much rather study Hope's curls brushing across her neck, or the way her lips parted when she said his name, decided to glance in Grace's direction as well.

"I do not know what, exactly?" He offered Grace a teasing grin, thinking she would share with him their customary expression whenever Hope ran away with her thoughts.

But Grace's lips remained pressed together in a grimace and she turned away. Odd.

A melodious laugh turned his attention back to Hope and her face beamed. "My incredible news, of course." She reached out and took both of his hands in hers, leaning forward in a conspiratorial manner. Jacob's heart barely had time to adjust its speed from the excitement of her nearness when she made her announcement, causing it to stop. "I am to go to the West Indies."

The room changed from warm and bright to cold and cramped. No, he must not have heard her correctly. Forcing a smile, Jacob managed to utter a one-syllable plea for the misunderstanding to be cleared up. "What?" He did not release her hands, squeezing them gently instead. She was real. The room was real. This was not a dream. Nor a nightmare. And Hope could not go anywhere —

"The West Indies," she said again, shaking his hands in her enthusiasm before she pulled away, executing an excitable spin. "Across the Atlantic Ocean, to the beautiful island of St. Kitt's. An adventure, Jacob. At last!

Jacob stared after her, his hands still hanging pathetically in the air as if to urge her back. He numbly turned to Mrs. Everly, who still studied her paper, then looked to Grace. He needed confirmation, unable to trust Hope's own words.

Grace turned just enough to glance over her shoulder at him, her eyebrows drawn down and her lips a straight line. She nodded once, correctly interpreting his unasked question.

"With the Carlbury family," Grace said, her voice barely loud enough to carry to where he stood. "They are going back for a visit, and Hope is to accompany Miss Carlbury." Though he could tell from the way she stood, stiff with her arms wrapped about herself, that this news was as poorly received by Grace as it was by him, she managed to keep her tone quite neutral.

He supposed he ought to follow her lead. Swallowing past a tight knot in his throat, Jacob tried to focus on Hope's joy. In all the time he had known her, Hope had been as daring as any boy who crossed his path. Her fearlessness, her desire for daring exploits, had landed even him in trouble a time or two. A trip such as this one would be something out of her dreams.

"That is wonderful," he managed to say at last, surprising himself with how cheerful he sounded. "You have always wanted to travel." He forced his mouth to form some semblance of a smile, but the facade was weak at best. Jacob stepped further into the room, determining that no one would remember to ask him to sit. "How do you fare, Mrs. Everly, knowing your eldest daughter is going on such a journey?"

Hope's parents could not be happy to have her out of their sight, could they?

"I would be a good deal happier about it if we could finish the packing list," Mrs. Everly said with a sigh. "Hope, darling, do you think you ought to take an umbrella or purchase one upon arrival? And ought you to bring one for the sun and another for rain? I should hate for you to take up too much space in a trunk with umbrellas. Do you suppose they have umbrellas for purchase in the St. Kitt's markets?"

Umbrellas. All his concern over Hope's safety and her own mother was fretting over mere accessories. When Hope flounced over to take a seat next to her mother to discuss the subject in greater detail, Jacob fled the seating area and went to the window to stand near Grace.

Always the levelheaded member of their little group, Grace would be able to tell him what was going on and why. She had turned back to the window, so he faced the same way, tucking his hands behind his back.

Quietly, he asked, "When does she leave?" Perhaps, if he had a few weeks, he might talk her out of going. Or at least give her a reason to stay.

"They go to Town next week," Grace answered, resignation in her tone. "They are finalizing her purchases in London, and then they will set sail." Shaking her head, Grace released a quiet sigh. "Her trunks are already packed. Mama is just worrying over final details now. The Carlburys will visit this evening and, I am certain, will put her mind at ease regarding the umbrella situation." The tiniest note of humor crept into the last of Grace's words.

He appreciated her efforts on his behalf, for she obviously saw his distress. But had anyone taken notice of hers?

Jacob took a step to the side, so their arms nearly brushed. "Are you going to be all right? You two have never been apart. Hope will be gone for —"

"A year," she supplied the term with reluctance. "Perhaps a little less." Grace released a shallow sigh and tipped her head to the side, regarding him with heavy eyes. "I cannot quite believe it, yet with Hope speaking of nothing else for the past two days, I have little choice in the matter."

Had they been alone, Jacob would have reached for her hand or put his arm around her shoulder. They were old friends, after all, and the ache in her eyes matched what he felt in his heart.

"I am sorry, Grace," he whispered, then turned his eyes back to the window. He did not truly see beyond the glass. "Sorry for us both."

How could Hope leave them like this?

"Jacob," Hope said, pulling his attention around to the woman causing his distress. His heart thumped sorrowfully as he compelled his features into another pleasant expression. "What should I bring on the journey? I wonder if you might think of something we have not. You are always so practical."

Was that how she saw him? Merely as practical? The word sounded so entirely her opposite at the moment. But then, she was right. A third son from a large family, he had learned to be practical and to make the best of things from a young age. Stepping away from the window and Grace, likely the only person as saddened by Hope's good fortune as he, Jacob endeavored to make himself useful by speaking of voyages, packing lists, and the sort of things a lady might expect to do while visiting the islands of the Caribbean Sea.

His visits normally took up a half hour or more of time, but with Hope fluttering about the room in her preoccupied state, he barely managed to remain a quarter of an hour. When he took his leave,

Hope gave him a brief curtsy, her mother a quick nod, and it was Grace who followed him from the room and down the stairs.

When they came to the entry, where his gloves and hat rested on a table near the door, Grace broke into his thoughts with her hesitant words. "This has come as a shock to you. I am sorry, Jacob." She reached her hand toward him, as though to place it on his arm, but then raised it instead to tuck a stray lock of hair behind her ear. Grace had always been less demonstrative than Hope, but just as compassionate.

He took it upon himself to lay his hand upon her shoulder, offering a gentle squeeze of comfort. "It is a shock. But given what we know of Hope, we can only be happy for her. Everyone in the neighborhood will miss her." He cleared his throat and stepped away, averting his eyes. He had no wish for Grace to see how much her sister's announcement affected him.

"Good day, Grace." He bowed and hastily exited, pulling on his gloves as he practically leaped down the stairs. His horse remained waiting for him, and that made it an easy matter to mount and hurry on his way. The future had seemed perfect that morning, ready as he was to take on a living that would at last allow him to also take a wife.

Kindly Mr. Spratt, who was aged two and seventy, was finally stepping away from the living and the parish. The vicarage would be Jacob's in June. Mr. Spratt had been an attentive spiritual leader for decades, never even entrusting his parish to a curate. His wife had passed two years previous, leaving the old man alone with a handful of servants to look after him. Ready to retire at last, the vicar planned to move away to live with a grown daughter.

The bright May morning sun hid itself behind clouds, much like his hopes and plans had hidden away behind the shock of losing Hope. She would not be gone forever, but a year was a long time. Especially when he had plans he had hoped to put in motion more immediately.

The living was the Earl of Inglewood's to give to whom he wished. The church and vicarage stood at the edge of the earl's property, near the village. When Silas, the current earl and a friend from

Jacob's childhood, learned of his friend's decision to take orders he had immediately promised him the position.

Once established, Jacob could obtain a respectable situation in society and afford to marry. Which was why Hope's adventure struck him as horribly ill-timed.

He clenched his hands around the reins and his horse, a spirited creature belonging to his eldest brother, protested with a toss of its head. Forcing his hands to relax and willing the tension from the rest of his body, Jacob attempted to find the equanimity he depended upon.

By the time he arrived home, two miles from the Everlys' estate, he had managed to stuff most of his emotions back into his heart where they belonged. He had waited this long to tell Hope of his admiration for her; he could wait a little longer.

Perhaps when she returned, her thirst for adventure would be sated at last. Not that he wished for that part of her character to change, but he would have a better chance of securing more than friendly affection if her eyes were not always directed toward the horizon and away from Aldersy.

Jacob left his horse in the stables with the grooms, too agitated to take the time to soothe the animal himself. Notwithstanding his outward calm, his mind had not stopped racing.

Hope, gone for a year. Too far for letters to even reach her regularly.

Inside the house, an airy 18th century construction his father had inherited from an uncle, Jacob went in search of the one person who might be able to calm him.

He passed his eldest brother on the staircase. "Matthew," he said, "have you seen Mother?"

"In the music room," Matthew answered without stopping in his descent, hat tucked beneath his arm and gloves in his hand. Perhaps he was going to pay a call on the lady he had been courting. Jacob shook his head, wondering how his brother had waited until the age of thirty-two to begin looking in earnest for a bride.

Turning around, Jacob went down the stairs to the music room, ignoring his brother's departure from the house. The music room was at the rear of the house, facing eastward, where there was a fair prospect of a dip in the land, full of long grasses and sheep. A few miles further than the eye could reach stretched the North Sea.

The gentle strains of a melody seeped through the door, his mother's talent with the harp easy to appreciate. For a moment, Jacob stood there, allowing the rich notes to wrap around him in a familiar and comforting embrace. His mother played a bright tune, reminding him of flowers and fairies more than the storm clouds gathering outside.

When the song drew to a close, Jacob pushed the door open and entered. "Mother, you play like an angel."

His mother, tall for a woman and as elegant as any duchess, cast him an affectionate glance from where she sat beside the window. The room was dim, thanks to the weather, and she had not lit any candles.

"You are a sweet flatterer, Jacob." She stilled the remainder of the vibrating strings, their almost inaudible humming stopped. "Why are you back so soon? Given when you left, I did not expect to see you until dinner."

Even with having six children to keep after, his mother always seemed to know where they were and what they were about. As a child, he had wondered if she possessed some sort of supernatural ability to track them.

"I was met with some unexpected news when I arrived at the Everlys'." He came into the room, his hands tucked behind his back. "And they were too busy to keep company today. Actually, I am surprised we did not hear of their news until now."

Arching an eyebrow at him, his mother folded her hands in her lap. "What news is this? You certainly are not pleased by it."

"Have you heard the Carlburys are to go back to the West Indies?" he asked, stopping a few feet from where she sat. Her deep brown eyes searched his, her blonde eyebrows drawn down. He had inherited his coloring from his mother, as had most of her children.

"I had not. I suppose that would send the Everly girls into something of a fit. They rather dote on Miss Carlbury." His mother seemed puzzled, obviously aware such news would not be the reason he had cut his visit short.

"The Carlburys are taking Hope with them," he said, the words escaping from him in a horrid rush. He looked away before he saw his mother's reaction, anticipating pity though he hoped for something more comforting.

She remained silent for a long moment before she stood, the swish of her skirts against her stool bringing his eyes back to her. Mother reached out a hand to him, laying it on his cheek. "I can see this is a blow to you, dear boy. You have not told Hope a word of what you feel for her?"

He shook his head slowly, not wishing to dislodge his mother's reassuring touch. "I have not dared. I wanted to secure the living first. She hasn't any idea—" He closed his eyes and took in a deep breath. At least he wasn't crying. As upsetting as the news was to him, it had not broken him. More than anything, he was overwhelmed by a sense of disappointment. "I will not say anything now. It would not be fair to her, for many reasons, to burden her with my feelings before she goes away on a grand adventure."

"Usually one does not view affection as a burden," his mother said, giving his cheek a gentle pat. When he opened his eyes and met hers again, she offered him a gentle smile. "But you are right. Telling her now would put you both under an obligation until she returned, to at least think on the possibilities of what could be. Perhaps it is best that she goes, and you take time to accustom yourself to your position as a vicar. Your calling is a demanding one, my dear."

His hopes further deflated, leaving Jacob nothing but weariness and disappointment. "You may be correct."

"I usually am." She reached out to offer him an embrace, which he readily returned. "You are a good man, Jacob. Any woman would do well to have your heart. Take this time to learn more about yourself and your duties. It might be that when Miss Everly returns you will both be ready for a conversation on the matter of marriage and love."

Though it was not what he wanted to hear, Jacob accepted his mother's words. She knew him better than anyone, and she knew

Hope quite well, too. The fact that she did not encourage him to try and speak to Hope right away, perhaps even try to talk her out of leaving with the Carlburys, showed that she had judged the situation as he had. Hope Everly would never give up the chance at a true adventure, no matter who asked or what they offered.

When his mother released him, she kept her arm around his waist, and he put his around her shoulders. "When will Hope leave?"

"Next week," he answered, his mother walking in the direction of the door.

"So soon." She shook her head, a blonde curl dislodging itself from the lace cap she wore. Though fifty years old, his mother appeared as elegant now as she did in the wedding portrait hanging in his father's library. "I am certain she will have a marvelous time. What I wonder," she added, her voice lowering, "is how Grace will do with the departure. Those two have ever and always been at each other's side. Grace will have to stand on her own."

"I worry for her." It was a relief to say so. The vision of Hope and Mrs. Everly consumed with Hope's journey, practically ignoring Grace's obvious upset, disturbed him. "They have always been different, and expressed themselves differently, but there was a balance with the two of them together."

His mother's lips pressed together, and her eyes narrowed. "You mean that Grace kept Hope in check, while Hope dragged Grace into all manner of trouble."

Although Jacob had not thought exactly that, he nodded. "Sometimes, yes. They are the best of friends."

"You know," she added as they went down the hall, "Some say the reason neither of them has married is because they will not be parted."

Jacob barked a laugh at that. "I think no man has been brave enough to attempt dividing them."

Releasing her hold on him, Jacob's mother went to the library door and paused. For a moment, she regarded him in a most puzzling manner, as though she debated with herself what her next words would be. "Now circumstances will prove they survive well enough apart. I wonder if any gentleman in the county will take notice of

Grace?" Then she shrugged the matter away and opened the library door. "Come, I wish to show you a new ladies journal I have received."

Jacob, somewhat amused by her thoughts on Grace's status as a single young woman, followed with steps less heavy than when he had entered his family's home.

CHAPTER 2

Obliged as Grace was to accompany her sister on visits, she had forborne to maintain a pleasant countenance and manner while Hope took her leave of the neighborhood. Hope and the Carlburys were bound for London in three days, and the Everly sisters had visited nearly every house in the county, or so it felt.

Again, and again, Grace listened to her sister speak effusively about her coming adventure. It seemed Hope had no regrets for anything or anyone left behind. The more she spoke of islands, potential storms at sea, and the unknown situations she might face when confronted with new people and places, the more excited Hope grew. Though it had been difficult to hear at first, Grace could not deny the joyful anticipation in her sister's eyes.

After visiting with the Kimballs, Grace stepped into their low phaeton with a lighter heart. How could Grace deny her sister anything that brought her such happiness? As Hope had said, this was the very adventure she had waited for her whole life. They could not always be together, though Grace may wish it. The time had come to part and lead separate lives.

"The Kimballs are such lovely people," Hope said as she took up the reins. They had two little ponies pulling them today, walking with high steps for their short legs. "I shall certainly have to find a gift to bring for them on my return."

"You shall have a whole trunk of nothing but presents upon your return." Grace chuckled and settled back against her seat. Her sister had a most generous spirit, for all her wildness. "Will you write all your adventures down while you are away so I might read of them later?" she asked, wistfully.

"I wish you could come and take part in everything with me." Hope turned enough to look around the edge of her bonnet, meeting Grace's eyes. That sparkle of life had not dimmed since the day she learned she would be on an adventure, nor had she stopped smiling. "I will write everything down in great detail. I will use the diary Mama gave me on our last birthday. I have left it woefully empty all this time."

Grace laughed. "If you could not keep one at home, where there is so little to distract you, how do you intend to keep a diary when you are facing new exploits every day?"

Adjusting herself to sit more jauntily, Hope answered with a decided air. "I wrote nothing at home because there was nothing but the dullness of everyday life to write down. My days will soon be full of such delight that I shall want nothing more than to record every moment so I can remember it. And share it with you." She nudged Grace with her shoulder.

The pair laughed, and for the first time Grace did not feel so abandoned by her sister. "I am glad it is you and not I who will go," she confessed. "I cannot imagine being away from all I know for so long."

"I would be such a dull creature if you left me behind." Hope shook her head, her eyebrows furrowing. "Forever imagining all that you must be doing while I was left here to my embroidery."

"Your embroidery, and your sewing club for the orphans, and your Sunday school for the little girls in the village," Grace said, easily listing the activities they worked on together.

Hope clicked her tongue against the roof of her mouth and affected a shocked expression. "However will you get along without me? Will you busy yourself with all *my* responsibilities?"

Her sister's cheeky response gave Grace leave to playfully nudge Hope's shoulder. "Oh, come now. You know everyone thinks those were your ideas. They might well fall apart when you have gone. I can plan and organize all the day long, but it is you who makes things happen. You make people excited to be part of your plans."

Hope put a hand to her chest, rather dramatically. "I am the fine actress upon the stage and you are in the orchestra, and behind the curtain, and painting the sets, and making certain I know my lines." She fixed Grace with a serious frown at last. "Perhaps this will be good for you. It is not right that you do so much of the work and I receive the accolades."

While it was true that Grace often planned what she and Hope would do, she did not mind her sister accepting the praise and compliments on behalf of them both. What did it matter which sister people attributed the work to, so long as Hope and Grace knew the truth of the matter?

"I haven't any use for accolades. I only want to see the success. I needn't be credited with it. You know the attention makes me terribly uncomfortable. I am quite grateful you relieve me from that burden." Grace adjusted the ribbons of her bonnet when a breeze tried to lift the hat away, her attention drifting to the lane about to converge with theirs. "Oh, look. It is Lord Neil and Lady Olivia." That ought to change the subject.

Hope groaned and gave the reins a quick shake. "I had rather not greet them, if we can avoid it. They were most rude on our visit yesterday."

"I do not think expressing their opinions of ocean voyages necessarily rude." Grace did not argue with the desire to avoid speaking to them, however. Lady Olivia and her brother were not the most pleasant people, though they exuded a strange sort of charm that apparently made them popular in Town.

"Lady Olivia suggesting that a gentlewoman who wished to protect her virtue would never sail was certainly not polite," Hope muttered, urging their ponies a little faster.

Their neighbors had seen them and hurried their own animals along in order to meet where the lane turned into the larger road. Lady Olivia drove, her phaeton a similar style to the Everlys' and made particularly for the use of women. Lord Neil sat next to his sister, his lopsided smile lazy and his eyelids half closed.

Lady Olivia hailed them, her voice raised and bright. "Good afternoon, Miss Everly. Miss Grace." She had adopted something of a lisp recently, and without explanation.

Hope's expression changed into a grimace and her eyes did not leave the road, so Grace took it upon herself to answer for both of them. "Good afternoon, Lady Olivia and Lord Neil."

The noblewoman was soon alongside them, handling her reins most expertly. "Are you still making your visits? Goodness me, I would have thought it would not take so long to visit the principal members of the neighborhood. There could not be above seven families worth visiting."

Grace sensed her sister growing tense beside her. She hurried to answer before Hope's impatience made her tongue sharp. "Hope has a great many friends and we could not think of her leaving without saying goodbye to all of them."

"Miss Everly is not so discerning as you in her choice of companions," Lord Neil said to his sister, his words slow and tone lazy. "Or perhaps people merely like her better." He met Grace's eye and offered a wink with those words.

His sister's hands flicked the reins and she pursed her lips. "Really, Neil." Her ponies stepped faster with her handling of them.

Hope smirked and flicked her reins as well, keeping pace with them. "Come, Lady Olivia, it is not as though friendships are a competition." Hope and Grace's phaeton pulled slightly ahead of the other. "Some have many acquaintances, others few."

Grace reached out and put her hand on her sister's arm, a quick and light touch, hoping to bring attention to their increasing speed. Though the ponies might never win a race against a horse of regular size, they could certainly go faster than Grace wished.

Lifting her nose in the air, Lady Olivia continued speaking as though she had not heard Hope. "I suppose when one puts herself forward constantly, she is bound to be known far and wide by such a reputation."

It took a great deal of control for Grace to keep her mouth shut over a retort on her twin's behalf. Unfortunately, Hope did not exercise the same restraint.

"Better my reputation than yours, Lady Olivia. Everyone knows you are a snob and make the very dullest conversation."

Lady Olivia's face flamed and she sped her ponies up faster. They were at a trot now, and soon would be at full gallop if someone did not put a stop to the competitive display.

Instead of coming to his sister's defense, Lord Neil started laughing and sat up straighter. "Touché, Miss Everly. What have you to say to that, sister? You are something of a bore."

"I say I have no desire to converse any further with such rude and ridiculous women." Lady Olivia had forgotten to use her affected lisp. Her eyes flashed as she sent a glare in their direction. Her nose wrinkled and her lips curled back in disgust. "In second-rate carriages with fly-infested nags." Then she fairly whipped her ponies, forcing them into a run.

"How dare she?" Hope gasped. She glanced briefly at Grace. "It is a race."

Grace's hands gripped the side of the phaeton, her fingers going numb. "Hope, no! Papa said—" She had to swallow the rest of her words when their ponies lunged forward at Hope's urging. For such short, stout fellows, they moved at an alarming speed.

Lord Neil's laughter floated back to them, and they could hear his sister screeching insults. Whether her unladylike words were directed at her ponies, her brother, or the Everlys, Grace did not know or care. She merely gripped the side and seat as they hit small ruts and dips in the road.

The lack of suitability of both the horses and conveyance, Hope had accustomed herself and them to riding about at a fast speed. She soon caught her rival, a broad grin on her face, and started to overtake Lady Olivia. Grace ground her teeth together and closed her eyes, hating every jolt of the wheels. Nothing good could come from this.

"Olivia," Lord Neil's deep voice shouted, sounding serious. "Stop!"

Grace opened her eyes, confused at why a man who exuded reckless confidence would call a halt to what had amused him but moments before.

A bend in the road ahead. At the speed they went, alongside each other as they were, it would not be a safe turn. "Hope, slow down," she yelled.

Neither woman listened nor yielded. "She will stop first," Hope shouted, leaning forward in her seat. "See if she doesn't!"

A closed carriage appeared before them, coming their direction and moving around the bend that already promised disaster. Grace opened her mouth, to reason with her sister, but it was too late. Instead, she screamed and grabbed at the reins herself.

Hope pulled at them herself, trying to stop her ponies. They tossed their heads and skidded, pulling to one side. Their phaeton went sideways on one wheel for an alarming moment, then crashed back down to all four wheels, a horrible crack sounding before the entire conveyance tilted heavily to the side. Something had broken.

Heart slamming against her ribs as if to escape the calamity, Grace could hardly breathe. She had hold of the reins with one hand and her seat with the other, her fingers gripping each so hard she did not think she would ever be able to unbend them.

A shrill scream brought her attention forward in time to see the other phaeton tilt sideways, and overturn into a ditch, the ponies' screaming covering any sound made by the people inside.

The oncoming carriage pulled to the side, its horses stamping and heaving, the driver struggling to obtain control of them.

Grace darted out of their phaeton where it listed to the side and hurried across the road. Her bonnet flew off as she ran, her shoes hitting the ground with force in her haste.

"Lady Olivia," she shouted, running into the ditch. "Lord Neil!"

"We are here," the man's voice shouted. The phaeton shook. Then she heard him muttering. "Crawl out, Livy."

Hope came stumbling down the ditch and then hurried past, on her way to check on the whimpering ponies. The other carriage driver appeared beside Grace, his face pale and his cheeks puffing with his breath.

"Help me lift here, miss," he directed, pointing to the side of the overturned vehicle before grabbing it himself. Grace took hold where he showed and added her meager strength to his greater effort in lifting the vehicle. They managed to create a few more inches clearance, and Lady Olivia's head appeared, her hair in her face and her bonnet hanging behind her. She crawled out, her gloves digging for purchase in the ground. Her face was covered in dirt and tears.

Lord Neil came out next, sliding out on his back and pushing with his legs. Bile rose in Grace's throat when she saw why he did not crawl as his sister had. One of his arms had been gashed open, the fabric of his coat split to reveal a terrible red slash of blood and flesh down his forearm. He held it against his chest with his other arm, protecting the injury.

The carriage driver cursed, without apology. "We need to get you to a doctor, sir." Then he stood and surveyed the women. "Is anyone else hurt?"

Sitting in the dirt with her arms wrapped around herself, Lady Olivia shook her head. Grace did the same. Hope shouted from the front of the wreckage, "One of the ponies is limping, but otherwise they seem well."

"Lord Neil's arm is injured," Grace shouted, aware her sister had not seen it. She swallowed and went to Lady Olivia, holding her hands out to help her up. Face pale and eyes unfocused, Lady Olivia allowed the assistance.

"Mr. Harvey," a voice shouted from the carriage. "What has happened?"

The carriage driver put his arms beneath Lord Neil and lifted him to his feet. "An accident, my lady. We need to get this young man to the doctor."

Grace put her arm around Lady Olivia's waist and guided her across the road to the carriage, following the coachman. Hope appeared at Lady Olivia's other side, her blue eyes wide with worry.

"Oh, Lady Olivia, I am so sorry," Hope whispered.

The dazed young woman did not answer. Grace shook her head at her sister. "Now is not the time."

The carriage belonged to a baroness making her way through the county to visit a friend. The woman brought the injured man and his sister inside the carriage, but Hope and Grace insisted on remaining with the frightened ponies. After promising to send help, the carriage went on its way.

Grace and Hope barely spoke to one another, the seriousness of what had happened, the tragedy that nearly occurred, weighing down their spirits and words. They removed the ponies, all four, from the phaetons and released them into a meadow near the road. Their phaeton's axel had broken, so they could not go home even had they wished to. Then they sat on a rise on the other side of the ditch, away from the wreckage.

"I am sorry," Hope whispered after they had sat silent for a time. "I do not know what came over me." The last word was accompanied by a choked sob.

Wrapping her arm around her sister, Grace sniffed back her own tears and tried to stop from trembling. "Oh, Hope." A sense of foreboding stole into her chest and she shuddered more violently. "I hope Lord Neil will be all right."

They waited in silence for help to come.

CHAPTER 3

Never, in all of Grace's years of witnessing her father lecture her sister, had she seen him turn the shade of red he was as he paced and shouted. His manner was normally subdued, as he was not given to a quick temper or shows of passion. Hope's actions had apparently broken the dam of his patience at last.

"—And all of this but days before you are given the reward of your life with the Carlburys." He ended with a shout, throwing his hands in the air. "Have you no brains, child? I have warned you about racing, for your reputation and safety. At the first opportunity you disregard everything I cautioned you against. And for what? Pride. Stubborn, inflexible, pride."

Grace dared not draw attention to herself by so much as shifting in her seat. She was in a chair in the library, her mother stood next to the hearth with pale face and pursed lips, and Hope stood next to Mama. Hope's cheeks were bright red, but with shame rather than anger, and her arms were wrapped about her waist.

"I am sorry, Papa. I did not mean—"

"Sorry?" he interrupted her, shaking his head. "You do not know the meaning of the word, given the number of times I have heard it, only for you to go about doing as you please. You have shamed our family with your conduct." He stopped pacing and glared directly at her, his nostrils flaring and his posture rigid. "But that I have born before. What I cannot countenance, what I absolutely abhor the thought of, is that you have caused harm to another person. Lord Neil's injury, should it become infected, could change his life entirely. Would you have him lose his arm as Sir Isaac lost his?"

Grace winced. The reminder of their friend, Isaac Fox, and his lost limb still pained her.

"You endangered yourself, your sister, our neighbors, a stranger on the road, a number of animals—" He broke off and approached Hope, his arms spread in a helpless gesture. "What, precisely, can I do to be certain you understand the seriousness of your actions? How can I trust that you will not act so foolishly again?"

Hope's lips parted as though to make her answer, her words trembling in the air. "I have learned my lesson, Papa. I will never act so thoughtlessly again."

The silence stretched as her father stared at Hope, his hands clenching and unclenching at his side. He looked to Mama who only raised her eyebrows, then he put a hand over his mouth and turned to regard Grace. "Grace. You were there with her. She could not be stopped?"

It would be easy to tell him how she had tried, how Hope had ignored her pleas, but Grace would not bring any more of his ire down upon her sister.

"It all happened so quickly, Papa," she answered, raising her shoulders in a slow shrug.

Papa narrowed his eyes at her. "I have one daughter who shows no restraint and another who shows too much." He went to the window, shaking his head. "This could not happen at a worse time. Your mother must leave to tend to your aunt—"

"Aunt Isabelle is unwell?" Grace asked, sitting upright again. She turned to her mother.

"She is doing poorly at the moment," Mama said quietly, the strain upon her face unrelenting. "I have agreed to go to her. I leave in the morning."

Hope's face paled. "Oh, Mama." She reached out, laying a hand on her mother's arm.

Mama patted Hope's hand with her own. "I am certain all will be well. Isabelle has always been a strong, capable woman."

"I have come to my decision," Papa said, drawing all attention back to himself. "I will not allow Hope to be rewarded for her inability to heed her parents. I cannot seem to impress upon you with my words," he stared fixedly at Hope, "that you must correct your conduct. Therefore, I will act. Hope, you are not going to the West Indies now or ever. Not so long as you remain under my care."

Grace put her hand to her throat to stifle her gasp, watching as Hope's expression crumpled from worry to despair.

"No," she whispered, covering her mouth with both hands. Her next words came out choked, almost indecipherable. "Please, Papa. It is all I have wanted, and Irene expects —"

"Your sister will go in your place," he said abruptly, cutting off her protests. "She will have your prize, the Carlburys will not be inconvenienced, and perhaps Grace will learn what it is to be confident enough to stand up to her own sister." He turned his hard glare in Grace's direction.

A voyage to the Caribbean, into the unknown reaches of islands and ocean? Grace shuddered. "Papa, I do not want —" She snapped her mouth shut, her protest unfinished, when he narrowed his eyes and clenched his jaw.

"You will both abide by my wishes." He pointed to the door. "Hope will write a letter, this very instant, explaining the change in plans. It will go to the Carlburys tonight. Then you girls will help your mother prepare for her trip and that is an end to it."

Hope lowered her head and rushed from the room, a sob breaking from her as she crossed the library's threshold. Grace stayed in her chair, watching her parents. Papa had crossed the room to Mama and wrapped his arms around her, tucking her against him. Mama's eyes were sad and she buried her face in Papa's shoulder.

Grace stood, averting her gaze, and left the room. In her thoughts, all she saw was a vast ocean of empty, unforgiving blue water stretching away from her.

She went to the stairs, going to her mother's room to help with the packing as she was bid.

Because Hope had gone too far, had tried to prove herself better than Lady Olivia, they were both facing punishment. Truly, Grace could think of nothing worse than being forced from her home into the unknown, on an adventure in a land foreign to everything she knew. Fear latched to her heart. To lose Hope had been a difficult enough situation to bear. To lose her home and everyone she knew?

Jacob's gentle aspect came to mind, but she swiftly pushed it aside. Letting any thoughts of him influence her decision would be foolish. They were friends, and given the way he often stared after Hope, they would likely never be more.

For once Grace had to put herself first in her thoughts. She could not sail across an ocean into uncertainty. It was not her nature and the furthest thing from her desires. Somehow, she must change her father's mind or….

An idea came to her, as suddenly as a bolt of lightning falls from the sky.

Grace said very little the remainder of the evening, though she watched her mother's expression with a heavy heart, and she could not ignore Hope's tear-stained face. With her lips pressed shut, she stayed in her thoughts, making her arguments and plans. As she considered the consequences to the action she would take, Grace realized something that nearly made her grin when she slipped into her bed that night.

Perhaps she and Hope were not so different after all.

CHAPTER 4

Mrs. Barnes rarely insisted that her children attend her when guests came visiting. But Jacob and his sisters, Elizabeth and Mary, were all present today while they bid the Carlburys farewell. It was not every day a prominent family left for voyages, after all.

The quarter-hour visit had not been extraordinary, and though Jacob wished to listen to their plans for Hope's sake, they did not say a word about her. Not until they prepared to take their leave.

Miss Irene Carlbury was bidding his sisters goodbye, taking their hands up in hers briefly, when she suddenly sighed. "Please, both of you, do visit Hope once we have left. She is gravely disappointed that she will not be joining us."

Jacob stiffened, hardly believing his ears.

"She is not?" Elizabeth asked, sounding as surprised as he felt. "Why ever not? I thought it was all decided." He would have to be certain to save her an extra tart for dessert, asking the questions he most wished to ask.

"Oh, did you not hear of the incident?" Miss Carlbury asked, looking between his sisters in a most dramatic fashion. "There was that terrible carriage accident, and then Mr. Everly said Hope's punishment would be to remain at home. Grace will accompany me instead."

Jacob heard no more, too busy with his tumbling thoughts.

Grace, on her way to the Caribbean? Such a thing struck him as almost cruel. Grace was quiet, unimposing, and happy with her place in her home and community. Hope possessed a wild spirit and a wandering heart, and being sentenced to remain home after setting her eyes so firmly on the horizon would be like clipping the wings of a hawk.

Mr. Everly had somehow managed to punish both his daughters in the most excruciating manner possible.

Jacob barely registered the Carlburys' departure enough to bow to them when they left. Mary and Elizabeth followed them from the room, still chatting about the excitement of the Carlburys' plans.

Hope remained at home for the foreseeable future. He had not lost her to an adventure beyond his ability to travel. Indeed, she would be home and heartbroken without her sister, her closest confidante. Though knowing how she would grieve pricked his heart, Jacob could not help but realize that her change in circumstances benefited his cause.

Jacob retook his seat, leaning forward with his elbows on his knees and his hands clasped before him as he pondered on the situation.

He had been praying for some time for help in securing Hope's heart, if she was the right woman for him. He had nearly given up on such a possibility when he learned she would be gone for a year, off on an exciting journey far from him. Perhaps his prayers had been answered, though not in the way he had hoped. The carriage accident—he had heard about Lord Neil's injury. Though they were not his friends, Jacob could not wish such harm upon anyone.

Mother's voice penetrated his thoughts. "I know exactly what you are thinking, young man."

Jacob blinked and looked up. She stood directly in front of him, her hands clasped and arms loose before her.

"Do you?" he asked, remaining in his hunched position. "And what do you have to say on the matter?"

Her lips turned down and she released a deep sigh. "I think it unkind to send Grace away. I cannot imagine she desired it. But her father has done what he thinks best. Hope will be rather upset, and likely so for some time. If you wish to be a comfort to her, be so as a friend first. Tread carefully."

He tilted his head to one side at that. "What do you mean?"

His mother bent double, bringing her eyes level with his. She studied him, the wrinkles on either side of her eyes deepening. "You have a good heart, Jacob. You are about to take orders to be a man of God first and foremost. Approach Miss Everly with compassion, because she is your friend. Be careful about making any declarations too soon. She has been hurt, after all, and disappointed."

"She will need time," Jacob agreed with a nod. "I can give her that."

"Good." His mother's expression did not relax as he thought it would. If anything, her frown grew deeper as she straightened her posture. "Poor Grace. I cannot imagine how she is taking this decision. Let us hope the Carlburys will be mindful of her. She hasn't the spirit for adventure her sister possesses."

Jacob leaned back in his chair, watching his mother carefully. "You have known the Everlys for a long time, but you have never tried to encourage me to pursue their daughters. Come to think of it, you have never encouraged any of us to make matches. Why is that?"

His mother's smile finally reappeared, though it was soft. "My dear boy, I know my children and I know your hearts. You will each find your way to a match and happiness in time. Why should I worry and fret over something that is not my choice, but yours?" She gave his shoulder a pat. "Do not brood for long, dear. You have an appointment with Mr. Spratt today, do you not?"

Jacob rose and straightened his coat. "I do. Thank you for the reminder." He checked the time on the mantel clock. "He is to show me the parish records today."

"I am proud of you for working so hard to be worthy of the position." She gave him a fond kiss on the cheek. "You had best be on your way."

Though he went to see Mr. Spratt, Jacob's thoughts remained on the Everly household and his two friends. Hopefully, with their change in plans, he would not be alone in the vicarage for long.

CHAPTER 5

The clock in the hall chimed the hour, and Grace counted each note carefully. After the twelfth bell, she slipped from her bed and wrapped her favorite green shawl around her. She did not bother with house slippers, as she did not have far to go. Hope's room was just across the hall. She did not take a candle with her either, given her familiarity with the house and the clandestine mission she undertook.

Entering Hope's room without knocking, Grace quietly padded up to the bed before she whispered, "Hope? Are you awake?"

Her sister immediately sat up. "Grace." Her voice was muffled by tears and sorrow. "Are you all right?"

Grace crawled onto her sister's bed and made her way to snuggle under the sheets beside her. "I am quite well, thank you. Have you been crying long?"

"Almost constantly since Mama left this morning," Hope admitted, shifting to pull herself into a sitting position. The room was full dark; there were not even shadows to make each other out. But they were accustomed to speaking in such a way. Until they turned eighteen, they had shared a bedroom and spent many a night sitting up with each other.

"I wondered why you would not leave your room," Grace admitted. "I have been going through what you packed all day today." She listened to the stillness beside her, trying to measure her sister's desperation in the way she sniffled.

"I know I keep saying it, and no one is listening anymore, but I am sorry. This is not what you wanted, Grace." Hope's hand sought Grace's on the bed between them, giving it a squeeze when she found it. "It might be wonderful for you, though. And you needn't have too many adventures if you do not wish them."

Grace's heart softened toward her sister and she scooted closer, wrapping Hope in an embrace. "Thank you, dear. You are kind not to be angry at me for taking your place."

A mirthless laugh escaped Hope. "How could I be angry at you? This is all my fault. You tried to stop me, and then you did not even tell Papa. I have never seen him so upset."

"Nor have I. But he is our father. He will be calm again soon." Grace bit her bottom lip, her heart picking up speed. She had to present her plan before she grew too nervous. "Hope. I have an idea. I have been thinking on it since our conversation in the library. Do you remember our governess, Miss Clark?"

"How could I forget her?" Hope asked, the faintest note of surprise in her words. She leaned back against her headboard, necessitating that Grace do the same. "She was excessively amusing. She never could tell us apart. Remember when we would purposefully switch places to confuse her all the more?"

"I would wear your hair ribbons and you would wear mine," Grace answered. "That was your idea. Remember?"

"No, but it sounds like something I would think of." Hope heaved a deep sigh. "It wasn't that brilliant a trick. Not very many people know how to tell us apart when we are dressed similarly. Only our brother and sisters, Mama, and Papa—"

"If Papa has his spectacles on." Grace's heart pounded all the harder. "And he loses them a great deal."

"I suppose." Hope's words came out slowly, uncertainly.

"Hope," Grace said, lowering her voice and attempting to sound earnest. "I would rather do just about anything than set sail for the

West Indies. And you would do almost anything to get that chance back, would you not?"

Quiet blanketed the room for what felt like an age, but Grace waited. Her sister would know what she meant. If Hope agreed with the plan, she would say so. If not, they would speak no more of it. But, oh, how much Grace wanted to stay home where all things were safe and familiar.

Finally, the words came, hissed out quietly. "We would be caught, Grace."

"Not for a time," she insisted. "Mama is gone for a fortnight at least. The younger ones will not be home to give anything away, and I am quite capable of pretending to be you until you are safely sailed from London. Once you sail, it does not matter. You will be away and no one can bring you back." Her voice rose as she spoke, eagerness coloring her words. "Think of it, Hope. All of your things are ready. Once you are at sea, you can tell Miss Carlbury. She will not give you away. She must prefer to have you on the voyage, as you will be a more animated companion than I. I will remain home, where I wish to be."

"Papa will be so angry when he finds out." Hope's words were discouraging, but her tone sounded the opposite. "Does that not frighten you?"

"I can weather our father's storm better than I can the ocean's." Grace spoke with more confidence than she felt. Her father's disappointment and anger, her mother's sorrow at her deceit, weighed on her heart. But she would pay that price when the time came most gladly. For she would still be at home when called to account. "We can switch in the morning. Come to my room, as if to help me dress. We will dismiss Susan." The maid would think nothing of their helping one another.

"Oh, that is clever. Then I will leave as Grace, and you will remain here, pretending to be me." Hope bounced a little as she spoke. "Do you think we can manage it? The Carlburys said they might remain in London a fortnight while they finish purchases and wait on the ship."

They had never switched identities for longer than a day, and that had been years before, and not more than a dozen times. Yet who knew Hope better than Grace? "We will manage perfectly well."

Suddenly, Hope's arms were around Grace. "Thank you, Grace. I had not even considered this idea. You have saved my adventure and given me another. How will I ever repay this?"

Grace's eyes filled with tears. "You are my best friend and my sister. I'm glad you will still have your chance at your dream." And she was more than a touch relieved that she could remain quietly at home.

They spoke for another hour, by turns advising each other on how to behave, giggling over memories, and occasionally wiping away tears for the months ahead without each other. Before Grace crept out of the room, Hope took her hand one more time.

"The only thing I am afraid of," Hope said in a whisper, "is being without you for so long. We cannot even write each other often. But I will write in my book for you, Grace. Every day."

They were doing the right thing. Grace knew it, and Hope's sweet words sealed the rightness of it in her heart. "Promise me you will be careful," she whispered. "If you do anything dangerous and it is my fault you are there—"

"Nothing bad will happen." Hope squeezed her hand. "Go to bed. We begin the finest acting anyone has ever seen tomorrow morning."

Grace barely stifled her laugh before slipping out of the bed, back across the hall, and between her cold sheets. Though her heart had been relieved of its burden, sleep did not come quickly.

As her sister had said, switching places would be an adventure all on its own. But it could not be too difficult, given how well Grace knew Hope's mannerisms. Her younger siblings might not be fooled for long, but she had every confidence she could win their silence if they guessed. There was also the matter that Hope, if she had been constrained to stay home, would not wish to talk or go about in society. This would keep Grace from having to practice her deception on too many people.

Deception. Dishonesty. Lies. She abhorred such actions, yet over the past day and a half had committed herself to performing them. It was a matter of self-preservation, she argued with herself, and doing the right thing. The terrible accident with Lord Neil and Lady Olivia should not rule the next year of her life or Hope's. People made mistakes, and Hope expressed true sorrow for it.

When her father realized what had happened, if he was angry, so be it. At least she would be home and not a world away on an island.

The sun rose at last, permitting Grace to do the same. Her head had started to throb, protesting her lack of sleep, but she fought through the discomfort. If she appeared haggard, it would help her appear more as a heartbroken Hope.

Susan, the maid who helped both young ladies prepare for each day, appeared with Hope right behind her. Hope's dark circles mirrored Grace's, proving that neither of them had been able to sleep. Hope was already dressed, too. Most plainly, in fact, with her hair pulled back and up in a simple style.

"Susan," Hope said after Grace's traveling gown had been laid out. "I wonder if you might allow me to help Grace today? Surely there are other things you must see to, and I would like to say goodbye to my sister."

The maid, only a few years younger than they, considered Hope with sympathy. "Of course, Miss Everly. I have sisters of my own. I understand what it is to have to say goodbye."

"Thank you, Susan," Grace said, another prick of guilt pressing into her. As soon as the door shut behind the maid, Grace and Hope met each other's gazes.

Hope came forward swiftly and embraced Grace. "This really is goodbye, for a very long time."

Grace held her sister close. "I know. But we will be together again, and we will have so much to talk about when we are." Tears sprang to Grace's eyes and when she parted from her sister, she saw Hope had started crying, too.

"We have no time for this," Hope said. "Hurry. Let's get you dressed as me first."

Chemises, stays, ribbons, and gowns flew about the room as they hurried to switch their identities. They whispered reminders to one another as they went.

"Remember," Hope said as she adjusted a pin in her hair, "that I cannot abide to eat parsnips, while you love them."

"Remember that Miss Carlbury knows of my simple tastes. Be careful what you purchase in London."

Back and forth they spoke their instructions until the transformation was complete. Grace wore the gown Hope had taken off, a deep green, striped dress more subdued than Hope's usual choices. Her hair had been styled by her sister as well. Hope wore Grace's periwinkle traveling gown, with a bonnet to match.

They stared at each other, inspecting the small touches that made the transformation complete.

"It will be fine," Grace whispered.

A knock at the door startled them both. "The Carlbury carriage has arrived. Cook has breakfast in a basket for you." Father's deep voice made Grace bite her lip.

"Coming," Hope answered quickly, giving Grace a crooked smile. "It's time. Hurry."

Hope's steps were light, though she managed to keep her expression neutral. Grace lowered her head and slumped her shoulders, easily able to appear dejected when she imagined it really was her who must leave that day.

Papa waited for them downstairs, without his spectacles in place. He tried to only wear them when he read or worked on his business letters. This worked to their advantage.

"Dear Grace," he said, raising his arms to take Hope's shoulders. "My sweet girl. I know you think me unkind to send you away, but this will be a good experience for you. You will thank me, in the end." Then he hugged her to him, kissed her cheeks, and opened the door to lead her out.

Grace followed slowly, hanging back as Hope stepped into the carriage. She raised her hand in farewell, calling out, "Goodbye, Grace. God go with you." Could God go with two women lying to their parents? Were their actions so terrible He might not hear their prayers?

Somehow, Grace had not thought to worry about such a thing until that very moment.

The carriage pulled away, Hope waving out the window, and Grace standing an arm's length from her father. He stood watching one daughter's departure, then turned slowly to look at the one left behind.

"Hope," he said, his voice slightly gruff. "Let this be a lesson to you, my girl. You will not be rewarded for acting as anything less than a lady. In time I think you will understand that this is for your own good. We must curb your behavior."

Grace lowered her eyes and nodded, whispering as though gravely disappointed, "Yes, Papa." He sighed heavily and walked past her. "Come, let us have breakfast."

Her adventure begun, Grace did not relish the challenge ahead as Hope had seemed to, but she gritted her teeth and followed her father. She would not give them away. She could not.

CHAPTER 6

Although Jacob's mother had cautioned him in terms of showing his growing affection for Hope too soon, he had no wish to leave her alone on the very day Grace departed for London and the West Indies. The poor woman had lost enough without being left friendless as well.

He took extra time dressing, though most of his clothing looked the same. The last several purchases he had made had been with his new position in mind. While it was not actually required that vicars wear all black, the somber and practical color was expected. He livened up his wardrobe only with waistcoats in blues and grays. Today, thinking of Hope's eyes, he chose blue.

Briefly he contemplated inviting Isaac to come on the visit with him. Isaac Fox, a baronet, and Silas, the Earl of Inglewood, were nearly as close friends with the Everlys as Jacob. Isaac's younger sister, Esther, had recently married the earl which made her part of their special circle of friends, too. Silas and Esther were in London in order for Silas to finish out the current session of Parliament. Isaac remained at home, putting things in order after his return from military service.

Though it was selfish, Jacob rapidly decided against asking Isaac to visit Hope with him. Perhaps, he told himself, it would be best to go alone and take her measure. He would invite Isaac another time, once Hope had adjusted to the thought of remaining at home.

Jacob took his brother's horse again, the fine golden gelding his favorite in their limited family stables. All the animals belonged to his brother, as Matthew had inherited everything five years past when their father passed away from a complaint of the heart. The vicarage and its attached farm would not support an animal of leisure, though Jacob meant to see about a few horses to pull a plow.

Thinking on the vicarage and all his plans for his future there made him lighthearted once again. Hope had remained, allowing him to dream of her company in the gardens on warm summer evenings. Surely he could have her cheered up and charmed before summer came to an end.

The tall, gray-stoned Refuge welcomed him as it always did, with glittering windows and its sweeping green lawn. Jacob rode up to the front doors, tied his horse to the hitching post, and took off his hat and gloves at the door.

Garrett answered, not so much as a black hair out of place. "Ah, Mr. Barnes. Good afternoon." The butler took his things as he stepped aside.

"Hello, Garrett. Is Miss Everly at home to visitors?"

The butler's eyebrows pulled down and he lowered his chin slightly. "She is home, sir, but I am not certain if she is permitted visitors. Would you care to speak to Mr. Everly on the matter?"

It had not occurred to Jacob that part of Hope's punishment might include restricting visitors. Hadn't keeping her from acting on one of her dreams been severe enough? Perhaps he would feel differently about it if he ever became a father.

Jacob followed Garrett to the library, where Mr. Everly greeted him with a book in hand.

"Ah, Jacob. Welcome. I suppose you have come to look in on Hope?" The man peered over the rims of his spectacles at Jacob, raising his gray eyebrows.

"Yes, Mr. Everly. If you will permit it." Jacob kept his face neutral, waiting for the verdict. He had never done anything to give the Everlys reason to distrust him or dislike his association with their daughters. When they were much younger, he had been attached a time or two to Hope's mischief and some of his own, but it had been years since he had done anything to earn a reproof from anyone's parents.

Narrowing his eyes, Mr. Everly tucked his hands behind his back. "As you are about to take orders and be our ecclesiastical leader, it would be foolish to deny you. Please, Jacob, as Hope's friend, do not let her bemoan her fate. I would have her grow from this, become a better person, and learn. By all means be kind, but do not allow her to act as though she is a martyr."

With the subject broached between them, Jacob dared to ask, "How is she taking it?"

"She has not spoken two words to me since breakfast. I believe she is in the gardens." Mr. Everly took a step back, ready to settle into his chair, and opened his book. "You may see her."

"Thank you, sir." Jacob took his leave and went through the house to a rear door that opened into the gardens. The gardens were not extensive. They did not stretch far from the house at all, as they might on a grander estate. He easily found Hope, sitting with her back to the house upon a stone bench, a book in her hands and a wide straw bonnet upon her head.

He walked slowly toward her, admiring her slender figure. Ever since he learned of her sentence to remain at home, Jacob had tried to decide what would be the best thing to say when he met her again.

He saw the moment she became aware of his approach. Her spine stiffened and she turned, peering over her shoulder with wide blue eyes. Almost as if she were afraid, or guilty. The poor woman. Jacob raised his hand and offered her his most charming smile—and she jumped to her feet, drawing the book in front of her like a shield.

Strange.

"Hope," he said, slowing his step once he was at an easy speaking distance. "How are you?" He tried to keep his voice gentle. "I know you cannot be entirely happy. I have come to see about offering you some company."

"Oh," she said, drawing the book against her middle. "I see. That is most kind of you, Jacob." There was no evidence of tears, no immediate storming about her situation. Had her spirits been so terribly shaken? Normally Hope acted with passion, speaking her mind and rarely withholding her feelings. She swallowed and then squared her shoulders. "It has been terrible, being sentenced to stay behind while Grace takes my place. I cannot believe Papa thought such an extreme measure necessary." Her chin tilted up, a touch belatedly.

Her actions and words were not quite what he expected, which made his response uncertain. "I am sure he did what he thought best. I hope Grace wasn't too frightened."

She tilted her chin higher and pulled her shoulders back. "Grace did not wish to go at all. But I am certain the Carlburys will take good care of her." Then she turned away from him. "You are a good friend to worry after us both."

"That is what club members do, is it not?" he asked, invoking the memory of their childhood fun. "We look after one another." He came closer to her, studying the gown she wore, the tendrils of hair that peeked out from her sun bonnet. "Hope?"

She peeked over her shoulder at him. "Yes, Jacob?" Something about the way she said his name was wrong, even for a disappointed and sullen Hope. She always spoke his name with a laugh, or with exasperation, as though she never quite took him seriously. That lilt to her voice was missing.

Could her spirits have been crushed that terribly? And if they were, what was she doing outside? Hope was rather famous for shutting herself away when in a morose frame of mind. Her reaction to the false news of their friend Isaac's death had been to drape herself in black and shut herself away until practically dragged out by Grace. Though no one had purportedly died this time, to see Hope appear so unaffected confused him. True, the roses had gone out of her cheeks, there were dark circles beneath her eyes, but she acted more skittish than sorrowful.

"What book are you reading?" he asked, taking a step closer.

She drew the book up, covering it with both hands. "Nothing of importance. I am merely trying to fill the time."

He tried to walk around her, but she turned again, keeping her back to him. He stopped, and she stared at him like a rabbit in a trap.

And then he knew, as abruptly as if a wave had swept his feet out from under him, what had happened. He moved without thought, taking her by the shoulders, forcing her to turn and face him.

Though the woman tensed in his grip, she did not pull away, nor did her expression turn mutinous. Rather, as he feared it would, her cheeks flared pink and her eyes met his with an open, pleading expression.

"Jacob," she whispered, "please, don't —"

He cut her off with one word. "Grace."

WHEN JACOB SPOKE HER NAME, Grace went cold inside and out. Her own father had not yet realized the wrong daughter remained at home. How had Jacob deduced such a thing in less than five minutes in her presence?

Judging by the way his face went slack, and how he lowered himself to the bench with slow, deliberate movements, he did not take the revelation well at all.

"How did you know?" she asked, watching him carefully. She could not afford to give herself away again. Not for two weeks, at the very least.

He groaned and dropped his face into his hands, muttering something she could not make out, though it certainly did not sound complimentary. He raised his head up, keeping his hands over his mouth, and narrowed his eyes at her. "Never mind how I knew. What in the name of King George are you doing?"

Jacob never swore. Invoking their mad king's name was the closest he ever came to it. Which meant he was angrier than he let on. She opened her mouth to answer, to tell him how she had no wish to leave home, could not imagine herself bound for the West Indies on a small ship atop a large ocean, but Jacob spoke first.

"I cannot understand how Hope could do this to you." Jacob thrust one hand into his hair in an agitated manner. "She runs off to do as she pleases while you remain behind to take the brunt of your family's displeasure when the truth comes to light. With the Carlburys, she faces little if any consequences."

He thought the whole thing Hope's idea? Grace understood the reasoning behind that. The most mischievous ideas in the neighborhood often came through her sister.

"Actually, I did not wish to go—"

"I know you did not," Jacob stated readily, shoving himself off the bench. "But circumventing your father like this, ducking her punishment and leaving you to take the full blame is hardly a sisterly act. She knew you would go along with it, too. You would do a great deal to please Hope even if it means denying yourself. It has always been that way."

Grace narrowed her eyes at him and held her book tighter. He made it sound as though she let Hope rule all her decisions. True, she often smoothed Hope's ruffled feathers and made excuses for her sister's sometimes thoughtless actions, but that did not mean Grace went along with everything her sister suggested.

"I ought to go right in there to your father and tell him everything." Jacob paced to the hedge marking the boundary to the fountain's courtyard, then came back to her. "She is only gone to London for now. There is time to stop her."

"No!" Grace surprised herself by shouting, and given the way Jacob stared at her he hadn't been expecting such an outburst either. Panic had taken hold. Jacob might ruin everything. "You cannot do that to me, Jacob. I know you are upset about this." And she knew why. His distress at Hope's decision to leave had been written plainly upon his face, as his anger was now. He had feelings for her sister and had been thwarted in retaining Hope's company not once, but twice.

"It has nothing to do with me," he insisted, stepping closer to her. "It has everything to do with what is right and honest. Hope has put you in a terrible position."

"No." Grace reached out, daring to lay a hand upon his arm. She could feel the tension in his body, saw it in the way his jaw tightened at her touch. "She has saved me. I could not go on that voyage. I'm frightened of the ocean, of being away from all I know. Hope did not do this for selfish reasons. If you tell my father, he will be angry at both of us and take me to London. He will force us to switch back. I cannot do it. Please, do not make me." Her voice cracked on the word *please* and she grasped his arm tighter.

Jacob stared down at her, wincing as though her words pained him. She could see the war within his eyes as he tried to decide what was to be done, where his loyalties must fall.

"Hope will not forgive you for interfering," Grace added, lowering her voice. "And I will suffer for it, too." She thought the former consequence more likely the winning one. If he had any desire to win her sister, if he wished to gain her favor and court Hope, revealing what she had done to their father would end all hope of such a future.

At last his shoulders sagged and he brought up a hand to lay over hers. "Hope has put me in a difficult position then, too. I would never do anything to harm either of you." He turned away, his arm sliding from her grip, and he ran a shaky hand through his hair. "How long do you think you can keep your deception going, Grace? There are those who will realize, as I have, that something is wrong."

The moment she had seen Jacob approach, her confidence had faltered. Jacob had been friends with both sisters for a long time. Having a particular affection for Hope likely made it easier for him to sense the difference in the sisters. Grace's private feelings in regard to him also kept her from acting as Hope did in his company.

For more than two years, Grace had watched as Hope remained oblivious to Jacob's growing tenderness toward her. Grace had been aware of it likely before Jacob knew what was happening. Grace had felt the difference in how he treated the two of them, how he looked at the two of them. The sting of her disappointment came shortly after noticing the change in Jacob. Grace had admired him, had held his friendship as the most dear to her, for many years. When she realized his preference for Hope, Grace also discovered she had fallen in love with him herself.

"The servants have yet to notice," Grace admitted, attempting to conceal her relief with a matter-of-fact tone. "My own father has not seen the truth, though I spent some of the morning in his company. Truthfully, I cannot understand how you realized it with such speed."

"You have different ways of expressing yourself," he said blandly. "You were not as outraged or as hurt as Hope would have been." Jacob walked away from her, his hands clenched into fists at his side. "I cannot be part of this, Grace. It is wrong and against my principles. My ordination is less than a fortnight away and participating in this kind of ruse is more Shakespearean than Anglican."

"I understand." Grace crossed her arms, hugging her book to herself. "But please, do not give me away. Hope will sail from London within two weeks. She will send me a letter the day they are to depart so I will know it's safe. As soon as I receive word from her, I will tell my father the truth. You have my word."

He did not immediately turn around. He stood with posture erect and every inch of his body stiff as a statue. As she began to despair, Jacob's shoulders dropped along with his head. "I will not say anything."

"Oh, thank you —"

He raised his hand, forestalling her from speaking another word. "I must go. Good luck, Grace." He did not so much as look at her as he walked back to the house.

Although Grace had not expected him to understand, she had hoped for at least some sympathy to her plight. Instead, she had disappointed him so greatly with her actions that he walked away as though he had no wish to even look upon her.

He had come to visit Hope. To cheer her up for being left behind. But he could not bring himself to offer even one friendly word to Grace, knowing that she took part in what he supposed was Hope's deception.

At least he did not know the entire thing had been Grace's idea. That would have likely made the situation worse. Perhaps he would have turned her over to her father had he not thought her a victim of

Hope's machinations. She had almost corrected that assumption. It would be one more thing to apologize for later.

For the moment, she made herself content with the fact that he would not reveal the deception.

Grace lowered herself back to the stone bench, facing the house this time. If Jacob had not taken her by surprise, perhaps she could have kept her act up longer.

The betrayal she had seen in his eyes erased any regret she felt over her poor acting. Hurting Jacob was not worth the ruse. Even if he had not promised to keep her secret, Grace wished no ill upon him. Perhaps, due to his feelings for Hope, he would have known no matter how well she mimicked her sister.

CHAPTER 7

J acob barely gave the horse any guidance and let the beast plod along home at its own pace. His thoughts were miles away, on the road to London with Hope Everly. The outgoing Hope would not maintain her ruse for long. Not if Miss Carlbury knew both sisters well. Hope did not have the patience her sister naturally maintained. Most likely, the Carlburys would realize they had been deceived and send Hope home within days. Such an occurrence would cause quite a scandal.

Poor Grace, caught up in the middle of the whole mess. Yet if she hadn't gone along with Hope's plan, leaving familiar shores for the ocean would have tormented her. But by giving in to her sister, Grace would eventually face her father's disapproval and the judgmental gossip of their neighbors.

How could Hope, a woman he held in high affection and esteem, do this to her own flesh and blood? How had she justified such an action, knowing it would hurt another?

He knew of her longing for adventure and of her dissatisfaction with the daily routine of her life in Aldersy. She expressed her desire to see faraway countries and learn of new things since childhood often enough. As a boy, he had eagerly gone along with her pretend expeditions as he had with Isaac and Silas's games of soldiers and kings. That's all it had been for him; fanciful games of pretend. Eventually, he had outgrown the playing and turned his thoughts to education and a profession. Hope, on the other hand, never stopped dreaming and took the steps necessary to ensure such dreams came true. At the expense of her reputation and Grace's.

Jacob had never practiced deceit in his adult life. He left off falsehoods in childhood when his mother and father drove home the lessons of honor and trust. Taking part in Grace's lies simply by omitting the truth turned his stomach. Soon to be a vicar, people expected him to be above reproach in all things.

If Hope and Grace were found out, and Hope's deceit scandalized the community, could he still wed her and maintain the respect of the congregants?

The horse nickered and picked up his pace when they came to the Barnes' lane, bringing Jacob out of his melancholy thoughts.

After seeing to his brother's horse, Jacob dusted himself off and went to walk in his mother's garden. Hers was smaller than the Everlys' cultivated shrubberies and flowers, and far more wild in appearance. His mother encouraged a natural look, which meant carefully planned disarray of long, decorative grasses and trellises of vines.

In a few weeks, Jacob would stand before a congregation full of his neighbors. People who had known him since childhood would sit before him, every Sunday, to weigh and measure his words against scripture and his own character. Some would see taking a wife with Hope Everly's personality and propensity to find mischief as a disaster.

Agitation building, Jacob went to a particular wall made from stone. As a boy, when he or one of his brothers misbehaved, his mother would send them outside to "rebuild the wall." She would come out with a parasol and fan and watch as they took stones from one side of the wall across the garden to another. They had to stack the stones carefully. The physical labor, though it seemed pointless, had done the job of wearing them out as well as forcing them into friendship again. The fight and bluster would be worked out of them, and the boys shared commiserating conversation while they worked.

Jacob unbuttoned his coat and laid it across a bench, then went to work on the stones. The steady, familiar movement of walking across the garden, the physical demand of carrying a small stack of the rocks along the way, helped him clear his head. For a time, he lost himself in the peaceful monotony of the familiar labor.

"And here I thought our days of moving rocks were long past." Matthew's clear tenor interrupted Jacob's flow and he nearly tripped on the paving stone. With arms folded and a grin stretched across his face, Matthew chuckled. "You must have done something unbecoming a vicar to be put to this old task."

Unable to laugh at the jest, Jacob continued his walk across to the other wall. "While that is not exactly how I would explain it, I suppose that statement is close to the truth."

Matthew took off his coat and dropped it on the bench next to Jacob's. "Sounds serious. Let me help you with your penance. I don't think any of us ever performed this task alone. We cannot break tradition now." He tromped over to lift a stone from the wall with an expression befitting a man dedicating time to a more pleasurable task.

Eyeing his brother, Jacob shook his head. "Suit yourself."

As the eldest, and with their father's death a few years previous, Matthew was the head of the family and carried the concerns of the estate upon his shoulders. He saw to their mother's needs and had committed to finding husbands for Elizabeth and Mary, their younger sisters. He allowed Jacob to stay on at the house until the vicarage became his home. Matthew also supported their brother, David, in his decision to take up business in London.

All of the responsibility due to Matthew's position had aged him, and given him a rather serious outlook on life for the past half dozen years.

Although, Jacob judged from his brother's light step and unconscious smile, perhaps that was about to change.

"You certainly are in a pleasant mood." Jacob's remark almost sounded accusing. He cleared his throat and added, "I'm happy for you."

"Thank you." Matthew passed him, holding a stack of three stone bricks. "I hope all the county may know the reason for my happiness in a few more weeks."

"Your courtship is going well?" Jacob asked, picking up three stones of his own.

Matthew stacked his rocks along the wall, his back to Jacob. "I believe so." He took an extra moment to align them. "Courting has not been as easy as I expected, but I am finally confident enough in the matter to be hopeful."

"That's good news." Though Jacob's circumstances in that area remained less than favorable, he could not resent his brother's better luck. "If the rest of us move on with our lives quickly enough, your bride might even have a home almost to herself." He dropped his rocks and cracked them together, lining them up along the top of the wall.

Matthew stayed where he was, an arm's length away from Jacob. "I'm in no hurry to see all of you away. You will have your living soon enough, and Mother will remain at the house for as long as she wishes. Elizabeth and Mary are not being courted by anyone at present. My prospective bride knows how I feel about the matter. Eliza is a practical woman."

Eliza Muir, a widow with two small children, could hardly afford otherwise. She lived with her late husband's sister in Aldersy village. Matthew's sweetheart, a pleasant woman and quite pretty even while wearing mourning colors for her late husband, had captured Matthew's interest as soon as she arrived. Though no one had suspected as much, including Jacob, until his mother had brought the matter to the family's attention at dinner one evening.

Their mother's uncanny ability to understand her sons' hearts never failed to amuse Jacob.

"But let us leave off talking of my present happiness," Matthew said. He turned and hoisted himself onto the wall, sitting upon the very stones he had laid in place. "Why are you out here executing such a useless task? I will help you in it all the day long, since you look as though you need the company, but it would be nice to know why we are out working in the sun."

"Physical labor is good for us." Jacob turned and stalked across the courtyard to lift the next stack of rocks. "And it helps me think. You need not stay. I am certain you have more pressing matters to attend to."

"Not at all." Matthew hopped down from the wall again and went back to hauling the pieces from one wall to the other. For several long minutes, neither brother said a word.

Jacob's thoughts went back to Grace, pretending to be her sister, and what a disaster it would cause when she was found out. Hope, with all her past antics, had never disappointed him in such a profound manner. Her trick would ruin her in the eyes of the community, would leave Grace in a difficult position, anger her parents, and all for what? For her to live out some childhood fancy to be a pirate or explorer.

He slammed down his rocks on the wall.

"Are you sure you do not wish to talk about it?" Matthew's question sounded less innocent and more concerned.

"There is little I can say that you would understand," Jacob said, not even glancing in his brother's direction as he glared at the stones as though they had given up his thoughts.

"It is Miss Everly, isn't it?" Matthew asked.

Perhaps their mother was not the only one in the family capable of seeing to the heart of a matter. That or, Jacob supposed, he did not hide his feelings so well as he thought. "It is I am —" What could he say without giving her away? "—Vastly disappointed in how she conducts herself of late. It is most unbecoming a gentlewoman and I don't know what to make of it."

"Mother hinted you might wish to court her." Matthew had the decency not to sound skeptical, though his neutrality was somewhat suspect. "Is that where your frustration lies?"

"Yes." Jacob lifted his eyes from the stone at last and met his brother's concerned gaze. "I have admired Hope for so long. And we are good friends. I hoped to build upon those things, but —" He broke off and threw his hands in the air.

"Ah. You have run into some difficulty." Matthew's lips quirked upward in a commiserating sort of mien.

"Indeed. I am beginning to wonder if I was wrong to even consider more than friendship between us." Jacob crossed his arms over his chest, ignoring the sweat upon his brow. Bending himself to a physical task had eased some of the tension in his body though it had given him no more peace of mind. "It's as though all the people I know have accepted they must grow into respectable adulthood, while Hope still thinks of the world as she did when she was ten years old."

"Not exactly the model vicar's wife, I suppose." Matthew rocked back on his heels. "I will not presume to tell you what to do, but might I offer some advice?"

Jacob chuckled. "If you think it will help. Though I must admit to some misgivings, since you are thirty-two and still unmarried."

Matthew cuffed Jacob on the shoulder, laughing as he did. "Come now. I am making progress; you must allow for that."

Although he doubted Matthew had any words of wisdom concerning his predicament, Jacob nodded. "Very well. I suppose if you have obtained approval from Mrs. Muir, you must have some idea of what you are about. What is your advice?"

"Stop worrying about whether or not Miss Everly will make a good vicar's wife. Instead, try to determine if she will make a good wife to Jacob Barnes." Matthew grinned as though he had said something particularly clever. "And come for a ride with me next time you are vexed. It is more productive than moving these old stones about." He retrieved their coats from the bench and held Jacob's out.

"Perhaps I will." Jacob accepted the coat and pulled it back on. Matthew's advice would be difficult to take if Hope's plan worked and she wound up thousands of miles away in the Caribbean Sea.

"There is a card party tomorrow evening at Mr. Greenfield's home. Will you come with me?" Matthew asked suddenly. The Greenfields were a respectable farming family, nearly neighbors to the Barnes family.

"A card party? I had not heard word of it."

"They are entertaining some cousin visiting from the north and decided a card party was in order. I received an invitation this morning. I think you might enjoy it."

A distraction would be most welcome. "I will come." But it was doubtful anything would keep his thoughts away from Hope and Grace for long. Grace's pleading expression surfaced in his mind, her eyes begging him to understand her part in the deception. For Grace he would say nothing, though it was Hope who had cracked his heart.

CHAPTER 8

Sleeping with a guilty heart proved impossible for Grace. She had taken herself to Hope's bedroom early the night before, pleading a headache and trying to maintain a sullen manner, only to spend most of her time staring out the window into the darkness. Though her bedroom was across the hall, her twin's room had nothing of the familiar about it. With Hope gone, and Grace unable to return to the comfort of her bed and belongings, she felt rather like an intruder.

The wind rustled the tree limbs outside Hope's window, creating a strange swishing sort of sound Grace could not ignore. Hope's linens smelled of lilacs while Grace preferred apple blossom soaps and perfumes. It was yet another thing, though small, that illustrated the differences between them. Grace loved the familiar scents of her family's apple orchards, while Hope longed for something entirely different.

Grace had finally fallen asleep, but woke again with the sun. Another day stretched before her in which she would wear her sister's clothes and try to avoid anyone who might notice that Miss Everly was not acting precisely as one expected.

She spoke little to her maid, hoping Susan interpreted her silence as continued melancholy. The kindhearted maid offered cheerful observations of the day ahead, noting the fine morning, that there were special biscuits for breakfast, and all manner of inconsequential pleasantries.

Grace's tired mind worked into a tangle over how she must behave as she took herself down to breakfast. Her father sat at the head of the table when she arrived, the dining room empty and nearly silent as he sipped at his morning coffee. His spectacles were upon his head and his newspaper lay folded to one side.

"Good morning, Hope," he said upon noticing her in the doorway.

She curtsied. "Good morning, Papa." Did she sound too subdued? Ought she to try and sound more belligerent? At least she need not pretend to have a great appetite. Grace imagined Hope, had she been left behind in truth, would not take much more than toast and tea. That was all she served herself from the sideboard before taking Hope's customary seat a chair away from her father's left hand. Habit nearly sent her to her own chair on the other side of the table, but she thankfully kept her head enough to avoid that mistake.

Her father said nothing as she nibbled at her toast, busying himself with his ham and eggs. Grace kept her eyes upon her plate, determined to eat swiftly and with as few words as possible.

"I must admit to some relief at your manner, Hope." Her father's voice intruded upon her frantic thoughts. "I expected you to either take to your room like some heroine in a Gothic novel, or else stomp about enough to shake the rafters loose." He chuckled.

Grace's fingers went cold and she swallowed her dry bite of toast with difficulty. Had she miscalculated the best way to behave as her sister?

"I am disappointed," she said at last, trying to keep her voice even. "But I do regret my actions."

"As I can see. I do hope Grace is handling her change in circumstances with the same sort of stalwart attitude." Her father shifted in his chair, but she kept her eyes down and held her hands in her lap, gripping her own fingers tightly. There was nothing and no one else to offer support. "I must admit, I had my misgivings," her father continued. "I know how much that voyage meant to you, my dear. Yet you must learn to let good sense rule your actions rather than your propensity to inact mischief."

"Yes, Papa." Grace did not even dare to reach for her tea. The slightest movement might betray her anxiety.

"I do feel for Grace, however." She nearly jerked upon hearing her name spoken again. "She has never desired to go far from home, to seek out new experiences as you always have. I think my decision to send her away may have frightened her."

It had terrified her. Grace's stomach twisted at the hated idea of stepping foot upon a vessel meant for the ocean. To hear her father express regret gave rise to guilt, however, which she liked no more than she had her fear.

"It is your opposing natures that leads me to believe you will have more opportunities in future, Hope. There will be other times, other experiences, which you will find and take advantage of. I know you well enough to realize that this one setback will not put an end to your sense of wonder." Her father's words were kind, spoken gently. Grace dared to raise her head, finding that her father stared at her with a softness in his features.

The guilt nearly erupted from her in a confession. Papa loved her. He loved Hope.

"Grace will never search for more from life than what it hands to her," he added, his expression as gentle as before though his words cut into her heart. "She is not as brave as you. I think this experience will teach you to temper your ways, but it will show Grace she cannot live her life timidly. You will see. Grace will come back with confidence and a new appreciation for the world outside our county."

Any desire she had entertained to confess the whole of what they had done to her father vanished. He thought her a coward, and he thought his punishment a boon to her. Grace bit her lip and averted her eyes. Did he truly know her so little?

"Yes, Papa," she whispered. Her stomach grew hot, the last few bites of toast upon her plate unappetizing. If only she had found a reason to take a tray in her room.

"As I have considered these things," Papa continued, "I have determined to allow you a few more liberties than we discussed before. I am attending the Greenfields' card party this evening and I should like you to accompany me."

Her eyes snapped up and she responded without thought, much as Hope might have done. "The Greenfields? Papa, you said I was not to go anywhere, nor see anyone, for weeks and weeks. You cannot change your mind now." She depended upon staying at home, staying away from any and all who knew her sister well enough to perhaps recognize the inconsistencies in character. "I cannot possibly go."

Her father's black eyebrows lowered. "What is this? Why not? Is the idea of accompanying your father so dreadful?"

"No, Papa." She shifted nervously, her hands sliding down her skirt as her palms began to sweat. What possible reason could she give to stay at home? "It would be humiliating." There was nothing Hope disliked so much as damage to her pride. "Everyone knows I should have gone away with the Carlburys. Facing our neighbors, having to explain the situation—"

"Would do you a world of good." Her father's eyes narrowed and he rose, tossing his napkin upon the table. "You are too proud, Hope. Everyone in the neighborhood knows of your accident with Lord Neil and that Grace has gone in your place. If your feather-headed friends push you for more information, it would serve you right. Humble yourself before our community, my dear, and learn your lesson fully."

"But, Papa—" She did not know what she would say, and he did not give her time to attempt another word.

"You will be ready to attend with me at seven o'clock this evening." He left no room for argument.

Grace gulped back her protest and lowered her head. "Yes, Papa." She did not look up as he left the room, listening to his retreating footsteps and then the slam of his study door. What was she to do? Feigning an illness would make him angry and he might call her bluff, or study her too closely, or any number of other unpleasant things. She would have to go to the party, as Hope, and pray that no one would realize she acted in any way out of character.

The nature of her punishment would account for any strange conduct. Even Hope might be subdued with such a great disappointment in her life.

Telling herself that no one knew Hope better than she did had given Grace the courage to propose the idea of switching places. Where had all that confidence gone? Was her father right about her nature? Did she truly lack courage?

Grace spent the day wrestling with her thoughts, sitting in Hope's room. She refused to pace. That was what Hope did when nervous or excited. Grace usually withdrew, sat in quiet contemplation, until her mind made its peace with whatever event put her into such flights of emotion. Somehow it was easier to maintain calm when she was in her own room or could be in the library. In Hope's chamber, decorated in bright yellows and pinks, it was difficult to settle her thoughts.

If only she had someone in whom to confide. But her regular confidante was in London, and Jacob had made it quite clear he had no intention of speaking with her while she pretended to be someone else. Pretended to be Hope, the object of his affection. Yet Grace wished she could speak with him, despite his obvious anger with her at the moment.

Grace settled herself on Hope's bed, holding onto the post with one hand.

Allowing Jacob to believe the whole thing was Hope's idea further nettled Grace's attempts at contemplation. It was wrong. She needed to tell him the very next time she saw him that she concocted the entire plan herself and persuaded Hope to go along with it. Not the other way around. If nothing else, it might soften his opinion of Hope a touch.

An ache that had become familiar to Grace returned to her heart. Though Grace despised feeling sorry for herself, her already rattled mind and guilt-stricken heart made it terribly easy for the pain to settle upon her.

She promised herself she would not think on Jacob as more than a friend. Not ever again. She had allowed herself to dream about it once, imagining what it might be like for him to court her. Then Jacob had begun looking at Hope, and Grace put her dreams aside.

Tracing the whirls in the bedpost with one finger, Grace saw the whole scene from the previous afternoon clearly in her mind. Jacob's shock, his disgust, his pain, at his loss of Hope.

Jacob did not see Grace as anything other than his old friend, likely regarding her with the same brotherly eye with which he watched over his sisters. Yet he stared at Hope as though he had never seen anything like her before.

Why did the one man who clearly recognized them as separate people have to be enamored with the elder Everly twin? Hope had never paid Jacob more attention than she had Silas and Isaac. Hope laughed at the idea of marriage, of being tied down to a home and family, but Grace yearned for those very things to call her own.

Grace did not realize she had started crying until a warm tear fell down her cheek, followed by another on the other side. She dashed them away quickly. Crying over Jacob Barnes had proved a useless action in the past.

The card party. She needed to create a plan of action, a mental script, of how to act and what to say while among other people in the neighborhood. Who might the Greenfields invite?

Rising from the bed, Grace went to her sister's small writing desk. After a few moments of digging about in Hope's things, Grace found pencil and paper and started making a list of possible guests. She focused on turning her mind to each person she knew and of Hope's opinions of them. Slowly she decided on the best course take when greeted by any one of them. No one at the party would ever know they had conversed with Miss Grace rather than Miss Everly.

The hours crept by until Susan came to help her dress for dinner and the evening's entertainment. Grace chose one of Hope's favorite gowns to wear, though the bright coral color made rather too bold a statement for Grace's liking. Hope *would* choose something like that dress, to show the whole neighborhood her punishment had not dampened her spirits.

Susan stood behind Grace at the dressing table, putting the finishing touches on her hair. "The curls look lovely, miss. They don't normally stay so well for you. Must be a bit of luck tonight."

Grace, preoccupied with what she might say if Lady Olivia made an appearance, barely heeded her maid's tone. "Perhaps. I will need all the good fortune in the world to get through tonight." She heaved a sigh and raised her eyes to meet Susan's in the mirror's and caught the maid frowning. "Is something wrong, Susan?" she asked.

"No, miss." Susan shifted and took a step back. "Just admiring your hair is all."

Grace's stomach tightened. Her hair. Hope was forever bemoaning that Grace's hair stayed put far better than her own. Could such a simple thing give her away?

Susan's expression cleared and she shook her head. "There now. Pretty as a picture. Dinner ought to be ready downstairs, miss. You mustn't keep your father waiting."

"Thank you." Grace stood quickly, instinctively needing to put distance between herself and the maid. As though being out of Susan's sight would be enough to put her out of mind, too. Dread inched into her thoughts. Why hadn't she considered her dratted hair?

Her father said little to her at dinner, though he did venture to compliment her gown. The silence at the table was necessary, though it made Grace more restless. Normally she and Hope would speak of their day, talk of their visits to neighbors with their mother and father, and when the younger children were home they would all chat at once filling the room with their cheer and affection.

But she could not risk conversation.

"I miss your mother," her father said near the end of the dinner hour. When she dared to look up at him, she saw he stared at her mother's empty chair. "I hope your aunt will be well soon. It is far too quiet around here at present." He sighed and stood. "And I cannot find anything when she is gone, besides."

Apparently, his spectacles had gone missing again. Perhaps that was another stroke of luck for Grace.

"I am certain Mama will have Aunt cured quickly, and will come home soon." Grace spoke the comforting words without thought, then bit her lip. Though natural for her to be mindful of her father's moods, Hope may not have said something such as that.

Her father walked away from the table and to the front door, hardly seeming to notice her words. "Come, the carriage will be waiting."

Grace took in a deep, steadying breath and followed. People mixed up Hope and Grace all the time. Dressed as the bolder sister, no one would think twice about which Everly sister attended the party that night. If anything, Grace reasoned, she might allow that truth to give her ease. Hope rarely thought before she spoke, and hardly cared for what others thought of her. For the first time in her life, Grace might allow herself that same privilege. After all, people would expect it.

Yet the whole carriage ride to the Greenfields all she could do was worry over every word not yet spoken and every gesture made in her sister's name.

⊛

JACOB DID NOT MOVE from his spot in the corner when Grace's familiar figure entered the drawing room. Clad in a bright gown that likely made her uncomfortable, Grace stood out at once in the crowded room. Most young ladies wore evening gowns in pastel colors, the matrons wore darker colors, and there stood Grace like a wild rose in a field of heather.

While he would not exactly call Grace shy, she never liked attention at events such as this, yet Hope thrived when all eyes turned upon her. As everyone in the room but himself believed Hope Everly stood in their midst, their neighbors obliged Hope's nature and immediately began to seek out the young woman's company.

Did no one else see Grace turn pale? Her eyes darted from one person to the next, never settling long enough to do more than give a brief greeting. She conversed deeply with no one, though she spoke to everyone who addressed her.

"Ah, Miss Everly has come after all."

Jacob glanced at Miss Hannah Keyes, one of the neighborhood flirts, standing at his side. She posed no threat to him, thankfully. Miss Keyes kept her sights set on much higher marks than a vicar. "Is that a surprise, Miss Keyes?" he asked, his stance remaining relaxed.

"Lady Olivia is in the very next room," Miss Keyes reminded him, nodding to the open doorway where conversation was more the thing than cards. "I should think even the brazen Miss Everly might be more sensitive to the fact that she nearly killed someone not even a week past."

"Are people to be punished for accidents?" Jacob asked, trying to sound curious rather than offended by the idea. Inwardly, he repeated verses in Ephesians. *Walk worthy of the vocation wherewith ye are called, with all lowliness and meekness, with long-suffering, forbearing one another in love.* Miss Keyes often brought out impatience in him. "It was my understanding that Lord Neil and Lady Olivia were also racing their phaeton."

The blonde beauty arched her delicate eyebrows at him and flicked open her fan. "I should have known better than to offer criticism of an Everly to you, Mr. Barnes. Everyone knows you are fairly wrapped up in their ribbons." A false, airy laugh floated from her while Jacob fought down the urge to answer her remark with a flippant word of his own.

"I have always been a friend to that family," he answered as mildly as possible. "Though I believe I would defend all my neighbors from undue censure, Miss Keyes."

"I am certain you would." She gave her fan another outward flick, the smirk never leaving her lips. "But one does wonder, at least when it comes to the Everly set, which young lady it is you favor. After all, they cannot go on sharing *everything*, can they?" She tossed her head and floated away, her graceful movements reminding him more of a slithering snake than anything else. She had been such a pleasant child but turned into one of the most conniving women of his acquaintance as she grew into womanhood.

Jacob's irritation made it difficult to remain standing still in the corner. He drifted around the edge of the room, conversing with neighbors, and trying to ignore Grace. The feat proved impossible, as no matter where he stood he remained aware of her and the knot of people around her.

Mindful that he could not avoid her forever, especially since everyone knew of his friendship with Hope and Grace, Jacob finally made his way to her side.

"Really, Miss Everly, you are not at all yourself this evening. I expected you would be as amused as I at the very idea of a boat race." Miss Johnson, a young woman who kept company more often with Hannah Keyes than the Everlys, peered at Grace strangely.

Perhaps he ought to intervene. Grace's cheeks had turned pale and she lowered her eyes in a most self-conscious and un-Hope-like manner.

"Oh, la. Perhaps we have reason to rejoice." Lady Olivia appeared and the gaggle of ladies around Grace parted, giving the earl's daughter a clear view of Grace.

Jacob moved around the women, coming to stand directly behind Grace. She turned her head enough that he knew she had seen him. Good. Then she knew she did not stand alone under whatever onslaught Lady Olivia had prepared.

"Whatever do you mean, Lady Olivia?" Miss Johnson asked, her eyes comically round.

Lady Olivia, dressed in greens and golds, looked like a strutting peacock when she lifted her chin. "I only meant that it would be a fortunate thing if Miss Everly gives up her fondness for racing. My poor brother remains at home this evening, nursing his wounds from the last time Miss Everly took up her favorite sport."

From where Jacob stood, he saw the back of Grace's neck turn red, along with the tips of her ears. Always, she suffered for Hope's decisions, whether it was the race itself or being held to account for something her sister had done.

He stepped forward, putting his hand on Grace's elbow. "I am certain Lord Neil is grateful that he took the brunt of the punishment that day." Jacob somehow managed to sound admiring rather than annoyed. "He would not have wanted any of you ladies injured in such a folly as a pony and cart race. I hear he bears it most bravely." He had not heard any such thing and, if he knew Lord Neil at all, the man likely complained of his broken arm to anyone within hearing distance. "Now you ladies must permit me to steal Miss Everly away. She has promised to be my card partner this evening."

Lady Olivia's smug smirk had turned into a frown, doubtless sensing an insult to her brother though none had actually been made. Grace's hand slid onto Jacob's arm, and he immediately forgot about the other women present.

All that mattered was seeing to Grace.

After he led her away, and into the card room, he bent close to her ear. "I did not think you would come out in society."

"Papa thought I had been punished suitably and rather insisted upon it." She barely raised her voice enough to be heard. "Jacob, what am I going to do?" she asked, her tone plaintive even if her expression was calm.

Though he had no wish to help in her ruse, Jacob could not bear to see Grace in such distress. Thankfully, an alternative to helping her lie existed. The Greenfield cousins did not know Hope or Grace. "Come with me."

The cousins visiting, Eugene and Jemima Standish, were a married couple about Jacob's age. And they stood near an unoccupied card table.

Grace came with him, her expression most serious and then relieved when they stood before the strangers.

"Mr. Standish, Mrs. Standish, I should like to introduce my friend to you. This is Miss Everly." That would be Grace's title honestly enough in the absence of her elder sister.

"How do you do," Grace murmured with her curtsy.

"Very well, indeed," Mrs. Standish answered. "Everyone has been so friendly this evening. I do so love parties."

"And being the guests of honor is always satisfying," her husband added with a teasing glance to his wife. "Tell me, Miss

Everly, what do you think of living so near the sea? I am convinced it must make life much more pleasing than living in the center of a crowded city."

They exchanged thoughts on conditions in London against Aldersy's quieter ways, and Grace relaxed beside Jacob. The tension left her face, the blush faded, and the hand upon his loosened its grip. As they stood next to the empty table, the conversation naturally turned to playing a game of Whist together.

Jacob helped Grace into her seat, then moved across from her. She and Mrs. Standish conversed with ease, even after they each had a handful of cards to see to. Grace naturally fell into her own habits, quieter and more contemplative than Hope might be, and more willing to listen to the stories of others than tell her own.

"Mr. Barnes, when we were introduced, you said you were about to take up the position of local vicar, did you not?" Mr. Standish asked as he played. The ladies quieted their talk to turn to Jacob, Mrs. Standish with eyebrows raised. Grace regarded him with her usual gentle smile.

"I am." He rearranged his hand after scowling at his cards a moment. "I look forward to my first day of sermonizing perhaps more than the community does."

"Do you think it might prove a struggle, to be in such a position over people who have known you since childhood?" Mr. Standish asked. "Will they hold you in high regard, as befits a vicar? Or will they only see the person you have always been before?"

Mrs. Standish leaned forward slightly. "Oh, that is a good question. I had not thought on that."

As Jacob had often wrestled with that very thought, he could at least answer it honestly and without hesitation. "I am certain it will be difficult for some, but with a little time they will grow accustomed to me in that position."

Without raising her eyes from her cards, Grace spoke quietly. "It helps that Mr. Barnes has always held himself to a high moral standard. I cannot think of a single incident after he started school that might offend anyone. He is kind to others, too. His character is what every good man's ought to be." She laid down her next card and raised her gaze to meet his, her blue eyes sparkling at him. "I believe we have won this round."

"Bad form, winning against a married couple." Mrs. Standish giggled and marked their point on the slate for keeping score. "Eugene, you simply must learn how to signal me better if we are to win."

Though they all laughed, and dealt the next hand, Jacob's mind stayed on what Grace had said. He caught her eye again as he put down his first card and the tender look she cast him was the visual equivalent of her gentle praise. She had never spoken of his character like that before, at least within his hearing. That she held him in such esteem humbled him. There could not be a truer friend in his life than Grace.

CHAPTER 9

The previous evening's card party, though begun with difficulty, Grace counted as a success. She spent most of her time in company with the Standishes and Jacob. Her father, never one to stay out late, had found them when he wanted to return home and had enough of a pleasant evening himself that he suggested Jacob and Grace go riding the next day.

"Hope needs more exercise than that pacing she does," her father had said with an affectionate sigh.

For the first time since the disastrous accident, Grace fell into bed with hopes for a good night's rest. But as her eyelids grew heavy, and her breathing deeper, a most unwanted thought tickled at her mind.

Why had Papa suggested that she and Jacob go for a ride? The party was one thing, but seemingly doing away with the punishment for Hope's misbehavior all together struck her as odd. Unless her father had another motive.

Perhaps he wanted Jacob to be a more steadying influence upon Hope? He often lamented that Grace could not temper her sister fully. Did he think a future vicar had a better chance of such a thing? While that made a little sense, she kept poking at the thought with dissatisfaction. Jacob had always been a steady influence on his friends, but never Hope. There must be something else behind her father's suggestion.

Grace tossed about in her bed for a time before the answer came.

Papa had never played at matchmaking before, but he as good as told the twins he wanted them both married, and soon, before the trip to the West Indies had even presented itself. Truly, the pressure had been mounting for quite some time. Insisting "Hope" spend time with Jacob, when he had been lecturing her for days about changing her ways, suggested that he thought Jacob Barnes might assist with that change.

The outing lost its charm as Grace laid in her sister's bed, aware that Papa wanted Hope to settle down and marry their new vicar.

She might be wrong. But given her father's frame of mind, his desire for Hope and Jacob to wed made perfect sense.

The night proved as restless as those that had come before it. When Grace finally climbed out of bed, she remained as tired as when she had entered it. Sitting before Hope's dressing table, with Susan again marveling over how easily she coaxed her mistress's hair into a stylish coiffure, all Grace saw in the mirror were the dark circles beneath her pain-filled eyes.

What made Hope such a better prospective wife than Grace?

Papa mostly ignored her at breakfast again, though with indifference rather than irritation. "How will you occupy yourself today?" He posed the question as he stood to leave the table, his newspaper folded and tucked under one arm, his spectacles in his study rather than upon his nose.

"I am not certain. I ride with Jacob in a few hours."

Her father narrowed his eyes at her. "Try and be productive. If your sister were here, I am certain she would have any number of domestic things to see to."

Grace agreed somewhat absently. If not for the need to act as Hope, she would have already met with Cook about preparing a special treat for her father. Hope rarely thought of such things. Yet now she had her father's encouragement to act more naturally.

"I could speak to Cook." She attempted to sound uncertain as she made the suggestion. "Perhaps put together a basket or two for a few families."

"Splendid idea. Best get a move on if you are to accomplish anything before Mr. Barnes arrives." He walked behind her chair and paused long enough to place a kiss upon her forehead. "You have all the makings of a fine lady, my Hope, if you will be attentive to the needs of others."

Grace bit the insides of her cheeks. The softly given reprimand hadn't really been given to her, after all. With her father gone, Grace threw away caution and added three of her favorite foods to her breakfast plate. Peppered eggs, a rasher of bacon, and baked apples. Hope favored sweeter foods at breakfast, but the richness of her sister's preferred pastries made Grace's stomach ache. With a morning ride ahead of her, she had no desire to feel as though she had swallowed mortar instead of more practical sustenance.

After eating as quickly as she could, and gulping down her cooling tea, Grace made her way to the kitchen to speak to Cook. As usual, Cook moved about her small dominion as busy as a bee. She flitted from sink to stove, hearth to table, with long steps and an air of impatience.

"Ah, Miss Everly." She wiped her hands on her apron when she spied Grace in the doorway. "Did breakfast suit this morning, miss?"

"Yes, it was delicious. Thank you." Grace came into the room, wondering how Hope might approach this situation. Likely with confidence, even though it was usually Grace or her mother who visited the kitchens. She tilted her chin upward and tried on one of Hope's larger grins. "Papa is in need of some cheering. I thought you might prepare him something special."

"Very good, miss. Will the usual do?" Cook asked, her black eyebrows raised high.

Grace nearly said yes before realizing Hope likely had no idea what treats were typically prepared. "What is it you usually prepare?"

For a moment, Cook's lips twitched but she turned her attention to organizing vegetables upon the table. "Oh, some combination of his favorite things. Mr. Everly enjoys ham, I know him to be partial to carrot soup, and at times, likes nothing better than my buttered rolls." She glanced at Grace from the side of her eye. "And you, miss, might choose the dessert."

Something about Cook's manner suggested suspicion. But how would Cook have guessed who Grace was if her own father had not noticed the switch? Perhaps Susan had shared something. If the servants had guessed her identity, why had they not said anything?

"I would enjoy your apple spice cake immensely." That was a dessert for which she knew Hope had a special fondness. "Papa also suggested I make myself useful by putting together a charity basket or two." There. Had she sounded reluctant enough?

Cook left the vegetables to retrieve baskets hanging near the pantry. "That's an easy enough task. Who will they go to?"

Drat. Hope would have no idea.

"I thought I might visit the vicarage this afternoon and see if Mr. Spratt could point me in the right direction."

With her back turned, Cook chuckled. "Sounds like a fine idea, miss."

Grace raised her head higher and squared her shoulders. "What sort of things usually go in the baskets?"

"Oh, day old bread. Preserves and jams that ought to be eaten or put out, or any extra things we might have. Sweets for the children. Nothing too extravagant." Cook placed the baskets on the empty end of her table. Her kitchen maid came inside, holding a basket full of herbs from the kitchen garden. Cook's attention turned to the young woman.

With some hesitancy, Grace approached the baskets. She knew exactly how to fill them best, but Cook's strange manner meant she must be especially on her guard. She picked up a basket and went to the pantry, biting her bottom lip and examining every jar and dried onion with perplexity.

She started putting things inside the basket, making certain fully half of her selections were not the normal choices. She even added eggs into the basket, wincing as she did.

She took the basket back to the table. "Is this right, Cook?"

Cook came back to the table and reached for her carrots, then stopped and stared at the basket. "Miss Everly." Shaking her head, she removed the eggs first, then the small crock of butter, and several dried onions. "Sweet child." She said the term of endearment the way one might lament a scraped elbow. Then she darted Grace a confused look before taking the basket up in her hands. "Let me show you."

Pleased she had erased the knowing smile from the servant's face, Grace had to bite her tongue and remind herself to frown as she accepted the woman's help. Whatever it was Cook had believed, Grace had thrown her off the scent.

Though Grace ought to feel guilty, as she had felt many times in the deception thus far, instead she gained confidence. The heady sensation did not dissipate quickly.

After blundering about the kitchen in search of a few things Cook asked her to gather, the baskets were finally prepared and covered. They would be put in the dogcart, which was the only vehicle Hope was permitted to drive. The little phaeton, with its broken axle and wheel, had been declared off limits to her for as long as she lived. Grace did not mind avoiding that equipage in the least.

She took herself to Hope's room to dress for her ride with Jacob, putting on her sister's deep purple riding habit with Susan's help.

Hope's penchant for bold colors irritated her anew. Not only did the deep plum of the dress stand out against nature, but Hope had added to the ensemble by requesting military epaulets and buttons upon the coat. Grace thought longingly of the forest green riding gown in her closet, with a more simple and sensible design, but kept a pleasant expression upon her face when Susan affixed the matching hat to her head.

"Pretty as a picture, miss." Susan offered her usual compliment brightly. "What shall I lay out for you upon your return?"

"Whatever you think best." The words slipped from Grace without her permission, or her clear thought. Hope always had an opinion on what to wear.

"Yes, miss." Susan did not even bat an eyelash, turning to begin tidying up the room.

Grace hesitated. Ought she to fix the blunder or not draw attention to it? Pride goeth before a fall, certainly, and her earlier happiness over confusing the cook melted into anxiety once more.

She left the room without another word, silently berating herself. At least she did not have to pretend with Jacob. As much as his early discovery had distressed her, his knowledge offered her relief.

A groom ought to have been saddled and prepared to accompany them on their ride, but the Everly sisters had always been together, chaperoning each other, when they went out with Jacob, or Isaac and Silas. Her parents never deemed a servant necessary. Though Grace recognized the oversight at once, she said nothing. After mounting her sister's chestnut mare, she guided the horse to the gate at the road.

Jacob, mounted on the tall hunter he favored, waited for her. The moment she caught sight of his form, waiting patiently at the end of the lane, her heart surged out of its normal rhythm into a gait far more appropriate for a running horse.

Grace had never been alone with Jacob, away from the house where anyone might watch them walk through gardens together. Hope had always been present. Or they were in a room or garden filled with people. Today, she had him to herself.

Her whole spirit lightened, she leaned forward and urged the little mare to move faster. She could not waste a moment of this time in his company. It might be the only hour she ever spent with him in such a way.

Except, as she drew closer, she saw Jacob's deep frown and rigid posture.

Of course, he did not feel as she did. He hated that she and Hope had lied, and he would much rather have her sister riding with him.

It would not matter if anyone else admitted to preferring Hope's company to Grace's. But why could Jacob not see or understand how wrong Hope was for him? She would never be content to live at the vicarage by the sea. The horizon beckoned her to explore each day with a vivacity few could keep up with, and even fewer understand. Hope's heart had wings, and Jacob's had an anchor keeping him safely at harbor. Jacob, always steady and sure, loved the people who would soon be under his care. For him, the sunset wasn't to be chased, but admired after a long day's honest toil.

Grace sighed as she drew up beside him. "Good morning, Jacob."

He nodded deeply to her, as solemn as if greeting a stranger. "Good morning, Grace."

Her shoulders slumped and she gripped the reins tighter in her hands. "If it is uncomfortable to be near me, we can forget about the ride. I have no wish to upset you any more than I already have."

"Oh, Grace. It isn't that." He blew out a frustrated breath. "Not entirely that. You are my friend, and even if I do not condone your actions, I understand them." He turned his horse around. "Come, let us ride while we talk. The horses need the exercise."

"I am not certain I wish to talk." Grace followed, staying near without drawing alongside him. "I have the feeling it will be more of a lecture."

Jacob snorted and craned his neck to peer over his shoulder at her. "That sounded remarkably like Hope."

Grace smiled despite herself. "I have had a few days of practice. And it is not surprising she resents your lectures; she receives them quite often."

He pulled up, forcing her to come nearer before he spoke again. "She thinks I lecture her too much?"

"Jacob." Grace studied the way his eyebrows were drawn down, wishing she could reach over the distance between them to smooth them out. Must he appear so disapproving? "You do lecture her. Often of late." She moved her horse forward again and he followed suit, staying parallel to her on the road.

Silence hung between them, the gentleman's head lowered. "I suppose I can be pompous."

"I'm not certain I would call it that." Grace held the reins lightly again, trying to give her attention to horse and road. Even with Hope physically absent, she managed to be present in thought. It took a great deal of restraint to avoid sighing over that fact. "You always mean well. But you sound very much like our father. He is forever reminding her to do or be different than she wishes."

Jacob's head turned in her direction, his horse moving closer. "Have I done that? It wasn't my intention. I always admired her more spirited ways. I meant to help her see what others expected."

As someone who had witnessed the lectures in question, Grace doubted he even understood how his words sounded to Hope. Though she knew he had not meant to stifle her sister, he certainly had made it clear he objected to Hope's actions a time or two. Yet even after voicing his disapproval, he stared after Hope, watched her every movement, admiring her.

"I understand, Jacob." Grace turned her horse onto a path off the road, one the three of them had frequently followed on their rides together. The horses knew the trail well.

"Thinking on it, I suppose I spoke more often than my place allowed. A friend should censure less." Jacob ducked to avoid a low-hanging branch that she had but to tip her head forward to pass. He was not an astoundingly tall man. Not like Silas or Isaac. But he carried himself with a confidence that made him seem larger than he was. He glanced at her, tilting his head to the side. "Do you ever take issue with your sister's behavior? I cannot recall you speaking ill of her."

"She is my sister." Grace offered him the barest shrug. "I have cautioned her at times, but it is not for me to tell her how to act. She does not always consider the consequences to what she does. But there is no one who would come to a friend's aid faster than Hope. I have never wanted to curb her liveliness."

Jacob turned his attention back to the road, his expression unreadable. "Even if most of society regards her liveliness as ill-mannered?"

"Why have we any worries over society? We are not often away from home, and here, people know and care for us."

"But what of the future, when you are gone from home?" Jacob asked, then his jaw tightened.

Grace knew the conversation had turned to something of a more delicate matter. Something she did not entirely wish to discuss with Jacob. It would hurt, if he said too much. The man had absolutely no idea how much it pained her to know how her feelings were overlooked.

"You speak of marriage," she said, watching him carefully.

Jacob's eyes darkened and he pulled his horse slightly away from her. "Yes."

Grace stiffened her spine. If he wanted to take this path in their conversation, then she would say exactly what he needed to hear, even if it was not what she most wished he knew.

"Hope and I have always agreed on one thing. We will not marry where there is not love. If a man truly loves Hope, he will see her for all her strengths and weaknesses, and not wish to change her. He will love her as she is." She adjusted her grip on the reins. "And I pray I find the same." Then she gave her horse a nudge, urging the animal into a faster pace.

Let him think on what she said and put together his response with care. How could he think himself in love with Hope when he saw fault when she acted in the way most natural to her? Hope could behave better, and the same might be said for most people, but nothing in her character posed any true moral difficulties.

At length, Jacob's horse drew even with hers again, matching her pace. He did not attempt conversation, riding at her side. Ignoring him, Grace tipped her head and leaned over her mare, enjoying the wind.

"To the beach?" Jacob shouted. A few miles away, it would make their ride long.

Grace almost cheered at the suggestion. "Yes, of course." They talked no more, but their horses raced along the paths that would take them to the shore faster than the road itself. Here they cut through the property of neighbors and friends, all the way to the Inglewood estate.

They slowed when they reached Silas's lands. Silas Riley, the Earl of Inglewood, and his bride, Esther, had gone away to London to complete his time in Parliament. The house remained shut up while they were away. With the earl and his countess in London, and Hope gone, the group of friends had been broken up again. At least Isaac had returned from the war, but he kept to himself a great deal.

"We ought to call upon Isaac soon." She spoke without thinking, their former conversation fallen from her thoughts.

Jacob glanced toward the north, where Isaac's baronetcy lay. "I have thought the same. We should not leave him to himself long."

They broke through the trees into the long grasses, then down the drop to the beaches. The rush of the waves and salted wind calmed her, though the breeze immediately took to teasing at the curls on the back of her neck. Most of her dark locks had been artfully pulled upward to fit beneath Hope's purple hat.

Grace shifted in her saddle. "Perhaps we could call upon him together?" She bit her lip after speaking.

"I will ask my mother if she might wish to come and see the gardens." Grace's confusion must have shown. Jacob chuckled before he added, "You need a chaperone now, Miss Everly. You've no sister to accompany you."

"Oh. I suppose so. I thought on that today, actually. But with my mother away and everyone so used to the way we do things, no one said a word about a groom following along." She watched a gull dip low across their path before it caught the wind and soared upward, over the water. "And we both know I am safe with you." Whether that was true due to his position as an almost-vicar or the lack of attraction he held for her, Grace did not allow herself to decide.

Jacob said nothing, and Grace kept her attention upon the birds.

THEY HAD TURNED HOME, and regained the path, when Jacob finally spoke the matter upon his heart. If it were anyone but Grace, he would say nothing, but she understood him and her sister in a way no one else ever could.

"I had thought of marrying Hope," he said, his words breaking through the silence of Inglewood's trees more abruptly than he thought they would. The sentence fell upon his ears as the sound of an axe against one of the birch trees.

Grace did not turn to him in shock, nor did she gasp or give way to any other dramatics. Instead her dainty chin jutted outward and her gaze remained fixed on the path before them.

"I know." The words were too clipped for him to find any sign of her thoughts on the matter.

"You do?" How he might coax more from her? She dipped her head in a brief nod, but her lips stayed pressed together. Certainly she had more to say on the subject than that. "I was terribly obvious?"

Grace ducked her head to avoid a branch, then kept her gaze down, avoiding his. "To me, yes."

Rather than embarrassment, Jacob felt relief at her admission. "My mother sorted it out as well. Perhaps my brother did, too. But Hope never acted any differently. I thought I had been circumspect." He removed his hat long enough to swipe at the thin line of sweat upon his brow. Though the weather remained mild, the heavy coat he wore kept him uncomfortably hot.

"She never said anything of it to me, if that is what concerns you." Grace's tone sounded disapproving. "Why did you never say anything to *her*?"

Jacob's mount snuffled, causing him to realize how tense he had grown. He bent his neck from one side to the other in an attempt to relieve that feeling. "Truthfully? I had no idea how she might react to the idea. We have all been friends for so long. I thought she might laugh at me." He studied Grace from the corner of his eye. Would Grace laugh at him? No, she had always been a compassionate sort, and kept her emotions well hidden beneath a mild, calm expression. Except at that moment, her lips were pressed together in what appeared to be an uncomfortably tight manner.

Jacob tried to ease the conversation into more comfortable territory. Perhaps his distress over the situation had wounded Grace's feelings, too. She was his friend, after all, and they discussed her sister's future too casually. "It was all for nothing, obviously. Hope is gone now." He put one hand to the back of his neck, rubbing at the knot at its base.

"She will return in a year," Grace said, bending to twitch at her riding skirts on the side opposite him. "You could begin your suit in earnest then."

While he had once tried to comfort himself with that truth, it had grown harder to do so of late. Speaking his doubts to Grace only brought his folly further into light. A wave of uncertainty that had lapped at his ankles had started to rise. As often as he tried to lecture Hope into doing things the proper way, into being the sort of person that he wished for rather than who she was, would she ever see him as more than a friend?

"Will you miss her?" Jacob asked, rather than continue discussing a possible courtship. "Her liveliness, her entertainments?"

Grace's expression softened and she faced forward, presenting him with a profile that might physically resemble Hope, though the gentleness in her countenance was something he'd never seen upon her sister's face.

"I will miss her companionship." That admittance came with a sorrow he hadn't expected. "She is my dearest friend. There is no one who knows me so well as Hope. As to the entertainments," Grace fiddled with her horse's mane and sighed. "I don't suppose there will be as many, with Hope away, but we will get on."

"Yes, as we must. I wonder who will take up her projects while she is away?"

Grace turned to him finally, her nose wrinkled. "Which projects?"

Hope had been involved in any number of charitable schemes. A redeeming quality, balancing out her sometimes more inappropriate actions. "The sewing group she started last month, to provide linens and clothing for the orphans of soldiers. There were several women interested in participating, I thought."

The woman at his side frowned and turned away, most abruptly. "Her conversation will be missed at that gathering, to be certain. But that was not Hope's project."

"It wasn't?" Yet Jacob had heard Hope in the churchyard, inviting women to come to her home to work out how best to go about organizing the work. "What of her championing a circulating library for Aldersy, then?"

"All that remains for that is collecting the donations and dues that have been pledged." Grace did not even bat an eye before answering. "I intend to see that done and then my father will lease a room in the village and hire someone to oversee the books."

"That is good, that you know what must yet be accomplished." Jacob regarded her closed expression carefully. "Did you assist Hope with all that she worked upon?"

For a moment, Grace pressed her lips together tightly enough that they turned white, as though she were forcing herself not to answer him. Odd. "I apologize, this subject seems to upset you."

She shook her head slowly. "It isn't that. Not precisely that." Grace pressed her gloved fingers to her temple. "You needn't worry over anything Hope has left undone. I am well prepared to manage the sewing, library, and even the proposed Sunday school class for the betterment of the working-class daughters."

Jacob had known that last one had been presented by both sisters to the vicar. They had asked for his opinion on teaching some of the younger children skills they might use to obtain better serving positions as they grew older. The vicar had consulted Jacob, as it must eventually fall under his supervision, and they had both been impressed by the plan.

"I'm grateful you will see to those things in her absence." Indeed, he was certain Grace's hard work might spare her sister harsher criticism later.

As energetically as Hope went about doing good for others, Grace had always seemed to stand as a quiet support to her sister, tethering the exuberance in a way that made Hope's efforts more focused. It was good to know that Hope's efforts would not be forgotten, that the community would remember her kind acts as they were carried on in her absence.

Apart from that concern, once people discovered what Hope and Grace had done, the lie told by them both, would anyone accept her as a clergyman's wife?

"Perhaps by the time she returns the gossip will have died down." He emitted a deep groan and rubbed at his eyes. "You are both going to face consequences for that, Grace."

Grace's posture stiffened and she turned to him, her face pale. "You do not think our neighbors might forgive such a thing? We haven't harmed anyone."

"But have you ruined the trust your friends had in you?" Jacob winced, imagining what the gossips might say. "A vicar's wife must be a reflection on him, and therefore above reproach. Courting Hope could prove difficult."

"I see." Grace's mount snorted and pulled abruptly to the side. Jacob eyed the mare dubiously. She was Hope's horse, and therefore a more spirited animal than the one Grace normally rode. Their pace had likely become too sedate for the creature.

Grace righted the mare, taking firm hold of the reins. "I hope things are not as bad as you fear, Jacob. You deserve to be happily settled in your new life."

Though the words were kind, something about the way Grace said them changed their meaning. Her tone bordered on satirical.

"I meant no slight to Hope," Jacob added quickly. "Or to you. I am only being honest."

"Oh, I understand." The horse danced sideways again. "If you will excuse me. I had better give this fine lady the exercise she wishes." They were nearly off the Inglewood estate and onto her father's property, but when Grace leaned over the horse's neck and gave the mare her head, Jacob's worry mounted and he tried to keep up with her, in case the animal proved too much for the young woman.

To his surprise, Grace proved she was as fine a horsewoman as her sister, which made sense, given that they had grown up riding together. Though he could not recall ever seeing Grace galloping across the country as heedless of speed as Hope. Even when she rode directly behind her sister, Grace exuded a calm and capable manner.

Grace had always kept pace with Hope, and not just while riding.

When they came back to the Refuge, Jacob expected Grace to slow down and bid him farewell. Instead she rode directly through the gates, and he remained on the road.

What had he done wrong now?

CHAPTER 10

"Mr. Barnes, take heed." The vicar's usual placid manner was overcome by impatience. "That book is two hundred years old."

Jacob hurried to support the text he had upset, before it slid from the top of the vicar's desk. He looked down at the book's spine. *Actes and Monuments.* John Foxe's Book of Martyrs. It must have been a later edition if it was only two hundred years old. Still. It was impressive their small seaside vicarage held such a book in its library.

"I am sorry, Mr. Spratt. My thoughts went wandering." Jacob put Foxe's book upon its stack again. "May I shelve these for you?"

"Yes, yes." Mr. Spratt waved Jacob toward the bookshelves. Though the top of the old man's head was devoid of hair, wisps of white still grew in a fringe over his ears. The elderly vicar would retire in three weeks' time, and Jacob would be ordained and take the position. In the interim, Jacob had helped Mr. Spratt go through the vicarage and the church, learning about the records of the parish, among other things. As he quite liked Mr. Spratt, he had also volunteered to help the old gentleman go through his personal belongings.

They were currently going through the library to determine

which of the books were part of Mr. Spratt's private collection and which belonged at the vicarage. Mr. Spratt had been the vicar for more than twenty years, so it was no surprise several of his volumes had been lost among the shelves. Most of the afternoon had passed in silence, with few comments shared between the men, the only constant sound that of the patter of rain upon the library windows.

"I do not remember if this is mine," Mr. Spratt muttered, peering through his spectacles at a particularly ancient looking book. "I studied poetry in school, but I thought I only kept the religious volumes." He handed the book to Jacob. "What do you make of it?"

"*Night Thoughts.*" Jacob opened the volume to check for a printer's stamp. "Seventeen forty-five. It is a trifle old, sir. When were you at university?"

"I finished my education in 1764." The man chuckled and rubbed at his forehead. "I shall say it is not mine. I was arrogant enough in those days to only purchase new books." He waved his hand at Jacob. "Go on and put it back in the shelves, then."

Jacob did as he was bid. "I cannot imagine you as an arrogant man, Mr. Spratt."

"It is incredible the change God can work in a man's heart in fifty years." Mr. Spratt groaned and lowered himself into the chair beside the old desk. He took off his spectacles and started to clean them. "God and a good woman. Ah, I miss her. It has been too long since my wife told me I am too high in the instep."

As Jacob had very fond memories of the vicar's late wife, that comment made him grin. "I cannot believe Mrs. Spratt was anything other than a saint of a woman. I remember her leading the children in hymns every Sunday."

"She was the very best of women." Mr. Spratt held his spectacles loosely in one hand, his eyes unfocused as he spoke. "An angel more than a saint. But you will recall, young man, that angels as often rebuked man as sang to their Maker. My Henrietta was the same. She could sing praises to heaven and then call its wrath down upon me when there was a need." He rasped a laugh and then settled his spectacles upon his nose again.

Jacob reached for another book. A roll of thunder in the distance brought his attention to the window. The skies grew dark. Were it not for the candles the men had lit earlier, even Jacob would have a difficult time making out the text printed in the books. "Mrs. Spratt? I do not think I ever heard her raise her voice to anyone."

"She did not raise her voice." Mr. Spratt picked up another book. "By the time you knew her, she'd accomplished her hardest task." He placed his free hand over his chest on the last word, clearly indicating what that work had been. "And she was a lady, true as could be. The youngest daughter of an earl, if you can believe it."

"A lady by birth? I believe that most readily, sir." Jacob remembered the woman's gentle gray eyes, the way she always had a kind word for the children. She knew all of their names. Even his, though he was surrounded on all sides by younger and older siblings. She never failed to greet him by name and ask after his studies or his play.

Mr. Spratt leaned back in his chair. "Believe it all. Henrietta and I were friends as children, you see. No one knew me better than she did. After I was ordained, I went about searching for a wife. I had a fine house all set up. On her father's land. It was a large parish, with one of those grand Elizabethan churches. My living was better than most."

Jacob shelved another book and paused, his hand still upon the shelf.

"I thought myself quite the catch," Mr. Spratt added, folding his hands over his middle. "And when I went parading myself about in drawing rooms, Lady Henrietta was nearly always there, watching me with those stormy eyes of hers. She let weeks go by before she spoke her mind. I will never forget it. 'Percival Spratt,' said she, 'you are no better than a peacock.' She told me I strutted about in my smock as though I expected the ladies of our county to fall at my feet and beg for the position of wife."

Jacob could not help the laughter that burst out of him, but he quickly covered it with a cough. Picturing Mr. Spratt as a young man was difficult, and imagining the wrinkled vicar before him *strutting* even more so.

Mr. Spratt took no offense. His lips turned upward, in fact.

"She was right. Though it stung to hear it. I had always admired her, you see. I knew her to be a good woman, a lady of intelligence. That she would say such a thing to me! I admired her more for it. In time, I came to realize we were a perfect match. Henrietta lifted my soul as much as she helped me keep my pride in check." His expression softened along with his voice. "And she was my very dearest friend. I could speak with her for hours, about anything."

Given Jacob's present difficulty with obtaining a wife, seeing the evidence of another man's joy proved both bitter and sweet. "It sounds as though you married the perfect woman, Mr. Spratt."

"Very much so." Mr. Spratt opened his eyes again and took up another book. "Have you given much thought to marriage, Mr. Barnes?"

"A great deal of thought, actually." Jacob went to the mantel where a clock rested and checked the time. Five o'clock. "I thought I had settled on a young lady, but I am beginning to wonder if we would suit after all."

A shuffling sound made him aware Mr. Spratt had stood, then the old man approached him. "It will happen from time to time. Being wrong." Mr. Spratt leaned closer to inspect the clock. "Ah, so late? And the rain has not stopped. Will you take dinner with me tonight, Mr. Barnes?"

Jacob did not bother to hide his pleasure at receiving the invitation. "Of course, sir." He knew well that the vicar spent many evenings alone, with no one but his butler to wait upon him. The old man's loneliness likely accounted for his retirement more than his age. When Mr. Spratt left, he would go to a daughter with whom he anticipated spending many merry hours, in company with grandchildren and great-grandchildren.

"Excellent. Let us put off this work for a time." Mr. Spratt patted Jacob on the arm and went to the door connecting the library to the parlor. Jacob followed. "Are you content with the vicarage? It is not as large as the house you were brought up in."

"It is not, sir, but I did not expect such when I decided upon the profession." Jacob came fully into the comfortable room, only half the size of his mother's favored sitting room. "It is a beautiful house, just the same. I am honored to be its keeper for a time."

"Very good." Mr. Spratt sat in a well-worn red chair, the nearest to the fire. "We loved it, Henrietta and myself. All our children were grown and away when we came here, so the house suited us well. Still, it has four bedrooms. Enough to start a family, if you ever find the right young miss."

Jacob settled on one end of the couch. "It will happen eventually. There are any number of suitable young ladies in the parish, after all."

"That sounded more like a lament than a hopeful statement." Mr. Spratt fixed him with a stern frown. "A man of your position and age ought to be more enthusiastic about such a pursuit, unless the first woman you mentioned left you with a broken heart. But you do not strike me as one greatly disappointed in love."

"No. I don't suppose that fits." A roll of thunder punctuated his words, the boom directly above them. Jacob started when a second crash overwhelmed the first. His eyes turned to the ceiling and his heart slammed against his breast at the exact moment a third crack sounded. "The storm is upon us, it would seem."

"Indeed. Not unusual at this time of year." Mr. Spratt turned to the table at his side, where a box rested. He opened it and took out a long-stemmed clay pipe, a box of tobacco, and began to stuff it. "So your lady did not break your heart? Well then. You must not yet be deeply in love with her."

The sudden return to that topic, and Mr. Spratt's pronouncement, startled Jacob nearly as much as the thunder had. Jacob stared at the vicar for several moments, until the man had his pipe lit, before he made his answer.

Wasn't he in love? Yes, he had enjoyed the idea of marrying Hope, had imagined what it would be like for some time. And it had hurt when she announced her plans to leave, taking away his opportunity to court her properly.

He had been hurt, then angry that all his plans had been frustrated.

Yet nothing had permanently broken inside him. If he had loved

Hope, wouldn't the hurt have lasted longer? And perhaps his passing idea to ride after her, to tell her what he wished for them, would have led to action. Instead he let her go, somewhat spitefully, with the thought she would fail at her act eventually and be brought back in shame.

Had he even worried over her properly?

"Perhaps I was not deeply in love." He admitted it aloud, to see how the words felt. Were they true?

The tension that had been growing in his heart and mind for the last several days eased enough for him to feel it, to let out a relieved breath. If he did not love Hope, then her going left him intact, heart and all.

"Good. Now go about finding someone you do love, with complete honesty and passion. Life is too short to spend it with someone you merely admire, whose faults you tolerate, and whose good points are a minor comfort." Mr. Spratt pointed the stem of his pipe at Jacob. "I've heard people from my generation call it a shame that so many marry for love these days. I say it is a fine thing. Be practical, by all means, but be passionate when possible." He put the pipe back in his mouth and puffed a few times. "Find a companion of the heart, Mr. Barnes, and you will find joy the rest of your days."

Although Jacob had never thought the vicar a romantic, he could not deny the way the old man's advice settled within him. The words circled about in his mind and distracted his thoughts for the rest of the evening.

A companion of the heart. Where might one find such a thing? And how soon ought he to start searching?

CHAPTER 11

O n the fifth day of Grace's deception, the morning post arrived with an invitation to dine at Sir Isaac's home the following evening. "A small dinner party," her father said after reading the card. "I cannot imagine how Sir Isaac gets on in that tumbledown manor of his. All alone now that his sister married." He handed the invitation to Grace across the breakfast table. "We will go, most certainly."

"Yes, Papa. Jacob and I were discussing how lonely it must be for Isaac." She read the brief script, obviously in Isaac's own hand. Many in their social circle had valued the handsome baronet as a guest at their tables, even though he was something of a flirt. Then Isaac went away to war.

"I suppose coming home after so many years he has a great deal of work to busy himself." Papa flicked open his news sheets. "And untangling that mess with his heir after the declaration of his death did not help matters."

"I imagine not." Grace lowered the card to the table and thrust another bite of Hope's favored breakfast into her mouth. She had no intention of giving Cook any reason to suspect her again.

Grace, along with everyone else she knew, had mourned Isaac dreadfully when the false report of his death arrived at the very end of the war. Thankfully, he appeared alive and mostly intact shortly after the news of his demise reached them.

"Have you written your brother and sisters?" Papa glanced over the edge of his paper, his spectacles in place. "Grace became an excellent correspondent with them, and they shall miss her letters. I will send a note of my own with yours."

Ducking her head, Grace pressed her napkin to her lips and rose. "I have not written yet, Papa, but I shall see to it this afternoon. If you will excuse me, I have more baskets to deliver today." Sudden nervousness compelled her to move; she did not know how well her father knew her handwriting. Would he at once recognize it differed from Hope's?

"More baskets? Hm. Yes. Good morning to you, Hope."

"Thank you, Papa." She darted forward to give him a kiss upon the cheek before hurrying away. She retrieved gloves, bonnet, and shawl before applying to the kitchens, where Cook had two baskets waiting for her. Apparently, her attempt to bungle everything had not impressed anyone. She hid her amusement as she ordered the baskets to be loaded in the dogcart.

In order to keep up appearances, she had to travel to the vicarage before taking her baskets where they belonged. The Wrights were expecting a new babe any day. Mr. and Mrs. Harper, an elderly couple who mended the nets of fishermen for their income, especially loved Cook's soft bread. But Hope knew nothing of those families and their needs.

Grace gritted her teeth. Everything about her ruse had turned complicated as soon as her father ended her imprisonment at home. Sulking in Hope's bedroom, while dull, would have been much easier.

A groom followed behind Esther, mounted on one of the carriage horses. He kept a respectful distance, for which she was grateful. She had no wish to make polite conversation while ruminating upon her difficulties.

Baskets to deliver to friends while acting as no more than a distant neighbor, a letter to write in another's style, and a dinner party to attend combined to give Grace a headache. Hope's note with word of her departure could not come soon enough.

She came to the vicarage at last. It was a large cottage, built at least three decades past, and nestled back from the road in a grove of oaks. If one walked directly through the house and out the rear door, an easy ramble of a few minutes would bring that person to a hill overlooking the sea.

After the groom assisted her in climbing down from the cart, Grace took a moment to tuck a few curls back into her bonnet. Hope's preferred way of dressing her hair, with frills and curls aplenty, was not at all practical for such an errand as this. Yet what was she to do? Insist Susan do her hair in Grace's usual manner? Pretending to be someone else was tiresome.

The door to the vicarage opened nearly the same moment she raised her hand to knock. Startled, she took a step back when she realized the person on the other side was neither the vicar nor his servant.

"Jacob." She blurted his name, then bit her bottom lip.

"Miss Everly." His formal tone gave her pause, but he spoke before she might question him. "I saw you come down the lane. Mr. Spratt said you are to take baskets to a few of our neighbors?"

"Yes." Grace tucked one hand behind her back, as she had when caught in mischief as a child. Jacob certainly stared at her as though she had done something which merited greater scrutiny than normal.

Though Jacob opened his mouth to make a response, Mr. Spratt's voice was the next she heard.

"Ah, Miss Everly. I am glad you have a fine morning for your ride." Jacob stepped aside, revealing the elderly vicar standing a pace behind him.

"It is a very fine day, Mr. Spratt." Grace met the kindly smile of the vicar with one of her own. "I hope this weather finds you well, sir."

"It does indeed. I came home from my own morning walk but moments ago. Yet I fear I ventured too far in my enjoyment of the day. This old body does not get around as easily as it once did." He lowered his head a trifle and released a tired sigh. "I am afraid I cannot accompany you as I did last time."

That considerably lifted Grace's spirits. Being observed by a man who had known her and Hope since infancy, and lying about who she was under the nose of the vicar, had made her previous visit almost impossible to bear.

"That is a shame, Mr. Spratt." Did she sound sorrowful enough? Likely not. And surely there would be some great, eternal penalty for deceiving a man of God. Yet how could she do otherwise? Switching places with Hope, accepting her father's sentence to sail far from home, had been out of the question.

"I think it best that Mr. Barnes go with you." Mr. Spratt came forward and put his hand to Jacob's arm. "It will be his place to make such visits in the near future, and he knows the business well enough."

Jacob's eyes bulged a moment, then went back to normal as he made his hasty agreement. "Indeed, Miss Everly, I would be delighted to accompany you. But are you certain you can do without me this morning, Mr. Spratt? I have only just arrived, after all, and we have not done any work."

"The work of packing up an old man's things is not nearly as important as seeing to the hungry and weary in our congregation, Mr. Barnes." The vicar had perhaps been taller than Jacob's height, a couple of decades ago, but stooped as he was now, he had to peer upward into the younger man's eyes. "This lady needs your assistance more than I do, at least at present."

Jacob's green eyes met hers, the color darkening as he stared at her. "Of course, Mr. Spratt. If Miss Everly has no objections."

What could she say to that? Although his reluctance to be near her made her tender feelings for him more bruised, Grace laced her words with cheer. "I would be most grateful for your company, Mr. Barnes."

"Excellent. You young people go on about the Lord's business." He nudged Jacob out the door. "Report back when you are finished with the visits." Then the vicar snapped the door shut, almost as though he could not wait to be rid of them.

Jacob glared at the door as though offended by it, then he turned toward Grace. She stiffened, prepared to receive a cool glare or disapproving frown. She did not give him the chance to speak, stumbling over her words in her haste to bring peace between them.

"I am sorry I did not bid you farewell properly when we rode yesterday," she said. "I know we did not finish our discussion. There is no excuse for my behavior. I—"

His hand closed around her upper arm, his grasp warm and firm. "Grace." He said her name quietly, nearly in a whisper. "It is not necessary to apologize. I know I caused offense with my words about your sister. I owe you the apology."

Grace pulled away, taking a step back from him and his distracting touch. Could she not be offended for her own sake? Must every conversation be about Hope?

"You do not owe me any such thing." She spoke stiffly. "I have already forgotten everything you said." Yet another lie she must tell. "We ought to start on our errand, Jacob."

His brow wrinkled. "It's obvious you are put out with me, Grace. I wish to make amends. How shall it be done?"

"Must you be so difficult?" she asked, puffing out an exasperated breath before turning. The groom remained with his horse, too distant to hear their conversation but near enough for propriety's sake.

Jacob made an amused sort of sound in the back of his throat. "Difficult? I am attempting to put our friendship back on even ground."

Grace gestured to the cart. "Come along, then. Help me deliver these baskets." She hurried to climb up, hoping he would not offer his assistance. But Jacob's nature prohibited such an oversight, and he was there, holding her elbow as she stepped up onto the driver's bench. Then he walked around the front of the pony, giving the shaggy little animal a thoughtful pat on the head, before swinging up beside her onto the narrow bench.

He sat too close for her immediate comfort. Grace's cheeks

warmed as she busied herself with the reins. They did not have far to go, but riding would see them to the Harpers' little house by the sea faster than walking with baskets in arms.

For several minutes they traveled without speaking, Jacob's elbow brushing against her forearm as she flicked the reins. He broke their tenuous silence first.

"Did you receive an invitation to dine with Isaac tomorrow evening?"

Speaking of another friend was a far safer topic than any she currently had on her mind. Grace snatched the subject up eagerly. "Yes, my father and I will both attend. Will your family be there?"

"Mother, Matthew, myself, Elizabeth, and Mary." Jacob listed all his family at home and leaned back, raising his face and closing his eyes against the morning sun. "It will be a cramped ride in the carriage if Matthew does not wish to ride."

"Why can you not ride?"

"The hunter belongs to Matthew," he reminded her, raising one shoulder in a shrug. "It would be presumptuous of me to use him if Matthew chose not to. At the moment, I can ride him all I wish when I know Matthew is seeing to estate business or is out with the carriage visiting Mrs. Muir."

Grace hoped the eldest Mr. Barnes would realize his brother needed a horse and offer one to him. Once Jacob became a vicar, his funds would not allow for too many expenditures, and he certainly did not think himself equal to affording a horse at present.

"I suppose that makes sense," she admitted. "At least it is not a very far distance. I wonder if Isaac retained his French cook when he went to the Continent? I do not think I have ever heard."

For a few minutes, they spoke of the staff at Fox Hall and how busy Isaac must have been when he returned, trying to see to everything at once. Their conversation turned to their other friend, Silas, and his bride.

"I do hope Esther is enjoying herself in London," Grace said during a lull in their conversation. "She seemed eager to go, though I cannot imagine why."

"Can you not?" Jacob opened one eye, tilting to one side the better to fix her with his incredulous stare. "I understand you not wishing to travel over the ocean, but have you no desire to tramp down London's fine streets?"

"None at all," she said airily. "The few times I have been to London I have not been impressed. The city is filthy, the streets crowded, the parties loud, and neighbors far too interested in gossip. I cannot understand the appeal of it."

The Harpers' cottage, which really was more like a stone hovel, came into view, skulking back into a hillside.

"I confess, I have no great desire to spend my time in London. But Oxford—I could have spent ten more years there and never had enough of that charming town." Jacob climbed down from the cart and came around to lift her down, his hands going to her waist rather than reaching for her hand.

She hesitated before allowing him to assist in such a way. The more familiar manner, one she thought he must have perfected while helping his younger sisters in and out of wheeled conveyances, allowed her feet to land more lightly upon the ground than if he had taken her hand for her to hop from her seat. Her hands fell quite naturally to his arms, and she felt the strength in them as he lowered her to the ground.

"I think you would like Oxford," Jacob said, staring down into her eyes, his hands still upon her waist. "It is a charming old town, and far less clamorous than London."

Grace's heart tripped along at a faster pace than necessary. He stood so near, the weight of his hands both inviting and somehow familiar. "Perhaps I will visit someday, given how highly you recommend it."

A horse's snort reminded Grace of the groom, their chaperone, and she stepped away. The moment she put distance between them, his hands falling from her waist, the air between them cooled. Still, her cheeks remained abominably hot. Jacob fetched the smaller of the two baskets from the rear of her cart. Hopefully he didn't see her blush.

The path to the Harpers' door consisted of well-packed dirt, and Mrs. Harper had taken pains to line the way with tiny white flowers.

Mr. Harper had painted the door a deep blue, giving the cottage another bit of cheer. Regardless of their age and humble circumstances, the two lived most happily together from what Grace could tell.

Basket in hand, Jacob led the way to the door. He knocked, and voices drifted through the old wood.

"Did someone knock?" asked Mr. Harper, voice raised.

"Yes, I think they must've." Mrs. Harper fairly shouted her reply.

Grace caught Jacob's grin and returned it.

Several moments went by before the door opened, Mr. Harper standing there, stooped over and smiling. "Ah, good mornin' Miss Grace."

She blanched and opened her mouth to correct him, to announce herself as Hope. But why bother? The Harpers wouldn't go about saying the wrong twin remained at home, as they likely had no idea either sister had left the county. Her lips closed over the denial of her identity and she curtsied instead.

"And the future vicar. Come in, come in." Mr. Harper allowed them inside and shuffled to the table where his wife sat, a net spread out before her on their old table. With a bit of thin rope in her wrinkled hands, she deftly finished off a knot in the mesh before standing and making her curtsy.

"Ah, Miss Grace and Mr. Barnes. A fine morning it is to bring such kind guests to us. Won't you sit for a moment? Might I offer you some cider?"

"You may, Mrs. Harper, but only if you allow me to take your place at the nets." Jacob bowed and slipped into her seat before she could say otherwise. "I have not forgotten your lessons." After he dropped his hat upon the table he took up more of her rope and started looping it through the mesh.

The old lady laughed and waved her hands at him. "Oh, you are a quick one. Mind your sider knots, lad." She looked to Grace. "And you, Miss Grace?"

As the cider had come from the Everly orchards, Grace knew it would be worth partaking. "Please, Mrs. Harper." She settled her basket on the small hutch that was sideboard and pantry both, then turned her attention to Mr. Harper. He whittled by the fire rather than work on the net. "What is that you work on, sir?" Though the pair were hard of hearing, Grace had to enunciate her words with a little more force than normal to be understood.

"Ah, nothin' of much prettiness, miss. Here, have a look if ye like." He held up the figure and she took it with delicacy. The wood, while still rough, clearly depicted two little birds huddled next to each other, one with a wing stretched over the other. "This is beautiful, Mr. Harper."

"Thank ye. They be two turtledoves." He took them back from her. "I've been makin' it as a present for someone. Not sure who yet. S'pose the next person of our acquaintance to wed."

Mrs. Harper shook her head with a fond smile deepening the wrinkles of her face. "He gives away most everything he makes. Everyone hereabouts has one of his little creatures." She came over with tin mugs full of cider, setting one before Jacob as she passed him. "Here, miss. It's really fine cider. Your father's crops did well last year."

"He will be glad to know you are enjoying it." Grace sipped at the drink, relieved to find it had been mixed with something less strong, perhaps dandelion tea.

Waving the large needle in the air, Jacob gestured to his work. "How is this, madam? Is it done to your satisfaction?"

"Likely not," Mrs. Harper answered with an amused sniff. "You cannot possibly know what you are about. You weren't born to the work." She came closer to him and peered at the net. "So you remembered your knots, but here." She reached out and with a quick pull had his rope dangling. "A good knot is a sure knot, Mr. Barnes."

His eyebrows shot up and his mouth dropped open as he stared at his work undone. Grace could not help the laugh that escaped her, though she swiftly covered her mouth and turned away. Mr. Harper's dim gray eyes were dancing with equal amusement to hers.

"Tell me, Mr. Barnes," the old man said, "are ye as handy with sermons as ye're netting?" He rested his gnarled brown hand on his knee and leaned forward. "There's a great deal of eagerness in Aldersy as we all wait to hear from ye."

Grace watched Jacob give his seat to the old fishwife. He took up his cider in one hand and came to stand next to her. "I should hope I'm better at my trade than I am at yours. Will you come and let me know how you judge? I make my first sermon the third Sunday from now."

"So soon? Aye, we'll be there."

"Unless it rains," his wife put in from where she sat. "Mr. Harper's rheumatism is awful when the sky's falling."

Mr. Harper straightened his stooped posture. "Can't let a little thing like a sore knee put me off hearin' from the new vicar."

The two of them argued the matter, she reminding him how it would be if his leg pained him and he insisting he would be just fine. Their words had the sound of an old argument between them, yet each point was made without heat and the two were smiling across the room at each other like young lovers instead of an aged couple.

Warmth tickled Grace's ear when Jacob leaned down to murmur, "We could leave now and they would never notice we were gone." She covered her mouth to hide her smile, then shot him a glare.

"Manners, vicar."

He chuckled and interrupted the argument in a friendly manner. "I think we must give way to Mrs. Harper's concerns, sir. I would not like you to displease her for one of my sermons. She would likely come to hold me in contempt."

Laughter trickled from the old woman, soft and light. "Never, lad. Though if you touch my nets again, it will be a near thing."

Jacob blushed to the tips of his ears and Grace, taking pity on him, laced her arm through his. "Thank you so much for the visit, Mrs. Harper. Mr. Harper. We have enjoyed the time with you so much."

Mr. Harper leveraged himself to his feet with a grunt. "Ye are a good girl, Miss Grace, to come lookin' in on us. And Mr. Barnes. Though I must tell ye, sir, that your visit is more enjoyable when ye come with this one." Then he winked, bold as brass. "Best make it a habit if ye can."

Grace's cheeks burned, but she confined herself to bidding the woman of the house farewell before Mr. Harper let them out the front door. The cool breeze brushed against her face, granting her some relief.

The groom remained at the road, letting his unmounted horse chew up the long grasses lining the way.

"They're good people," Jacob said, coming along beside her. "It has been too long since I visited."

Grace focused her attention on that idea rather than dwell on any more uncomfortable thoughts. "I did not know you had ever been before. It took me by surprise to see you so familiar to them." As they walked to the cart she nudged his arm gently with hers. "When did you visit last?"

Jacob tucked his hands behind his back and turned his face into the breeze. "About a month ago, with Mr. Spratt. He took me around to all the cottagers and tenants he could think of to introduce me as his replacement." A lock of his dark blond hair fell into his face and he combed it back with his fingers. "Is the wind picking up?" he asked, putting his hat upon his head once more.

"Not enough to worry over." Grace came to the cart and rushed inelegantly to climb up without Jacob's help. "And the Wrights do not live far."

"Half a mile down the road, if I remember correctly." Jacob went to his side and stepped up. "What made you think of them? Mr. Wright is employed at Inglewood, is he not?"

"Yes, but they are expecting a child soon, and Esther is away or else I am certain she would make this visit." Grace took up the reins and with a gentle slap of leather to the pony's back they were on their way once more. "As this is their third child and Mrs. Wright certainly knows what she is doing, they will appreciate a few little things to make the time go more easily."

Jacob folded his arms before him and angled his body enough so he could look at her fully. "You are most thoughtful, Grace."

She had no wish to color under his praise, mild as it might be. Grace tilted her chin upward. His words meant very little, of that she assured herself. "I have always liked visiting with my neighbors. That is all."

"Indeed? For what purpose?" He lifted one of his eyebrows at her, and a corner of his mouth twitched upward as well. "For the local gossip?"

"Why else? I especially enjoy hearing all the tittle-tattle about the new vicar." Why had she said that? Grace pressed her lips together tightly and busied herself with the reins to avoid looking at him. She was ill-equipped to tease and flirt. Those were Hope's tools, not Grace's.

"I hear he is a tiresome fellow." Jacob tilted his hat back upon his head. "All his sermons shall be dull and his prayer-making long and drawn out. Half the parishioners will fall into a stupor and the other half will call for his resignation." He released a deep, dramatic sigh.

"Never," she said firmly. "Unless he reads directly from a book. I understand he is not a very great reader. Lacks the voice for it." Her attempt to tease surprised her, and when Jacob laughed it took her a moment to join in his amusement. She had not heard him laugh at all since he discovered it was she and not her sister who remained at home. Perhaps he might one day overcome his disappointment.

Or else he had cheered himself by thinking on Hope's return in a year's time.

Jacob corrected his posture, and his hat. "Thank you for that, Grace. I will always have you to keep me humble, I hope."

She nearly promised that he might. Except Grace knew, before long, it would no longer be her place to speak to Jacob in such a manner. She answered more circumspectly. "I am certain you will do well enough without me to tease you." She slowed the horses before the Inglewood tenant cottages. "There is a great deal of interest in what subject you will choose for your first sermon. It will set the entire path for your time as a vicar."

"I have given it a great deal of thought," he admitted as he swung down.

With the memory of his hands on her waist, Grace tried to lower herself to the ground before he could touch her again. Unfortunately, as one foot hit upon the dirt, her hand slipped from its hold on the seat and she fell backward, directly into his chest.

Jacob caught her around the shoulders and they both stumbled backward, but he acted quickly enough, pushing forward again, to settle Grace firmly upon her feet.

He kept a firm hold upon her.

"Are you unharmed?" Jacob asked, bending down to her ear as he had in the Harpers' cottage. She nodded, mutely. "Wait next time," he said softly, giving her shoulders a gentle squeeze. "Let me help you."

Her heart fell back into its normal rhythm, though it ached as he let her go to fetch the basket.

Why, after years of successfully burying her feelings for Jacob, was she so undone by such a simple thing as his touch? For so long she had kept her heart still in his presence, had betrayed nothing of her feelings, and Grace would not risk their friendship now. Not when she needed his support, his care.

Perhaps if Hope had been present, Grace needn't have struggled. Hope had been the perfect buffer, a barrier wall to combat the rising tide of Grace's admiration, without even realizing how she protected them all. If Grace gave a hint to how she felt, it might make things awkward for Jacob, who preferred Hope. He had seemed amenable to the idea of courting her when she returned, if the gossip died away.

Grace mulled this over in her mind as she followed him to the tenant house door. She stood mutely by his side as he knocked, eyeing his profile discreetly.

What did Hope have that Grace lacked? How could Jacob not see, not understand, that Hope would never be the complacent wife of a vicar?

As Hope's sister, what was her duty to them both? She could not encourage Jacob, with his heart set upon her sister. Not when she knew how wrong they were for each other. Hope had never said anything to indicate she cared for Jacob as more than a friend. But if he approached her as a suitor, things might change.

It took a great deal of strength for Grace to get through the visit with the husband, wife, and small children of the Wright household. In every tender look the couple shared, she saw what she could not have. With the two younger children playing near their hearth, and Mrs. Wright's hand upon her child-swollen middle, the entire scene of domestic felicity was more than she could bear.

When they took their leave at last, Jacob insisting on helping her onto the cart, Grace wanted nothing more than to bid him good day. Perhaps give in to another bout of crying. But she kept a pleasant countenance, and if Jacob noticed anything amiss, he said nothing.

His thoughts were likely too occupied with Hope to pay much attention to Grace. She clung to that thought, though its barbs pierced her heart, for the remainder of their time together that afternoon.

THE DRESS GRACE wore to Sir Isaac's dinner party was one of Hope's particular favorites. The yellow satin fabric was perfectly complimented by a deep purple shawl. At least, Hope had always thought the two perfect together. For Grace's part, she much preferred softer colors to bold. Perhaps the bright colors gave her sister an added measure of confidence. Perhaps they drew the eyes of others more often, making Hope stand out as she wished.

Perhaps one of the reasons Jacob had more affection for Hope was due to her cheery wardrobe.

Grace stepped into Sir Isaac's foyer, releasing her father's arm to make her curtsy to her friend. Had she been herself, Grace would have shared a quiet smile with him before exchanging greetings. As Hope, she instead had to beam as though vying with the chandelier for brilliance.

"Sir Isaac." She imitated her sister's fond manner of speaking to their dear friend. "I am thankful you invited us, as it saved me from having to storm your home in a quest to ascertain your well-being. I have not seen you in such a long time."

Isaac grinned back at her, his spirit as adventurous as Hope's. "When one goes to war, it leaves a great many things undone at home. I am attempting to put everything to rights and I've had little time for visits. Soon, though, I should like to call upon you for one of our rambles."

"That would be delightful." She waited for her father to make his greetings to the host. Then she looped her arm through Papa's and walked into the parlor off the dining room. Isaac's mother had been the last woman to decorate the house, which meant a great many of the rooms were out of date in terms of fashion. The familiar pink and gold furnishings did something to steady Grace's nerves, however, so she could not think ill of them.

Mr. and Mrs. Parr were present, with their daughter, Miss Bettina Parr, newly come out. Although not part of Miss Parr's set, to see another young lady present gave Grace leave to relax. In fact, since Miss Parr did not know Grace or Hope particularly well, that gave Grace more room to make mistakes.

She had barely exchanged greetings with the Parrs when the Barnes entered the room, followed by Isaac. Mrs. Barnes, tall and stately, floated gracefully into the room. Matthew Barnes, the head of the family, escorted his mother with easy confidence. Then came Miss Elizabeth Barnes on Jacob's arm, her sister Mary behind them.

Jacob. He cut a fine figure in his dark blue waistcoat, a pristine white cravat at his throat. When she met his eyes, he winked.

Her heart stammered and stuttered, though her mind immediately berated it. The wink was naught more than a friendly offer of support, meant to bolster her confidence. Still, she had to turn away to keep her composure.

Nothing about the ruse she acted out met with Jacob's approval. Not really. Believing that Hope had orchestrated the entire switch was the only reason he had ceased to speak against the plan. Had he known Grace was behind it, he surely wouldn't look upon her with any measure of friendliness or offer support.

Isaac drew Matthew and Jacob into conversation, speaking with them on a matter regarding the vicarage. Mrs. Barnes drifted away from her sons, but rather than go to the other matron in the room, she came across the carpet to where Grace stood with her father.

"Mr. Everly, Miss Everly, I am delighted to see you both. I understand Mrs. Everly is away visiting her sister?" She looked from one to the other with a genteel smile. The two women had been friends for many years. "You must miss her, given Miss Grace's absence, and the children away at school."

"We do, Mrs. Barnes." Papa sighed deeply. "The house is far too quiet of late. Occasionally, I fancy stomping through the passageways merely to make some noise."

"Ah, I understand. I have felt that way a time or two myself. It is somewhat distressing to know Jacob will be out of our home soon, though I know he looks forward to taking up his place at the vicarage."

Grace's eyes drifted to where Jacob stood, admiring the broad grin he wore as he spoke with animation to his brother and Isaac. He said something she could not hear and the two men laughed. Jacob's head turned in her direction and she swiftly dropped her gaze, as she had been doing for months, so he would not know she gave him any more attention than she ought.

When she attempted to return her focus to Mrs. Barnes, her gaze collided with the older woman's piercing stare. Mrs. Barnes raised an eyebrow at her. "And you, Miss Everly. Do you miss your sister?"

"Terr—" She broke off and cleared her throat when her voice emerged hoarse. "Yes. Terribly."

"Hope has born the separation better than I thought she might." Pride tinted Papa's words.

Guilt wormed its way further into her heart. All that pride would evaporate the moment he knew the truth. Yet she would not tell him until she absolutely must. She would not take Hope's place aboard that ship, and until she knew her sister successfully made it out of port, she mustn't say anything.

The butler came into the room, announcing dinner. The men and women fell into place, each by order of importance, by marital state, by age. Grace went before the other unmarried misses, on Mr. Parr's arm. Jacob took up the rear with Miss Parr, as he was the only unmarried and unlanded gentleman in the party. When everyone took their chairs, the foot of the table unoccupied, Grace found herself seated directly across from Jacob.

He shared a friendly smile she had no choice but to return, and then the soup was served. Seated between Mr. Barnes and Mr. King, Grace conversed with them on the subject of horses. Though she did not know as much as Hope about the beasts, she held her own well enough.

"I have heard you are a fine horsewoman, Miss Everly." Mr. King addressed her with polite interest. "Sir Isaac is most adamant that we go riding together while I am visiting."

"Ah, now there is a dangerous thing," Matthew Barnes said at her other side. "Miss Everly has had the most unfortunate luck in her races of late. The last resulted in an injury."

Mr. King's eyes widened. "I am sorry to hear that, Miss Everly."

"Oh, it is not as terrible as it sounds," Miss Parr said from across the table, soup spoon held delicately. "The local rake was the injured party."

Grace spoke up quickly, trying to infuse her words with humor. "I think that makes it sound rather worse than before, Miss Parr."

"The whole of the story," Miss Barnes said from Mr. King's other side, "is quite diverting. Miss Everly and her sister, Miss Grace, raced the son and daughter of a marquess, in phaetons pulled by ponies." She covered her smirk with her fingertips.

"Ah, that does sound like an interesting tale." Mr. King leaned toward Grace, over the arm of his chair. "And the gentleman, I assume, is still alive to tell his version?"

Jacob at last entered the conversation, firm voice carrying across the table. "Lord Neil is well enough."

Miss Parr giggled and glanced at Jacob from the corner of her eye. "Mr. Jacob Barnes does not particularly care for Lord Neil."

From up the table, Sir Isaac spoke, his manner sardonic. "Lord Neil never ran in our circle, and none of us wished him ill. Still. I have heard he is healing well and perhaps his injury will prove instructive to him."

A quick glance in Papa's direction gave Grace every reason to attempt to make herself smaller. He glared at his soup in as fierce a manner as he had glared at Grace when he learned of the accident. He said nothing, and though Grace watched him, no one else seemed inclined to seek his opinion on the matter.

"I understood it was Lady Olivia who initiated the race." Mrs. Parr joined the conversation, her tone mild. "I cannot approve of young ladies behaving in such a manner. I hope the accident curbs the desire for gently bred women to take part in such sport. It is neither safe nor seemly."

"Miss Everly's sister was with her," Mr. King said, coming back to that point. "I have yet to meet her. Is she not yet out?"

"Grace is Miss Everly's twin." Miss Parr's knowing smirk made her far less likable than Grace had previous supposed. "A very quiet young lady."

Isaac put down his spoon. "Very quiet, but a particular friend of mine." Something like a warning flashed in his eyes at Miss Parr, and her superior look dimmed. "Miss Grace has left us all behind to have an adventure. She is on her way to the West Indies with friends."

"Indeed? I have always wanted to travel. She must be an adventurous young lady." Mr. King's pleasant expression fell when he saw the knowing smirk of Miss Parr return. But it was not the self-important young woman who elected to correct him.

It was Grace's own father.

"Adventurous? Not Grace." Papa leaned back enough to allow the footman to take his bowl and lay down a dish with the next course. "My dear girl has no liking for exploration or excitement. It is the wish of her mother and myself that she will gain some spirit from her journey. Hope is our adventurer." He nodded to Grace and everyone at the table turned to study her, as though they had never seen her before. All except Jacob. He kept his eyes upon the dish in front of him.

What would Hope do with so many stares upon her? She certainly would not quell beneath the curious eyes of her neighbors. No. She would sit taller, tilt her chin up, and dare them all to disapprove of her. Grace tried. Assuming a stiff posture, and the haughty expression she had seen her sister wear on any number of occasions, she did her utmost to challenge them to speak ill of her.

"Poor, dear Grace." Mrs. Barnes met Grace's eyes with a heaviness in her own. "It will not be easy for her to be so far from home." Her eyes flicked to Jacob, then she turned her attention to her meal, slicing her meat delicately.

"No, it will not be easy," Papa agreed. "But I think it necessary. The Carlburys will keep her safe. What better way for a young person to learn about the world than to step out into it?"

He and Mama rarely left the familiarity of their lands and the village. How could he wish for her, the child who shared his love of their home to such a degree, to go far from it?

Grace needed to speak. Silence did not suit Hope. Not when opinions of her character and her sister's were bandied about so easily at a dinner table. Contradicting her father in front of their neighbors would prove unwise, however.

The irritating Miss Parr spoke again, after sipping from her cup of wine. Hopefully it was well-watered, the girl hardly seemed mature enough to step out of the school room. "We are lucky, Mr. King, that you have come while the adventurous Everly is at home and her sister gone away to learn to be more interesting."

"Bettina," her father said, the warning low from his place at the other end of the table. His daughter flushed and lowered her cup to the table.

Learn to be more interesting? What a horrid thing to say. Grace did not go about over-turning carriages like her sister, or pushing irritating gentlemen into ponds, or climbing up trees to fetch lost kites, but did that relegate her to the position of a wallflower?

She held to the arm of her chair, squeezing the wood tightly enough she might see the whorls of it in her hand if she looked closely.

Mr. King started talking again and everyone laughed. Grace did not pay enough attention to know why.

Their neighbors did not regard her as highly as they did Hope. Though she and Hope were nearly inseparable, attending every public and private function with each other, Grace had noticed the enthusiasm with which people always greeted her twin. Especially their friends and the younger set. Hope knew how to play every game, knew the steps to every dance, and told entertaining stories.

What did Grace do, but stand in her sister's shadow and play the pianoforte? Sometimes she held conversations, quietly and politely, with the matrons. She made certain to include those young and old who stood on the outskirts of the festivities, like herself.

Stabbing at the lamb on her plate, Grace struggled to remain silent. Had she become a wallflower without realizing it? Did no one think of her when they wished for entertainment? How would they change their opinions if they knew it was always Grace who planned Hope's popular parties and picnics?

The thoughts tumbled about in her head, mingling with her guilt. What would they say if they knew it was Grace and not Hope in their midst? Perhaps they would make excuses. They might even pay her a compliment of some kind, the polite sort of thing one says to just about anyone.

"Miss Everly."

Grace raised her gaze and found Jacob watching her, his eyebrows drawn tightly together. Forcing her emotion back, she gave him her attention as best she could. "Yes, Mr. Barnes?"

Jacob pressed his lips tightly together a moment, then hurried on. "Perhaps you might arrange one of your famous picnics while Mr. King is visiting?" He winced after the words, then cleared his throat. "The orchards are perfect for such activities at this time of year."

"I do love a picnic," Miss Parr said, bouncing once in her seat. Had no one taught the girl to avoid putting herself forward in such a manner? It was not as though Grace had extended an invitation. If she did, she must now include the young woman. Drat Jacob, bringing up such an idea.

"I am not certain. Papa, what do you think?" Grace turned to her father, hoping he would recall his anger with Hope and tactfully refuse the request. Hope was to be punished, after all, for her willfulness and inability to think her actions through. Gifting her with a picnic would be preposterous—

Without much of a pause, her father nodded once. Most firmly.

"Splendid idea. You ought to organize a picnic. A most excellent way to pass the time before your mother returns, and the children come home for the holiday."

"Yes, Papa." She swallowed her dismay and replaced it with a cheerful grin. "This will be lovely. And I will need everyone's help to plan it, after dinner."

"A glorious idea," Sir Isaac said, raising his cup as though to toast her. "You always put on the best entertainments, Miss Everly. I remember the last party of yours I attended, before I purchased my commission."

Grace barely listened as he described an adventure Hope had arranged which had them traipsing all about Everly Refuge, searching for items that corresponded to riddles she handed out. Yes, the party had been Hope's idea, but Grace had written the riddles. And Hope had planned any number of picnics, but it was Grace who put together the menu and arranged the guest list.

"I will admit, I worried over the entertainment I might find in the country, but it sounds as though Miss Everly is an excellent hostess." Mr. King tipped his head to her.

"I do my best, Mr. King." Grace lifted her glass and drank as much as she dared, having nothing more intelligent to say.

Mr. Parr spoke, his blustery voice drawing attention to his end of the table. "I say, Mr. King, if you are in search of entertainment, might I offer you the use of my stream? It is the same as the Everlys' brook, but has considerably more fish in it on my property before it gets to theirs."

"You are forever saying you catch the largest fishes." Grace's father leaned back in his chair and one corner of his mouth tipped upwards. Mr. Parr and her father had always had a competitive friendship. "Given what I have pulled from my water, I cannot think it so."

"Why fish in the little streams when we have the whole of the sea?" Isaac asked. "I have been thinking of purchasing a yacht, especially for fishing trips and to make my way to London with greater ease."

"There are some beautiful boats I have seen in the Cumberland

Fleet." Mrs. Barnes leaned toward Isaac, waving her hand in the general direction of London. "Are you interested in joining any of the clubs?"

The next course was brought in amid the general conversation on the subject. Some were for the idea of a yacht, others thought them a nuisance and waste of money.

Grace, barely listening, kept an amused look upon her face. Hardly caring whether or not it appeared as false a mask as it felt. Everyone else might have put aside the idea of a picnic, but she could not so easily dismiss it.

The eldest Everly sisters had worked together on everything, and that made Hope's endeavors successful. Always, Grace had assisted her sister's plans. Grace supported her sister, and Hope made certain Grace had a say in each activity.

But no one had seen Grace, working furiously behind the curtain, putting the final touches on each detail. Then Hope pulled back the drapery and reveled in the attention Grace did not enjoy.

Hope received the praise and accolades while Grace received the gentle, pitying smiles. It had never bothered Grace before. She and Hope were a set. The accomplishments of one were celebrated by both.

Without raising her head, she peered up at Isaac. Despite his brush with death, and his missing arm, he carried on as he had before the war. He spoke pleasantly to all and laughed without reservation. Together, he and Hope had arranged many exploits, launched campaigns which put the five of the Silver Birch Society's members in harm's way and earned their parents' disapproval. Try as Grace might, she could not think of a time when Isaac praised Grace's more levelheaded nature.

Jacob sat across from her, and when she glanced in his direction, she found him staring rather bleakly at his plate. Doubtless he was thinking of Hope, too unaware of his feelings to yearn for his company as he must yearn for hers. Grace might be the one to share knowing glances with him from time to time, but it was Hope's approval he looked for.

Had it always been that way? If she could show him, prove to

Jacob she could be sociable, capable of putting people at ease, he might see she had the qualities he admired in Hope.

The picnic she arranged would need to be perfect. In fact, it needed to be the very best outing she had planned. That way, when all her friends and neighbors realized it was Grace and not Hope who had done all the work, they might pause long enough and reconsider whether they truly knew the Everly sisters at all.

CHAPTER 12

No one in the neighborhood appeared to possess the ability to truly observe another person. The previous evening, Jacob had watched, with mounting frustration, as not a soul at the dinner table had noticed something wrong with Miss Everly. Were the sisters so interchangeable to everyone else that they did not see how quietly she sat? How stiff she grew when they spoke of Grace Everly as though she was of little consequence?

He walked the dusty road to the Everly house, as early as propriety allowed, to meet with Grace. She could not be expected to organize her picnic alone, especially since it was his fault she had to plan it.

Grace's grip had tightened around her fork, her expression had turned wooden, while the people who claimed to know both sisters discussed her unobtrusive nature.

She had rarely spoken the whole evening. Yes, it was more than typical for Grace, but far less than Hope. Usually at such a dinner party, Hope would regale them with stories and keep a great deal of the attention upon herself. She thrived with all eyes upon her, while Grace contented herself in joining the audience rather than be its focus.

"How does no one else see it?" he muttered as he kicked a particularly irritating pebble out of his path. Isaac should have noticed the difference. He knew Grace and Hope nearly as well as Jacob. They had all grown up together.

Though he waited all night for a word from Isaac, watched for a look of confusion or sudden comprehension, he never saw it. Which led his mind down another disturbing path. Isaac, even with his generous attentions as host, had been distracted. Catching up on all his estate business did not seem a suitable reason for such a neglectful frame of mind, either. The war had to have altered more than Isaac's physical appearance and abilities. As his friend, and the man about to be made shepherd over the local flock of Anglicans, Jacob ought to find a way to help.

Everly Refuge, though made of somber gray stone, never failed to bring Jacob peace when he set eyes upon it. Even with his thoughts muddled, the house did its duty that morning. The deep green shutters at the windows and the fine gardens surrounding the house made it a cheerful prospect. It helped that Jacob had visited the Refuge enough to practically call it his second home.

He went to the front door and gave his customary knock, removing his hat before it even swung open.

"Good morning, Garrett." He greeted the butler with easy familiarity. "How is everything at the Refuge?" He tried to keep his tone light, as chipper as ever.

"Entirely too quiet, Mr. Barnes." Garrett took the hat and gloves away, giving Jacob barely any time to glimpse the puzzled frown the butler wore. "Miss Everly is in the upstairs parlor, organizing the picnic." Garrett disappeared without another word or backward glance.

"Thank you, Garrett," Jacob called to the butler's retreating form. With Mrs. Everly and Hope gone, and the younger children away at school, the house seemed most forlorn. Jacob quickened his steps as the silence thrummed in his ears. As unsettled as he was by his thoughts and the difficulties of his friends, the strange, empty air of the house made him irrationally uncomfortable.

He fairly vaulted up the stairway and into the hall, as though outrunning the silence was an actual possibility. The door to the parlor was shut, but he pushed it open without thought of settling his nerves first.

When he entered rather more like a hurricane than a gentleman, Grace jolted to her feet. She stared at him with wide eyes and open mouth.

"Jacob?" she asked in her customary, soft voice. A tone he had never heard from her sister. "Is something wrong?" She came three steps toward him and stopped, not quite within arm's reach, and her clear blue eyes swept him up and down with concern.

"Yes—" He cut himself off, putting a hand to the back of his neck. "I mean, no. Nothing is wrong. A bit of foolishness on my part is all." He dropped his hand and tapped his fingers against his thigh. "I am not entirely sure what came over me."

Her dark eyebrows drew together and one corner of her mouth pulled back, her confusion tempered with amusement. "After being near Isaac last night, I think it must be something catching. None of us have been ourselves lately."

"You less than anyone," he added, trying to tease her. But his words fell flat, and somehow sounded like an accusation to even his ears.

Drawing herself up, though her height was nothing impressive, Grace gave him a most indignant glare, but said nothing. She merely turned and went back to her table, sitting as she must have been when he rushed into the room. She took up her pen and dipped it into the ink.

As she had not invited him in, Jacob hovered uncertainly in the doorway. Why did it always feel as though he was wrong-footed of late? It had started when he learned Hope planned to leave on her voyage. At least that no longer stung as it had before. He could think on her being away and wish her well. After speaking with Mr. Spratt, Jacob's heart hadn't been troubled by Hope's absence.

Truly, his only present difficulty was the role he played in Grace's deception. That reminder brought him back to his purpose for arriving at such an hour. It was barely past breakfast for most households.

"I am sorry for my part in the conversation last night," he said at last.

Grace's pen stilled but she did not look up. "Your part? I cannot think of anything you said that you need apologize for."

Encouraged by even that much consideration, Jacob stepped further into the room. "I believe it is my fault you are now proving yourself with a picnic."

Her nose wrinkled as she looked up at him. Most would think that wrinkle a sign of disgust, but Jacob knew well enough it indicated her confusion.

"A picnic is hardly an imposition. I have planned dozens of them, after all."

"You have?" He took another step and tucked his hands behind him. "I thought the picnics were Hope's ideas."

"Some were." Grace stared at him as if he were spouting ridiculous nonsense. "But whether I planned an event or she did, Hope sends the invitations, then she plays the hostess. I always do everything else. That is how we divide all our projects, because people are more keen to do a thing if Hope suggests it." She went back to working on her list, completely unaware as to what her explanation had done to Jacob.

All their projects, she had said. Not just picnics and parties. All. Perhaps like the Sunday school for the village daughters, or the sewing club for the orphans of soldiers killed in the line of duty, or the lending library meant to benefit those who could not afford to purchase books of their own. Hope had voiced each of those ideas within his hearing, and Jacob assumed they had been her ideas.

Before he could decide whether or not to discover the truth, Grace sat back in her chair, laying her pen down upon her paper. "Can you think of any picnic you enjoyed in particular?"

Asking him a question regarding his opinion ought to be as good as an invitation to stay. He settled himself on a spindly-legged chair near where he stood. "There was that one where we all played games. That was so long ago, we were only children. I don't suppose that it is a helpful memory, but it is one of my best."

Grace's eyes gleamed and her lips turned upward. "Can you

imagine ladies and gentlemen running about in the gardens, having three-legged races?" The amusement in her manner turned to enthusiasm. "Oh, this is a wonderful idea. Thank you, Jacob."

"I cannot see how it helped you at all." He had to admit, though, that imagining his brother playing leapfrog, at his age, would be cause of amusement. Yet the humor in the situation fled when he noticed Grace's expression.

Grace stared at the floor, nibbling at her lower lip, her blue eyes distant.

"Is there something else troubling you?" he asked, studying the weary tilt of her head. If planning the picnic had not worried her, what did? Acting as Hope? How much longer would she have to play that role?

Grace emitted a deep sigh and the wrinkle on her nose appeared again. "Everything is changing, Jacob. I knew it must happen, but that does not mean I have to like it. Silas is married and spends part of the year in London, Isaac has not really come all the way home from the war, Hope is gone, and you are to be our vicar."

"What of you?" he asked when she did not continue her list. "How are you changing?"

The corner of her mouth tipped upward again, but it was more sardonic than amused. "I suppose I am going to have to change from a dull, quiet woman into someone more interesting. More like Hope, perhaps. Without her here to amuse and entertain, someone must take up the position." Her shoulders slumped and she lifted her pen again, rather listlessly.

Frankly, Jacob thought one Hope was enough, no matter where she might be in the world. And Grace—they needed her, too. Did she really wish her nature away? He knew of no one more kind, no one as thoughtful and gentle, as Grace Everly. When she was a child, she helped calm temper-fueled spats and found compromises in their games. Hope blew through their years together as fierce as a sailing wind. Grace twirled about them like a summer breeze, familiar and temperate.

"I cannot think you would enjoy living that way." He made

certain he spoke kindly, so she could not mistake his meaning. Her grip tightened on the pen, but she made no effort to write.

"Might it be too difficult for me to be like my sister?" her voice rose unnaturally, making the question sharp.

Without thought, he picked up his chair and moved closer to her. So close, their knees nearly touched, and he could use the writing desk as easily as she. "Grace." He spoke firmly, and honestly. "I have seen you do incredible things, good things, without betraying your true self. There is no one like you, and it would be a shame if you cast off those parts of yourself when there are so many who admire and love you just as you are."

She drew in a slow, deep breath, not meeting his eyes. "Thank you." Grace shifted, turning fully to her paper and dabbing her pen into the ink again. "You are a good friend, Jacob. I know it is difficult for you to sit by while I pretend to be Hope."

It hadn't been. Yes, it smote his conscience when he was required to act as though he did not know of the subterfuge, but Grace had somehow managed to keep him from needing to say much. The dinner party had proven trying. He'd wanted to speak up for her, to defend her or keep the others from commenting in a way that implied Hope held the position of favored twin. Yet he could say nothing without it seeming strange to others. He had spent most of the evening thinking of all the things he wished to say, and some of those thoughts cropped up again.

"Do you miss her very much?" Grace's question drew him out of his thoughts.

"Hope?" She could mean no one else. *Did* he miss her? She had left a week ago. "I suppose I find it strange to know she is not about." But he did not pine for her. After his initial frustration with the way she manipulated her sister into deceit, after the momentary pain of being left behind for grander things, he had accepted her absence.

Grace's pen moved swiftly across the page. "Perhaps when Hope returns, she will not wish to go away again. It will only be a year." She bit her lip again and bent slightly over her page, so he could not see her eyes. "She may finally settle down."

Again, Jacob wondered where Grace saw herself in a year's time. What would she do with her sister away for a year? Grace's next birthday would bring her to four and twenty. Most young ladies would be married or betrothed at her age. Yet neither of the sisters had ever entertained suitors. But Grace had told him they thought upon it, that they spoke of marrying for love.

"Do you wish to settle down?" he asked, less interested in Hope's future than he had been days before.

Her cheeks turned pink. It appeared she had entertained the notion. "I have not given it much thought. Papa seems to think no one paid us any attention before because of the oddity of being twins. I'm inclined to think that there is a lack of suitable young men in the neighborhood who could tell us apart long enough to express an interest." She finally looked up at him, amusement in her eyes. "And I must say, I could never entertain a suitor who might confuse the two of us. Can you imagine? What if he came to call and took the wrong young lady by the hand?"

Jacob chuckled and leaned closer still, his nose only inches from hers as he pretended to confide in her. "Such a man would be a great clod, not to recognize the woman holding his heart. I never understood why people have such a difficult time telling the two of you apart. Even I, who know nothing of women's fashion or hair, can see your personalities in your curls." He reached out and caught one of the spirals peeping out from behind her ear and gave it a gentle tug.

Grace's lips parted as she inhaled sharply. Jacob stilled. He had not been so familiar with either of the Everly sisters in many, many years. Slowly, carefully, he withdrew the offending hand. The tip of one finger grazed her cheek, which blossomed with a dark blush.

He sat as far back in his chair as he could without tipping the thing over. "What are you writing?" The question came out desperate, and had he been a few years younger he knew his voice would've broken on every syllable.

Something had shifted. He did not know what it was, or how to put a name to it. But somehow—with one casual touch—he'd thrown their friendship off balance. He felt it. Given Grace's glowing cheeks, she had too.

"I am writing a list of possible activities for the picnic." She pushed the paper at him, heedless of the wet ink her finger smeared on the page. Perhaps his action left her as befuddled as he was. The sooner they stood on familiar ground, the better.

Taking up the list gingerly, Jacob tried to focus on what she had written. The slant of her hand was quite like her personality. Subtle, but elegant. After he stopped thinking ridiculous thoughts, he studied the list and nodded with approval. "All fine activities. Except Blind Man's Bluff. I do hope you will not play that one."

She raised her eyebrows. "It is a children's game."

"Will children be playing? I was under the impression this would be a picnic for the young people of our community." He looked over the sheet of paper at her, frowning. He had heard of even innocent games growing compromising, but a game with an individual chasing about members of the opposite sex while blindfolded sounded like a sure way to disaster.

Grace plucked the paper from his hand. "We shall see." She pointed at another item with her ink-stained finger. "I also thought we might have an informal archery tournament. Yet I wonder — Isaac always loved the bow, and I should not want to remind him of his inability to shoot."

"He will not expect everyone to forgo that pleasure merely because he cannot join in." Jacob folded his arms across his chest, leaning away from her again. "Why not include Charades?"

"Because it will be a glorious day and charades is a game for inside a house when it is miserable without." Grace spoke with decision. "We could play hide and seek."

He raised his eyebrows. "Can you not think how that could go wrong?"

"Stag Out, then?" she asked playfully. "King of the Castle?"

Jacob groaned. "Must we play games at all?" At least the awkward, strange moment between them had passed.

"You sound like a vicar of sixty, instead of a man not yet six and twenty." Grace laughed, and he could not help but join her.

"I am going to have to be an upstanding, stodgy sort of fellow after I take my orders." He pretended to adjust the lapels of his coat. "Who would take a vicar playing Leap Frog at all seriously?"

"I suppose you might be right. Although I am more likely to trust a vicar who jests and laughs than one who is perpetually gloomy." She tapped his arm with the tip of her pen, then immediately put it down on the table again.

Rather than allow another difficult moment between them, Jacob threw out his own suggestion. "What if you let some of your guests name their favorite games? We might get more variety that way."

"That is not a terrible idea." Grace tapped her bottom lip with her inky finger, and he watched carefully to see if it left a mark. The ink had already dried, so her lips remained perfectly pink. For some reason, that disappointed him. "I will ask for suggestions but keep my selections at hand in case people are not quick to remember their nursery days." She pursed her lips thoughtfully.

Jacob started, realizing he still stared at her mouth. What had come over him? He had thought the strangeness in the air a product of their conversation. But now, meeting her gaze, Jacob came to an incredibly different conclusion.

No. He couldn't allow his thoughts down that path. Wouldn't allow them to wander in that dangerous and tempting direction. Changing affections from one sister to another—Grace would be insulted. Besides, it had been folly to allow himself feelings greater than friendship for Hope. He'd known both Everlys too long.

Prudence urged him to leave, before he said or did something to cause any more strange tension between them. He cared about Grace too much to make her uncomfortable. He needed to get hold of himself and stop acting like a fool.

"I had best go, now that you have this sorted out." He stood before she could respond. "I have other visits to make today." Not precisely true, but he could stop in and see Isaac or Mr. Spratt. Or any number of people. Paying visits to others, looking in on his neighbors, was precisely what he needed to put his thoughts back in order.

The wrinkle appearing just above her nose again, Grace rose

from her chair. "I am sorry to see you leave so soon, but thank you for stopping in. I will see you at the picnic tomorrow."

"Yes, of course. Tomorrow. Good day, Grace." He bowed and fled the room. Almost immediately after clearing the doorway, he skidded to a stop.

Mr. Everly stood in the passageway, spectacles on the end of his nose and hands behind his back. He did not appear surprised to see Jacob.

"Mr. Barnes," he said, more precise than usual. "I did not know we were to expect a visit from you today."

Unaccountably, Jacob's stomach dropped in the manner it had when he was a boy, about to be taken to task for misbehaving. Had Mr. Everly heard Jacob use Grace's name instead of Hope's?

"Mr. Everly." He bowed after a brief hesitation, his heart thudding rapidly with his guilt. "I only meant to see if Miss Everly needed help with the picnic. It seems she has things well in hand."

"Does she?" Mr. Everly glanced over Jacob's shoulder to the open parlor door, then back to Jacob. "I am pleased to hear it. You are a good friend to her, Mr. Barnes. A good man. Thank you for coming."

"Yes, sir. Thank you." It did not feel like the correct response but remaining in the hall another moment would likely lead to disaster. "Good morning, sir." Jacob bowed again and stepped around the older gentleman, hurrying down the steps.

The day had turned strange, and his mind with it.

CHAPTER 13

Despite Grace's confident conversation with Jacob, she could hardly stop her fingers trembling given her nervousness on the day of the picnic. She stood in the garden to greet her guests, who were brought through the house by the butler and a footman. Wearing one of Hope's day dresses, the color of which reminded her of a cherry tart, Grace prepared for her place at the center of all the attention.

The servants had worked all morning, under her direction, setting up tables for lemonade and refreshments, and laying out blankets, cushions, and chairs beneath the apple trees for those who wished to rest out of the sun.

Mr. King and Sir Isaac were among the first to arrive, the two of them nearly as fidgety as she was. Perhaps it came from being in the army so long; they were used to movement and action, not the quieter life of the country.

"You will enjoy the orchards," Isaac said to his friend. "They are the finest old trees."

"It is a pity it is not late enough in the year to pick apples." Mr. King glanced in the direction of the orchards and then back to

Grace. "I wish to sample their fruit for myself, after hearing Sir Isaac talk of spending every fall eating his fill of them."

Grace did not even try to conceal her amusement, one of her favorite childhood memories immediately coming to mind. "He made himself rather sick one year. He challenged our friends, Lord Inglewood and Mr. Jacob Barnes, to see who could eat the most apples in one afternoon."

"Not one of my finest hours," Isaac admitted, his eyes dancing merrily. "That was the same summer Inglewood fell out of a tree after challenging us to see who could climb the highest."

"The summer of young male stupidity," a new voice said, drawing their attention to Jacob as he came down the steps from the house.

The trembling started up again, necessitating that Grace swiftly take hold of her skirts to keep her fingers hidden. Jacob came closer before making his bows, then shook hands with the other gentlemen. "Mr. King, I hope the day is to your liking."

"It has been far too long since I have enjoyed a country picnic. I look forward to putting myself in our hostess's capable hands." Mr. King's tone, warm and genuine, did nothing to ease Grace's anxiety. What if she muddled the whole thing by being an inferior hostess? Then the gentleman turned to her. "Miss Everly, I hope you will give me a tour of the orchard this afternoon."

The question startled her, but Grace nodded her agreement without reservation. "Of course, Mr. King. It would be my pleasure."

His eyes lit up and he touched the brim of his hat before following Isaac out of the garden and to the orchard.

Jacob stepped closer to her side, turning to face the house. "He seems a good sort of fellow." He spoke the compliment with an odd lilt in his voice.

"I suppose so. If Isaac likes him, that speaks highly of his character." Grace faced the house as well, waiting for her next guests. Why was Jacob standing so close? Why had he not gone with the other gentlemen? His nearness did nothing to alleviate her anxiety.

Tucking his hands behind his back, Jacob shifted as though settling into his stance. "No parasol for you today?" he asked.

"Hope abhors parasols even on days when they are necessary,"

Grace answered, watching him from the corner of her eye. "And this bonnet ought to be all the protection I need." She reached up to touch the wide brim with her gloved finger. "I produce all my own shade while wearing it."

He met her gaze a moment, amusement twinkling in his eyes, before he turned his attention back to the house.

The chattering of more guests announced the arrival of Jacob's sisters, his elder brother, and his brother's particular friend, Mrs. Muir. When would Matthew get on with it and ask the beautiful widow to marry him? She greeted everyone properly and they went on to the orchard, but Jacob remained at her side.

Miss Parr and the Ashworths, a brother and his two sisters, arrived next. Then the Kimballs and the Keyes. There were seventeen young people in all, including Grace herself, and her guests were divided evenly between men and women. A few parents had come as well, including Mr. and Mrs. Parr, Mrs. Keyes, and Mrs. Kimball. They would act as chaperones for the group, taking their ease beneath the trees with glasses of lemonade.

After the last guest arrived, Grace gathered all her courage and confidence.

Jacob had remained at her side. "You look as though you are marching into battle." His words were colored with humor, though he spoke them gently.

"I feel as though I might be." Forcing a cheerful expression, Grace touched the ribbons at her neck nervously.

"Come now. Everything will be fine." Jacob offered her his arm. "We will enjoy the afternoon with our friends. Everyone will have a splendid time." Grateful for his encouragement, she rested her hand upon his arm, accepting his escort. At last her fingers stopped their anxious shaking.

The familiar sight of the hundreds of trees, planted in neat rows years ago by her grandfather, lightened her step. This was her home, her land, her beloved orchard. The weather was glorious, and friends surrounded her. It did not matter that everyone, saving Jacob, thought she was Hope. She was perfectly capable of giving them all an afternoon to remember.

They started with refreshments as Grace made certain everyone had been introduced to Mr. King, the only new face in their midst. Jacob remained at her side, walking with her from one guest to another, his presence steadying her as it had in the past. His pointed attention would likely go unnoticed by the others. Most of the neighborhood was used to seeing him in company with Hope and Grace. Grace appreciated the kind gesture and unspoken support.

"Let us come to order," she said at last, raising her voice as Hope would, to be heard over all their conversation. "Thank you all for coming. The order of the day is to recreate our fondest childhood games. On the table over there—" She pointed to a smaller side table beneath a tree. "—there are slips of paper and a bowl. Please write down your favorite game and put it in the bowl to be drawn out at random. Some of our entertainment will come from the suggestions, and other activities I have planned for later."

The little crowd made its way to the table, the ladies chattering with pleasure while the gentlemen began to brag of childhood achievements. No one had thought the idea silly, it would seem.

It took time for everyone to think of something and scribble upon the slips of paper with their pencils. At last Grace took up the bowl with sixteen suggestions waiting inside. She eagerly took out the first and read aloud, "Two Hats." She blinked at the paper. "I am afraid I am not familiar with that one."

"Ah, it is my suggestion." Mr. King stepped forward. "It is one we played all the time in the village where I grew up." He glanced around, but no one else appeared to know the game. "I am happy to teach it to the group. It is best if we sit in a circle."

"To the trees, then." Grace pointed to the cushions, chairs, and blankets prepared for their use. "Mr. King can teach us a game about hats." There was a smattering of giggles, but everyone complied. The Misses Ashworths hurried to claim places on either side of the gentleman about to explain the game.

They all took seats upon the ground or in chairs, Mr. King standing in the middle of their ill-formed circle. "This is a game in which you are required to be contrary." He pointed to his hat. "And it is called Two Hats because two people play at a time until a winner is determined. Everyone need not take part, but I think you will all be amused. Miss Everly, as our hostess, would you assist me in demonstrating how to play?"

Grace, on the ground between Jacob and his sister Mary, pretended to consider. "I suppose it is my duty. Very well." She held her hand out and Mr. King came forward to take it, assisting her to her feet. He led her into the center of the circle again.

"This is how the game is played. There is one person who is the first hat." He touched his chest and bowed theatrically, the little group clapped their hands while Grace shook her head. "And another who is the second hat." He held his hand as if presenting Grace to an audience, and she curtsied.

"The first hat says a common phrase, or performs a gesture, and the second must react in a manner completely opposite of what is expected and proper." He took two empty chairs and placed them in the middle. "For instance. If I sit—" He demonstrated. "—Miss Everly stands. And if I stand, she sits." He stood, and Grace did as he directed.

"If I say good day to you, miss, you say—"

Catching the idea, she did not hesitate to answer. "Good evening to you, sir."

His expression was most approving. "That is the game. The winner is the last player who can be contrary every time. Should Miss Everly respond appropriately, instead of contrarily, she is out. Would you like to try a real round?"

Grace glanced about to make certain the others liked the game. Miss Keyes appeared bored, and Jacob... He was frowning. But as everyone else seemed interested, she agreed. "Very well. Everything contrary. I am ready."

Mr. King grinned and began at once. "The weather is fine today."

That one was easy. "I believe it shall rain tonight."

He looked up, she cast her eyes down, he moved to the left, she to her right. He commented that the lemonade was refreshing, she told him it was boiling, he asked her to dance, she refused, he bowed and she saluted as she had seen military men do. Grace, while enjoying herself, began to fear that no one else might have a turn.

"Do not shake my hand," he said, holding out his. She quickly put her gloved hand in his palm. Then he bent and kissed her knuckles.

Grace froze. The impertinence! Yet it was a compliment. Or was it part of the game? She did not know what to do and stood, gaping at him, until he grinned and turned to the others at the same moment he released her hand. "I won. She hesitated too long, would you agree?"

There was laughter and applause. No one seemed to think the moment strange. Grace went back to her seat, still uncertain. She met Jacob's eyes to see his frown had deepened.

He leaned toward her to mutter, "I'm not sure I like this one."

Although she agreed, she knew Hope would most likely laugh such an awkward moment away. She must endeavor to do the same. "It was entertaining."

He made a sound in the back of his throat that did not sound like an agreement. Mr. King had another gentleman up next, and then allowed others to take turns as first hat. Everyone who wished a turn had one, and Grace clapped along with the rest when someone at last could not keep up. Sometimes it was the first hat who ran out of ideas, most often it was the person playing second hat. The best moment was when Sir Isaac and Matthew Barnes faced each other.

"Would you like a punch in the nose?" Sir Isaac asked, all politeness.

Matthew hesitated. The truthful answer must be no, the contrary answer would be yes. He tilted his chin down, as though presenting a better target, and said, "I would very much enjoy one, thank you."

Everyone burst out laughing and Isaac gave up with a wave of his hand.

They played a rhyming game after that, and then a short game of riddles. Most of the group seemed to be in good spirits when Grace suggested they play a game of Fox and Hounds.

Jacob's frown reappeared, but she studiously ignored it. A game of chase could not be nearly so improper as a game of Blind Man's Bluff or one that necessitated hiding in tucked away places. It had been a favorite in the neighborhood for as long as Grace could remember, but she explained the rules for Mr. King's sake. She retrieved a handkerchief from the reticule she had kept tied to her wrist.

"The game starts with one hound and the rest of us are foxes. The foxes all carry handkerchiefs in their hands by the corner, like this." She demonstrated, holding just the corner of the linen square between thumb and fingers. "The hound chases the foxes and, if he catches their handkerchief, turns them to his side. If a fox makes it back to where the game began still in possession of his or her tail, the fox is safe and wins the game." She pointed through the trees. "Foxes must run to the brook and back to this spot."

"I elect Mr. Ashworth," Miss Parr said, "as the first hound."

Matthew Barnes seconded the election, and the grinning Mr. Ashworth started to preen. "I shall have a pack of hounds on my side in next to no time. What are the limits of the playing field?"

"The orchard. No other place will serve," Elizabeth Barnes said with a clap of her hands. Everyone agreed, as it had been the proper place to play many years before.

"The hound must count to ten before he begins his pursuit," Mr. Barnes added as he helped a smiling Mrs. Muir to her feet. "And no cheating. Everyone must have their handkerchief where all can see it."

Jacob stepped close to Grace, standing just over her shoulder and close enough she could feel his breath on the back of her neck. "I am not certain this is the best idea," he said. "We ought to play in an open field. There are too many trees—"

Grace did not immediately answer him, but instead her gaze took in all of the people around her. Thus far, her party had been a triumph, *without* Hope. Calling a halt to this game, one that every miss and gentleman about her did not mind, could undo the success she had thus far enjoyed.

She looked over to where the chaperones were seated, talking and laughing amongst themselves, and then stepped away from Jacob, making her way deeper into the trees. "I think the orchard will do splendidly."

Without waiting for his response, she called out, "Begin your count, Mr. Ashford." Then she darted into the trees, smiling all the while, her handkerchief clasped in one hand. She glimpsed the others darting about on the paths marking the rows of apple trees. The orchard rang with laughter and challenges issued by her guests.

She looked back once, seeing no one behind her, then forward to the line of trees. The brook was not far. One could walk through the orchard to the water, from this position, in five minutes at a stroll. There was a shout somewhere to her right, startling her, before it was followed by laughter. Had the hound caught someone?

"Miss Everly," a voice shouted. She looked behind her, one hand clutching the handkerchief and the other holding her skirt.

Mr. King, handkerchief in hand, cut through the trees toward her. "I thought that was you. I neglected to ask where the brook is located! And I—"

"King, I have you," another voice shouted. It was Mr. Ashworth's voice.

Grace hesitated, but Mr. King grinned and motioned for her to run before he took off in the opposite direction. The man was drawing his pursuer away from her. She almost laughed at the show of gallantry in the midst of a children's game. Giving it no more thought, she continued to the brook. Breaking from the trees, she went to the bank and then turned, not hesitating before running back beneath the branches.

She took a serpentine route. If someone caught sight of her, someone not wearing a dress, she had no hope of outrunning them. She went around one of the older, larger trees a trifle more slowly, endeavoring to make her feet fall lightly.

A hand snatched at her wrist, above her handkerchief, and she stumbled sideways. The hand kept her upon her feet, and another came around her waist, halting her downward momentum.

Her chest constricted and her gaze shot up to identify her captor.

Jacob held her; his eyes so dark in the shadows they were more black than brown. They stared at each other, he still and firm as the tree at his back, and she trying to make sense of their predicament.

Hurried footsteps from the other side of the tree made her head turn at the same instant Jacob pulled her toward him. His back hit the tree and she bumped into his side. Miss Kimball ran by, pursued by a laughing Miss Parr and Isaac. They were too intent on their chase to see Grace and Jacob standing there, pressed against the tree and each other.

Grace slowly tilted her head to peer up at Jacob. He was staring into the trees, and she could see his pulse beating rapidly in the strained vein beneath his jaw.

"Jacob?" she whispered, aware of his hand at her waist. "They are gone."

He dragged his attention back to her, apparently with great effort given the amount of tension she saw in his expression and felt in his body so near hers.

They stood so close together that, for a wild moment, she thought of what it would be like to raise up on her toes and kiss him. No one would see. No one would know. Except for Jacob. Her aching heart would be laid bare before him at last.

It would be the end of their friendship.

No other thought could have removed her from him at that moment as violently as that one did. She put both her hands to his chest and pushed him, hard, causing Jacob to stumble back a step.

He blinked at last, as though coming out of a stupor, and then his expression changed from a blank and stony aspect to a deep frown.

"You frightened me," she whispered, putting as much force into the words as she dared. Perhaps he would forgive her the shove if he thought his actions startled her. "What are you doing, snatching at someone like that?"

"I—" He uttered the single syllable before clamping his mouth shut, then he turned to glare at the trees again. "This game was a bad idea, Grace. It is not appropriate."

She countered quickly, her poor heart still racing. "Everyone is enjoying themselves. Now come, before we are caught."

Jacob's eyes lowered a moment to her hand with the handkerchief, then darted back up to her face. He stepped forward, his hand circling her wrist more gently this time. Then he bent slightly, toward her. Grace's lungs constricted, the air around them crackled with energy and her foolish hope.

"You are already caught," he whispered. His hand dropped from her wrist to her handkerchief, pulling it gently from her grasp.

All he wanted was to get her handkerchief. Jacob's actions were nothing more than a ruse, for the game. Her cheeks flamed with embarrassment and she lowered her head, unable to meet his gaze. She had been ready, had anticipated something else when he bent closer. More the fool, she, after thinking of giving a kiss to then believe she might receive one. He did not care for her like that. It was Hope he wanted, and Hope was too far for him to reach.

Mortified, she did not know what to do. The handkerchief had slipped from her fingers, but he lingered, nearer than any man ought to stand to a lady not his wife. Did he mean to drive home his opinion on the impropriety of the game? She hardly cared anymore.

"Grace," he said, tone still low, as though he meant to share a secret.

What sort of sister was Grace, what sort of friend, to entertain the idea of a kiss when she knew Jacob would court Hope upon her return? Even though Grace sincerely doubted Hope would entertain him as a suitor, it was not for Grace to decide. She swallowed, demanded courage from her wounded heart, and lifted her head.

Jacob had come closer. He leaned down, lowering his head to hers. After her disappointment, Grace could not entertain the notion of kissing him again. Shoving him away had worked before, but this time she stood still, waiting. Grace searched his expression for his intent, her heart breaking.

After a moment of hesitation, Jacob cleared his throat, and backed away. Brought to his senses, somehow. While Jacob had never struggled to tell Hope and Grace apart, perhaps he had momentarily thought to replace one sister with the other.

She could never allow that, no matter how much she cared for him.

He took another step away, then another, and Grace saw the look of shock upon his face. Finally, he realized his mistake. She lifted her skirts with both hands as high as she could without risking indecency, and she ran. Back to the start of the game, to safety, leaving Jacob behind.

By the time Grace broke through the trees, most of her guests had returned and were laughing. She forced away her hurt. Pasting a pleased expression upon her face, she slowed to a walk.

"Who has been caught?" She called loudly enough to gain attention. Only a few people were missing, and they arrived shortly after she did. The only couple who appeared as though they might have spent extra time in each other's company was Jacob's brother and his Mrs. Muir. They were holding hands, neither with a handkerchief. Grace bit her lip and ignored that intimacy between them.

Mr. Ashworth had four handkerchiefs, Isaac one, and Mr. Keyes held six. Jacob, at the edge of the party, did not announce he had caught Grace's. She did not bother to bring attention to it, either, and avoided glancing in his direction. Mr. King had made it back with his handkerchief, along with several others.

Grace counted the game a success, and she called their attention to the refreshments. She led the way, head held high, planning the next entertainment. Something much more subdued was necessary. Like charades.

CHAPTER 14

I t took the better part of the afternoon for Jacob to stop calling himself a fool. He withdrew to the shade where the chaperones conversed, where he ought to have been all along.

The frivolous games his friends played without thought would do nothing for his reputation. He owed it to his future to distance himself from all of it. A vicar ought to hold himself to higher standards of conduct.

He watched Grace lead the way from the table of lemonade and tea, taking everyone across the newly-mowed field to the bowling green. She moved with confidence, giving no one reason to suspect she had been through an unpleasant experience.

What had come over him? Jacob had wanted to kiss her. Had been ready to do so. He ought to have known, after she pushed him away when he caught her, that she would not welcome the idea. Yet in that moment, alone with her and admiring the pretty blush upon her cheeks, he had wanted to take her up in his arms as he had to pull her against the tree.

His mind warred with the desire, reminding him that such an action was the very reason he had protested the game of fox and hounds. But Grace, flushed and breathing heavily while her eyes gleamed up at him through the shadows, had presented too tempting a picture. He had come so close to kissing her.

Jacob did not stir from the chaperones the rest of the afternoon. Instead, he kept up conversation with them, asking after the Parrs' school children, the Kimballs' married daughter, and trivial matters which barely served to distract him from Grace's movements. He knew where she was, though he tried not to look, and he took himself away to his family's carriage as soon as he sensed the end of the picnic drew near.

He had ridden Matthew's horse so his brother could escort Mrs. Muir and their sisters in the carriage. He mounted the hunter the moment his family appeared for the return trip.

Every time he came in contact with Grace of late, he did something that he immediately felt the need to apologize for. It was impossible to continue laying the blame for his actions on his confusion over Hope's disappearance and the subsequent lies Grace must act and tell. Something entirely different troubled him.

When he arrived home, Jacob took himself to his room. At least, that was where he intended to go. He met his mother in the hall leading to the family's bedchambers.

"Jacob," she called upon seeing him, coming as she was from her own chambers. "You are returned from the picnic. How was the event? A great success, as always?"

His guilt at making Grace uncomfortable made it difficult for him to answer at first. "Everyone seemed to enjoy themselves."

His mother came down the hall, her brow puckered. "Everyone but you?"

How did she do that? Though he limited his words, twisted his expression into cheer, she knew his mind seemingly better than he did.

"It occurred to me that it might not be the best way for a vicar to spend an afternoon." There. That was partly the truth.

She stopped a few paces from him, searching his face. "You are not a vicar yet, and you were among friends. Did anything happen to put you out of sorts?"

He glanced at his door, wishing he had made it inside before she found him home. His mother would not pry, not if he asked her to leave him be. But the strange mixture of guilt and desire he felt, the difficulty of his position as friend to Grace, roiled inside his mind in a most unhealthy manner.

"I cannot tell the whole of it," Jacob said at last, the promise he made Grace to keep her secret binding his tongue. "But something did happen."

His mother joined her hands before her, appearing completely relaxed and ready to hear anything he had to say. With six children to look after, how Mother had managed to remain on good terms with them all impressed him. It was due in part to moments like this, when she invited them to share their burdens with her.

After a moment of arranging his thoughts, Jacob attempted to explain. "Something odd happened, Mother. I know we have spoken of my feelings for a certain friend." He shifted from one foot to the other, not looking his mother in the eye. "Lately, however, it is another woman we know who has my attention. Today, in the middle of the games, I almost did something that would make you ashamed."

"I very much doubt that. You are a good son, and I have never been ashamed of you." Her gentle words made it harder to admit his guilt.

"I almost kissed this woman." He winced with the admission.

She stared at him a moment. "And? I am afraid the notion of you stealing a kiss is not enough to shock me. Do you think I kissed no one until after my betrothal to your father?" She shrugged when he gaped at her. "Come now, dear. If you care for a lady, it is only natural. Though I am surprised such a thing would happen when it was not long ago we were speaking of that *certain other* lady."

Jacob's ears grew hot. "I know. I cannot understand it myself."

"And what you feel for this new miss, this other friend. Is it genuine affection?" his mother asked, raising her eyebrows at him. "Or a passing fancy? You said you did not kiss her. Why is that?"

Jacob released a deep breath before answering, a bit sheepishly. "I am fairly certain she wants nothing to do with me, at least in a romantic sense." He ducked his head, the rejection of her pushing him away stung, even if his own motives confused him. Was he that disgusting to her? Even after she knew of his former wish to court Hope?

His *former*—Had he ever told Grace he'd given up his desire to court her sister?

With that thought, realization came. Jerking his head up, Jacob met his mother's concerned gaze. "Lud, I am twice a fool. I bungled everything."

"Jacob, you are hardly making sense. Whatever do you mean?" Mother eyed him suspiciously, a perplexed frown in place.

"I need to think on this more, Mother. But rest assured, I will let you know what comes next." He stepped forward and gave her a kiss on the cheek. "Thank you for listening to my nonsense."

"I am always here for you, Jacob. I do hope everything will turn out well for you." She shook her head at him, but Jacob barely noticed as he went back down the hall. Locking himself away in his room would do him little good. He needed to walk. The fresh air would clear his mind faster than anything else.

CHAPTER 15

Dawn found Grace already awake and sitting on the edge of Hope's bed. Since beginning her ruse, she had not slept well. The previous night, she had barely slept at all. Over and over in her mind, she saw the scene between herself and Jacob in the orchard as though she watched a play. A rather tragic play, at that. Her longing for his attention had finally brought about the very scene she desired, but nothing in that moment with him had felt right.

What if he had kissed her? The idea sent a blush into her cheeks, but as quickly as it came it left, wondering if he only saw her as a replacement for Hope. The thought made her stomach lurch unpleasantly.

When Susan came to help Grace dress, the maid found her mistress had done most of the job. All that was left for Susan was to tie up a few things and assist in the arrangement of Grace's hair. Grace, distracted, barely said a word to her servant. The quiet hovered between them, an almost impenetrable curtain.

"Miss?" Susan at last brought Grace from her thoughts. "Your hair is finished. Do you require anythin' else?"

Meeting her maid's eyes in the mirror, Grace studied Susan carefully. The maid had stopped exclaiming over her hair, had not made another comment about anything that struck her as odd. Yet Grace could not think she had completely fooled Susan. The woman helped her in and out of the bath, for goodness sake.

"No, thank you." She rose from the chair and went to the door while Susan went about tidying up the room. Though it was too early for breakfast, she went downstairs. Putting something in her stomach might stop its odd behavior. Perhaps she could beg toast from Cook.

Grace passed through the silent house, her ears listening for the busy sounds of her family even though she knew no one but her father was at home with her. She missed Hope. Missed her mother. And her younger brother and sisters. Edward, Charity, and Patience would come home from school soon. At least then some of the old liveliness would return to the Refuge.

She entered the kitchen, the sound of her footsteps on the wood floors lost amid the clanging of a pot and fussing of the cook.

One of the kitchen maids spotted Grace first and hurried over, wiping her hands on her apron. "Might I help you, miss?" Molly asked.

"I wonder if I might have a bite of toast before breakfast." Grace offered the servant a smile and received a quick nod in return.

Grace, with no work to do, did not presume to sit at the table this time. She had no wish to be underfoot.

Garrett appeared and stopped upon seeing her. "Miss Everly. You are up early this morning, miss. May I help you?"

"I am only come to sniff out some toast. Molly is tending to me."

He nodded and bowed, then took himself off to the shelves near the back door. He reached into a nook and drew out several folded papers. The post. Someone must have run to town for it.

"Here is your toast, miss." Molly offered the small plate with the dry bread and a little crock of marmalade.

"Thank you." She took the food and turned to leave, intending to take herself off to her mother's sitting room. The familiarity of the room might do something to help her rather woebegone mood.

"Miss Everly?" Garrett said, and she turned around again. "There is a letter for you, from your sister in London."

What little appetite the toast and marmalade had coaxed forward immediately vanished. A letter from Hope meant only one thing. She had set sail and posted the note as one of her last acts on English soil.

Grace held onto her plate with one hand and held the other out for the letter. "Thank you, Garrett. I-I am glad she wrote." Was she? It meant things were final. It meant she must tell the truth, at last.

The butler placed the folded and sealed paper in her hand, his eyebrows drawn down. "Are you worried it is bad news, miss?"

"No." She attempted a brighter expression, though she doubted her ability to be convincing. "I miss her, though. It will be good to have news." She left without another word, tucking the letter into the bosom of her gown. Grasping her plate with both hands, she ran to the first room where she knew she might have privacy.

The music room was across from her father's study, as he claimed he enjoyed hearing his children practice and play upon their instruments while he worked. That morning, all was silent when she entered. She had not practiced the pianoforte once in Hope's absence, though she had longed to do so a time or two. Hope sang. Grace played the piano.

Grace was forever in the background while her sister performed, in music and in life. Truthfully, she preferred it that way. The picnic had been entertaining, but exhausting.

She put the plate down on a chair and went to the window, pushing the heavy curtains aside, allowing the morning sunlight to illuminate her letter.

It was as she thought. Hope's part in the masquerade had remained undiscovered, and she had set sail the previous day after giving the letter into the care of a servant.

Hope was gone. Beyond reach of their father, beyond Grace's help.

She lowered herself to the wide windowsill, paper in hand, and leaned back against the glass. Her plan had worked. Neither of them had been discovered, both had what they wanted. Why then, with her triumph confirmed, did she feel so lost? She dreaded telling her father. Who knew what he would say, what the punishment for her actions might be? But that was not what left her heart empty.

Her sister was gone. The sister she had never been apart from, since before their birth. They had done everything together, excepting brief separations lasting no more than the space of a day or two. All this time, pretending to be Hope had wearied her. Thinking of how her sister might act in every situation had kept Grace from truly recognizing the hole in her life with Hope away.

Grace raised her free hand to rub her eyes, trying to plan what came next. That was what she did; Hope took off on whatever wild idea came to her while Grace planned each moment of her day with care. She knew Papa ought to be told soon. It was wrong to go on lying to him any longer than necessary. Yet she hesitated.

The person she most wanted to speak with, to share her feelings, to mourn the loss of her sister for an entire year, was Jacob.

The awkward moment beneath the apple trees would have to be addressed. She must let him know she thought nothing of it, that it was forgotten. Even if that might be another lie.

With a groan, Grace put her face in her hands, heedless of pressing Hope's letter into her cheek. What a mess. Though she had won the ability to stay at home, remaining near those she loved, everyone she cared for would have reason to be cross with her once the whole truth came out.

She had to think carefully about how to reveal the truth. It certainly needn't be done right away.

Tucking the letter back into her bodice, she found her plate. The toast, though cold, would be all right with the marmalade. Forcing down a few bites, Grace's mind kept busy, examining each of her options.

The day passed, and she through it, as silently as it began. Grace ate breakfast with Papa and then retired to sew. Hope sewed sometimes, after all. Then she strolled through her mother's garden, inspecting the plants carefully. She took tea in to her father when she thought he might be peckish but had little in the way of conversation with him.

All the while, as she went through her normal daily tasks, she tried to put together the right words to tell her father what she had done. To tell Jacob it had been her idea, not Hope's.

Every time she thought of Jacob, however, her memories took hold. How many times in the past year had she caught him admiring Hope? How often had she wished he would turn and look her direction instead? Everyone thought Hope to be exciting and clever, given all the interesting things she might do or say at a given moment. Some thought her brash. All would agree that she was a bold, bright creature.

The same could not be said of Grace. Content to be quietly working in the background, Grace was calm. She was the sea on a clear day, lapping gently against the shore. Hope's personality held the potential of a hurricane.

When Grace settled back into Hope's bed that evening, she still had not found the precise words to use when she spoke to Papa, or Jacob. Tucking her feet in the sheets Susan had warmed for her, she pulled the blankets up beneath her chin and tried to find some comfort. Sleep would doubtlessly elude her again.

Had it been wrong to switch places? Every moment since the idea struck, Grace had justified her actions. She had granted Hope the ability to go off and have an adventure the likes of which she had only dreamed of before. But Grace's motives began with selfishness. She had wanted to protect herself from that sort of upheaval as much as she wanted to gift it to her sister.

As she tried to sleep, one thought she fought against since the beginning materialized clearly in her mind. Saving herself, and giving Hope what she wanted, had not been Grace's only motivations.

When Jacob took orders and moved to the vicarage, Grace knew he would ask to court Hope. He never said as much, but that would be Jacob's way. He would wait until he had a future to offer the woman he loved, then he would make his intentions known.

Hope wouldn't have agreed to it. Grace couldn't imagine her sister ever entertaining the idea of marrying a vicar, of living a quiet and simple life. But what if she was wrong? By preventing Jacob from trying, had she ruined his chance at happiness?

Within the deepest corner of her heart, Grace knew if he only gave her the chance, she might prove herself the better match for him. Through her machinations, her deceit, she had sent Hope away and created the perfect opportunity to show Jacob what he had not seen before.

Tears burned at her eyes and she dashed at them before they could wet the pillow. They were hot, shameful tears, condemning her selfish conduct. Did she have to confess this to Jacob, too? It had pained him to lose Hope. It was Grace's fault he had been hurt. Confessing feelings she had only ever acknowledged in the privacy of her heart and thoughts, revealing everything to him, frightened her more than any ocean voyage ever could.

Groaning, Grace pulled the blanket over her head. Jacob would hate her. He would despise her for lying, for her selfishness, and she would lose his friendship. Through that, she would likely lose the rest of the Birchwood Society. Isaac and Silas would not look at her the same way again, she was certain, when they learned of what she had done. When Hope returned and learned the truth, whether or not she considered Jacob a possible match, she would be hurt Grace had thought to manipulate her.

Though Grace tossed and turned for hours, she finally snatched a little sleep. When the sun rose, she woke again. It hurt to open her eyes. She had finally given in and cried, and now her eyes ached. Susan would likely see them, swollen and red, and think Grace ill.

Without much cheer, she rose and bathed her face in the cool water of her basin. She pressed a damp cloth against her eyes and laid back down, willing the swelling to go away. When she finally heard Susan at the door, she snatched the cloth from her face and dropped it between the bed and the table at its side.

A whole day had passed since receiving the letter. Another day of falsehoods.

There was no choice. She must tell Papa at the first available opportunity.

Her stomach sank. Well. Perhaps after he had finished his

morning work and she took in tea to him. Then they would be in his study, a private place away from the servants. Yes. That would be the best time. Because, she reasoned, after she told him everything, he would forbid her access to her friends. And she must confess to Jacob, too.

Grace made plans for visiting Jacob's home to seek an audience with him. It would be indecent to call upon his household before ten. That was when she would leave.

Her mind made up, Grace went to breakfast and greeted her father as warmly as she ever had before. Once she told him everything, it might be some time before he allowed a kiss and embrace from her.

CHAPTER 16

Adjusting her gloves as she walked out the front door, Grace did not at first notice someone standing beside Hope's pony and the dogcart.

"Mr. King," she said, unable to disguise her surprise. "Good morning, sir. I did not expect you to call today."

The handsome, dark-haired man turned from studying her conveyance to face her. "Miss Everly, good morning." He came to her and bowed, a rather dapper grin in place. "I realized yesterday, Miss Everly, that you never did give me a tour of the orchards. I hoped to beg one from you today. But I can see you are going out and I am no more than an inconvenience." He sighed dramatically, his eyes twinkling at her. "Might we arrange it for another time?"

There would not be another time, she well knew. As anxious as she was to speak to Jacob, delaying the inevitable look of betrayal upon his face appealed to her. "I think I can spare you a quarter of an hour this morning, Mr. King. The orchard is not large, but a turn beneath the trees might do both of us good."

His countenance visibly brightened, and he held his arm out for her. "Nothing would be better for me, I am certain."

Grace took his arm, realizing she had no need to pretend with

Mr. King. He did not know Hope, only the stories he had heard of her, and yet he seemed to like Grace. Perhaps being in his company would give her the measure of confidence she needed to face Jacob. Walking beneath her father's apple trees never failed to settle her nerves, either.

"Then we had better take our tour, Mr. King." She waved to the groom. "I shall need the cart in a quarter of an hour." She kept her voice cheerful and light as she explained the importance of orchards to Mr. King, who proved an engrossed audience.

The diversion, the delay, was what she needed before she sought out Jacob for a much less lighthearted conversation.

※

JACOB HAD SPENT the whole of the previous day pondering his feelings for Grace. Now, on the second day since the picnic, he needed to speak to her. Not to make any sort of hasty decisions, but to see if he had imagined the possibility of more between them.

The uncomfortable conversation wasn't something he looked forward to, but what was a little discomfort if it led to lifelong happiness? Even if Grace did not see things as he wished, it would be best to find that out before he spent any more time romanticizing a friendship.

He asked Matthew to borrow the hunter and wasted no time in leaving once permission was given. What would he do when he could no longer use his brother's mount for his own errands? While the vicarage afforded a fine living, and some farmland came with it, he certainly couldn't afford such a fine horse. Whatever mount he used would have to pull a gig and likely a plow.

The bubble of pleasure in his chest, knowing the vicarage would be his in less than a fortnight, nearly burst within him. He would leave for a meeting with the bishop soon, to be ordained. Then, finally, his life would be on an established path where he had a place that belonged to him and a vocation to work upon.

As much as he had attempted to delude himself, entertaining the idea of courting Hope, Jacob easily recognized his folly now. Hope, though one of his dearest friends, could never be content with the life of a country vicar. She longed to see the world, to never be still, and she tended to act without thinking. He admired her fine spirit, and always would, but they would make each other miserable as husband and wife with their disparate ways.

He urged the horse into a longer, smoother gait, enjoying the summer air.

Grace, thoughtful and kind, aware of the people around her, and content in the familiar, would be an excellent wife. They were two of a kind, really. Often, Jacob had shared a look with Grace and instantly knew her thoughts were his own. He had attributed that strange phenomenon to their many years of friendship. How had he not seen how perfect they were for each other?

Jacob arrived at the Refuge and could not help grinning when he saw the pony and dogcart waiting for its mistress, a groom standing by. He dismounted and took the reins in hand.

"Is Miss Everly going on a visit?" he asked the servant.

"Yes, sir," the young man answered. "After she shows t'other gentleman the apple trees."

The other gentleman? Arching his eyebrows, Jacob tied his horse to the post near the front door. Who could possibly want to see the orchard? At least they would be easy to find. He took the path around the house, skirting the gardens. He came to the hedge, the orchard in sight, and heard Grace's laugh.

"I am in earnest, Miss Everly," an unfamiliar voice proclaimed, sounding anything but earnest. Jacob paused, the hedge keeping him out of sight. "You would far prefer London if you knew it as I did. I should love to see you try and convince a room full of peers to play games in the park."

Grace laughed again. "I cannot imagine it should end well, for me or the peers, if I were to make such a suggestion. You were fortunate to be part of that afternoon, Mr. King. To have grown men and women cheerfully playing those games is a rare sight, even in our quaint little neighborhood."

Of all the people he had thought of taking a stroll with Grace, Mr. King's name had not been one of them. Since he was friends with Isaac, and had fought in the war, Jacob had not stopped to consider the gentleman much beyond their initial introduction, except when irritated with him for flirting with Grace during her picnic.

They would come upon him eavesdropping in another moment. Jacob took the final steps around the hedge and raised his hand in greeting. "Miss Everly, Mr. King. Good day to you both."

Grace, on Mr. King's arm, drew up short and turned pale, no greeting passing her lips. Mr. King grinned hugely, however.

"Ah, Mr. Barnes, good day. We just took a turn about the orchard. Beautiful trees. I begin to wonder why my family never planted fruit trees. We have too many patches of vegetables." He sighed and lowered his head with an unnecessarily dramatic air.

Grace's color returned and she regarded Mr. King with a raised eyebrow. "We grow those too, Mr. King. Having one does not necessitate doing away with the other."

Mr. King, with his dark good looks and easy charm, regarded Grace with an overly familiar fondness. "I thank you for the education, Miss Everly. As you have another guest, I will take myself off and call upon you again another day. Perhaps you might show me the vegetables next time." He released her arm and bowed. "I shall say farewell to you both."

"Good day to you, Mr. King." Grace curtsied politely. She kept her gaze pointedly away from Jacob.

"Yes, good day." Jacob had to remind himself not to glare as the man took his leave. Grace stared after Mr. King, until he disappeared around the hedge. Then she dipped her head, not meeting Jacob's gaze.

"Jacob, what brings you here today?"

Had he bungled everything between them that terribly? At least he knew where he must begin. "I have come to apologize to you." He clasped his hands behind his back and then bent, enough to glimpse beneath her bonnet's brim. "I did not behave well at your picnic."

Her cheeks reddened and she shook her head. "Let us not speak of it, Jacob. I would rather we both forget about the whole thing."

"Forget?" He repeated the word stupidly. How could she wish to forget the moment that had made him rethink everything? Change everything? "Grace, you must at least let me explain."

She turned from him, folding her arms across her middle. "I would rather not hear another word about it. There is nothing to forgive because nothing happened. You see? Now we can go on as we always have."

That was the last thing he wanted. To contradict her might be impolite, but after all the time he spent preparing his speech, he could not remain silent. "You don't understand, Grace. I need you to know—"

"I received a letter from Hope." The words tumbled from her mouth, cutting off his attempts at an explanation. "She has left England. The letter says as much, that she would leave it with a servant to post after they boarded ship. Hope is gone." She shuddered and her arms tightened still more.

The news did not disturb Jacob. Not in the least. He did not feel sick, nor did he experience the horrible clenching in his gut as he had when he first learned Hope might leave. Love was not meant to be that fleeting and changeable. His own response to Grace's news served as evidence that he had come to his senses about Hope at last. She was not the woman for him, and he had never truly been in love with her.

But the news disturbed Grace. As her friend, first and foremost, he must do what he could to comfort her. "I see. What are you going to do?"

"I don't know. I was hoping to speak to you, to ask your opinion." She shrugged and opened her arms, then untied the reticule at her wrist. "She does not say much." Grace withdrew a folded paper —the letter from her sister. "But she is well, and happy. Would you like to read it?" Grace thrust the letter toward him with nearly as much vigor as she had thrust him away from her the day of the picnic.

Jacob looked from the letter to Grace's clear blue eyes, noting the way she stared at him when she had avoided looking at him moments before. She was searching him, a slight tremble to her lips as she pressed them together.

He slowly shook his head. "I don't need to read it, Grace. I'm glad that Hope is well." He steadied himself and relaxed his stance, hardly realizing how stiff he had become in his urgency to speak with her. As the tension left him, he managed to curve his lips upward again. "Would you like to take a walk to talk things over?"

The line appeared at the top of Grace's nose, her lips fell open again in that look of surprise he had seen when he came upon her and Mr. King. "A walk?"

"Yes." He stepped closer, gazing down at her. "To the orchard? Unless you grow tired of that particular path."

"No." She put the letter back into her little bag, then moved in the direction of the apple trees.

Jacob took two quick steps and snatched up her hand, startling her. He threaded it through his arm, then continued on as though nothing was amiss. They had not walked that way very often. Most of the time, if he offered an arm to Grace, Hope took the other. Alone with her now, her hand upon him, he took a moment to enjoy the sensation. How often had he touched her, as her friend? Helping her in and out of carriages, escorting her across a ballroom floor for a dance, and playing together as children, there must have been thousands of times in the past. Lately, however, he'd become more aware of her. More aware of the peace which settled in his heart when near her.

Distracting her with conversation struck him as the strategic thing to do, lest he give something of his feelings away too soon. "When did you receive the letter?"

She stared up at him almost plaintively, then turned so the brim of her bonnet blocked his view of her eyes. "Yesterday morning."

"Yesterday?" That surprised him. She had let another entire day go by without admitting the truth to her father. "Are you afraid of what your father will say?" Grace had never exactly been timid. Only quiet. Yet she had done her part in a trick that would lead to great heartache and disappointment for her parents.

"Not precisely." She paused a moment, and then spoke her next words clearly. "I think whatever punishment he gives will be worth the peace I have won by remaining home."

That did not sit well with him. "Wrongdoing is to be weighed against the consequences? You do not care about the response to your deception because you feel it was worth it?"

Grace sighed as though disappointed. "You cannot understand. You are a man." Her hand tightened briefly upon his arm, as though to soften her words. "You have choices. And I, even though I am of age, have none. Were I a son, my father would not attempt to send me away against my will. As a daughter, I am to be moved about as a pawn on a chessboard."

Jacob's feet scuffed to a stop. "A pawn? Grace, your father loves you."

"I know," she said. "But that does not mean he always does what is best for me. Sending me with the Carlburys was a punishment. But does a year away from all I love seem like an appropriate response to something *Hope* did wrong? He did not ask if I wished to go, or how I viewed the situation. He demanded it of me." Grace spoke softly, adopting a tone he had heard used before, by nurses and mothers when they explained difficult concepts to children.

"You have taken part in a lie, Grace. An act of disobedience. You may not have wished to go, but your father must have had his reasons for sending you." Jacob shook his head and began their walk again, though her steps seemed reluctant to match his.

Grace released a deep sigh. "Whatever wrong I have done does not compare to the wrong my father would do to me. He made a pronouncement when he was out of temper and no one would speak against him. I acted as I felt I must, and I am not sorry for it."

He had not expected such a response from Grace. While she had never been a contrary child, or a willful one, she had been stubborn. Just in a gentler way than most. "Very well. Then you will not apologize to your father?"

"No. But I will tell him the truth." They were nearly to the shade of the orchard when their progress halted again when Grace tugged at his arm. "And I must tell you the truth, Jacob."

"What truth? I knew of your identity from the beginning." Thankfully, he had never struggled to tell Grace and Hope apart.

Grace's hand fell from his arm. He watched as she raised her chin and squared her shoulders, gathering her words and her dignity like a shield around her.

Dread stilled his breath. She intended to tell him that his advances from the previous day were unwanted, and she did not feel for him anything beyond friendship. What other reason would she have to appear so grim? His fists clenched, as if he could fight away such words.

"None of this was Hope's idea."

Surprise replaced his fear. "None of what?"

"I came up with the plan to switch places." Her words emerged clear and strong. Unashamed. "I could not bear the thought of leaving home, of journeying to the West Indies. I have never wanted to leave here, and Hope was desperate to have her taste of adventure. I went to her the night before I was to leave and told her my plan. I had thought on it for days before I presented it to her."

Utterly confused, Jacob started shaking his head. Her declaration made no sense. "I thought you said Hope persuaded you—?"

Grace cut him off, her words spilling out with urgency. "I never said that, though you assumed it. Everyone thinks that Hope's propensity to rush into things headlong shows some sort of courage, and I do think she is quite brave. But it takes a different sort of bravery to plan all that I did. I had to do something to save myself, because no one else would." She took in a deep breath and stared at him, her eyes wide and pleading.

Pleading for what?

Everything had been her idea. She had no intention of apologizing for any of it, for admitting all she and Hope had done, all their lies, was wrong. And he had thought—had entertained the idea—of courting her.

"Grace," he said, taking a step away from her. "I hardly know what to say. I feel—it's as if I don't know you at all."

Tears glimmered in Grace's eyes. "Perhaps that is true. But I know you, Jacob. You are my dearest friend, and I have watched for the past year as you have done nothing to ensure your own happiness. You must excuse me, for I could not sit so long as you have when action was needed."

Her words reverberated through his mind, condemning him for acting a coward and not speaking to Hope of his desire to court her. It did not matter. Not really. He could brush aside Grace's anger, tell her his hesitation had saved them all from heartache, ask if he might try to get it right this time by courting *her* instead.

But to what end? He'd thought he understood Grace. Yet this conversation had shaken him, left him uncertain.

What was left for him to say? The silence stretched longer between them, the rustling of the leaves and far-off calling of birds the only noises which disturbed the stillness.

At last, Grace spoke. "I know I have upset you. I am sorry for that. But please, Jacob. Do not judge me too harshly. I did what I must to make certain of my future, and to give my sister the chance at one of her dearest dreams."

Jacob said nothing, the conflict in his heart and mind forcing him to keep still until he worked out what to do. His feelings for her, he realized, remained the same. But what was he to say about her actions?

"I am going to speak to my father now. You likely will not see me for some time." She lowered her head, the bonnet obscuring his view of her expression. "I hope you can understand, someday. I know you cannot condone my actions, and that is all right. You will make a fine vicar, Jacob."

Grace turned and went away, ignoring the path and cutting through the long grass in a direct line for the house. She did not look back, though he watched until she disappeared from sight. She never ran. Never faltered. In fact, she marched with the same determination he had seen in the soldiers who had practiced their drills marching through Aldersy years and years ago.

Yes, Grace had courage. But what of her integrity?

He dared not examine his heart's reaction to how terribly wrong the day had gone.

CHAPTER 17

Though Grace hadn't lacked the ability to tell Jacob exactly what she thought of her father's plan to send her to the West Indies, her determination started withering as soon as she entered the house. Her bonnet and gloves, her reticule, she handed to a maid. "Please let Charlie know I will not need the cart and pony after all," she said, realizing she had kept the boy and animal waiting for at least half an hour. She would need to make it up to them both.

As she walked down the hall, approaching her father's door, Grace wanted to continue on by and save her revelation for another time. But when would it be best to confess? No matter the time, her father's disappointment and anger would be the same.

Her feet stopped directly in front of the study. Her hand raised to knock, and she hesitated again.

Had she not just told Jacob there were different kinds of courage? She had to bear up and do the right thing. She had accepted the consequences when she chose to switch places with Hope.

Grace knocked.

"Come in." Her father's voice came through the wood, rich and warm as ever. Rarely had he ever lectured her, or raised his voice, as he had to Hope. Grace had never given him much reason to be displeased with her.

That is certainly about to change. She opened the door and entered, closing it carefully behind her. Her father's study was not overly large, but it was a comfortable room, full of elegant reds and golds, and dark stained wood. Papa was not behind his desk, as she thought he might be, but standing at the window behind it. He glanced over his shoulder.

"Ah, dear me. Is it time for refreshment already?" he asked, checking the time by the clock on the mantel. He wore his spectacles.

"No, Papa. At least, it is not your usual time. But if you would like something, I might fetch it for you." And give herself a few more moments of torment, facing the temptation to delay her confession.

"I am well enough," he answered with a grateful nod. "Is there something I might do for you, daughter?" He raised his graying eyebrows and came away from the window, around his desk. "You look as though you are troubled."

Grace crossed the distance between them, stopping at the chairs on the other side of the desk. "I have something I need to tell you." Although she wanted to stare at the floor, she kept her chin level with the ground. "I have done something that will disappoint you."

Papa stared at her, his face giving nothing of his thoughts away. "Have you? You had better tell me what it is, so we may go forward from there. I can see it upsets you, whatever the matter may be."

It had been much easier to be brave when she explained herself to Jacob. Would Papa care to even hear the reasons for her actions?

Curling her hands into fists at her side, Grace put her resolve in each word she spoke. "Papa, I am not Hope. I am Grace. We switched places the morning I was to leave."

Silence. The snapping fire, the slow tick of the clock, hardly made an impression upon her. All Grace could hear was the deafening muteness. Papa stared at her, his expression unchanging.

Until he sighed, and the corners of his eyes wrinkled as he grimaced. "I suspected as much."

Had he announced he wished to disown her, Grace could not have been more taken aback. "You what?" she stuttered the words out, her voice squeaking. "You could not—" She grabbed the back of the chair for support. "Papa, if you did—?"

"Why not say anything?" he asked for her. "Because I was not sure. I had hoped no daughter of mine would perform such an outrageous farce." His shoulders sagged. "Grace, how could you lie to me?"

As much as she hated the idea of him shouting at her, this unexpected reaction was somehow worse. "I could not go, Papa," she said, her voice weak. "I could not board a ship and be away from all I love for a year."

He took off his spectacles and rubbed at his eyes with the other hand. "Grace. This is a serious thing you have done. You have disobeyed my wishes, committed a deception not only upon your family but upon the entire neighborhood. Do you grasp the consequences to your actions? Have you any thought as to how this will change you in the eyes of all who know you?"

Grace opened her mouth to speak, but he cut her off again.

"I do not imagine you do. Your selfish performance, your lies, have stained you." He turned away from her. Why was he not shouting at her? Why not offer punishment and be done? "I had a letter yesterday from Mr. Carlbury. He wanted me to know they had sailed. Did you know Hope was gone?"

"Yes." She could have left it at that but told him the whole truth. "We arranged for her to send a letter before disembarking."

Lifting his eyes, he fixed her with a disbelieving stare. "Clever of you." He spoke the words flatly when he ought to have railed at her, or at least sounded disappointed. "This is serious, Grace. Your mother wrote to tell me she is staying another week. Perhaps you ought to write her your confession while I think upon this. I cannot decide how best to handle this situation. She may have greater insight." And then he went back to his chair, sitting and picking up a book. "Good day, Grace."

The dismissal did nothing to ease her shock. How could he have no reaction, nothing to say, other than to put her out of his way again?

"Papa?" She twined and twisted her fingers. "Do you not wish to know why?"

He put down the book and leaned back in his chair. "I can imagine. Hope wanted to have her adventure. You desired to stay home. You did what suited you best, never mind who you hurt or the trust you broke."

Although not technically incorrect, it was much less defensible than how she had worded it to Jacob. "No one should be forced to leave their home if they do not wish to go," she said at last, voice nearly a whisper. "It was not what suited me best, Papa. It was not fear of going."

"Doubtless those were strong motivators. I have excused you to your room, Grace. I no longer wish to speak of the matter." He did not lift his book, but kept his eyes on her, a furrow appearing in his brow.

Grace closed her eyes. "Papa, can you not see? There are precious few choices for a woman. To order me halfway across the world as some sort of punishment—"

He interrupted, tone at last stern. "It was an opportunity for growth. One that might never come your way again. It is true, you had no choice in the matter, but I acted as a concerned father. You are content to let life happen all around you, Grace, without actively seeking to better yourself or the world in which you live. Hope, though she can be over-exuberant, is not afraid of the world or of leaving home. She would make adventure for herself anywhere she goes. But not you." He released a long-suffering sigh, a sound which bruised Grace's heart. "You are timid, you are content for things to remain unchanging, and it concerns me. Now. Go to your room."

The command given firmly, Grace had to obey. She sucked in a quick breath and turned, each footstep falling heavily. Which of them was right? She thought it her. But that Papa could not understand her, and he saw such weakness in her character, hurt deeply.

There were arguments she might have made. Her parents hated traveling and rarely ever took their children to London, for the

Season or anything else. They remained happily at home. Why was it wrong for her to wish for the same?

And timid? She could not think herself so. Especially given the difficulty of pretending to be Hope in such varied situations. Jacob had not thought her timid. He thought her willful and rebellious.

As for the neighbors, why should they care which twin went where? Or which they had been talking to? Few of them even bothered to ascertain which sister they spoke to before beginning conversations.

No one would care at all.

For the first time since Hope had gone away, Grace entered her own bedroom. The familiar greens and blues, the soft rug by her hearth, immediately comforted her bruised heart. She settled upon her bed and took down her hair. At last, she could be herself again.

⚜

JACOB PACED BACK and forth after dinner, eyeing the writing desk in the corner of the parlor.

His mother noticed. "Whatever is wrong with you tonight, Jacob?" He pulled his gaze away from the paper and pen, fixing it upon his mother instead. She sat in her favorite chair, her little terrier in her lap. "You hardly said a word at dinner and now you are attempting to wear a path into my best carpet."

His feet stopped.

"I think it is one of two things," Matthew said from the other side of the room, newspaper open in his lap. "He is either nervous over the ordination or anxious about a lady."

Elizabeth and Mary both giggled where they sat upon the couch, organizing a box of buttons.

"Jacob, anxious about a lady?" Elizabeth's eyebrows arched high. "I cannot imagine it. He has never courted anyone."

Mary, younger and more intrigued by the interaction of men and women than not, peered at him through narrowed eyes. "Jacob does not even dance often. I cannot think it is about a lady."

He looked from one family member to the other, hardly knowing if he ought to be insulted or amused. Unfortunately, given his present state of mind, he was merely tired. "I happen to enjoy dancing, and I will thank you all not to speak of me as though I am not present."

Matthew turned his newssheet over. "You had better tell Mother what is bothering you if you wish for the rest of us to stop speculating."

"It's nothing." Jacob took one of the empty chairs near the couch. "I suppose I'm anxious to be on my way tomorrow." He could not tell them about Grace. He did not know if she had spoken to her own father yet.

He felt his mother's stare, as he had many times in his youth. When she spoke, he was unsurprised. "Perhaps you ought to go and visit Sir Isaac before you leave. He is one of your oldest friends, after all, and may wish you to take your leave of him."

Jacob answered without thought, "I will only be away a week."

"Jacob." When his mother spoke in that commanding tone of voice he had to look directly at her. It was not the voice of gentle coaxing she had used before, but one of command. When he turned to her, she considered him a moment with pursed lips before issuing her edict. "Go visit Sir Isaac."

"Yes, Mother." He stood and went to the door.

"Why does he have to go? And at this time of night?" Mary asked, her curiosity sweetly innocent.

It was Matthew who answered. "Because he will talk to Sir Isaac if he will not talk to us."

Jacob shut the door behind him and went for the stairs, smiling at how well his family knew him. Perhaps they were right. He could trust Isaac with Grace's secret, and someone ought to know in case she needed assistance. Whether or not she had revealed her ruse to her father, things would get more difficult for her.

He rushed through getting dressed, not bothering to call a servant. He might not look tidy when he arrived at Isaac's door, but his friend did not care about such things. Once his dinner clothes had been properly replaced with riding boots and the rest of an ensemble suited to such an activity, he went for the stables.

It was dinner time for most of the neighborhood, or just past the hour for such. Isaac, a bachelor with a friend to entertain, would not think the hour too late for a visit.

When he arrived at the baronet's house, Woodsbridge, there were enough windows lit from within for him to know his friend was home. Woodsbridge was an old establishment, consisting of only two floors and the attics and cellars. It was not a large residence and did not give away that the family was old and well-funded.

Isaac's home had always been comfortable. One did not feel they must be on their best behavior or wear their finest clothing when visiting.

Upon Jacob's arrival, he was shown to Isaac's billiards room. Mr. King and Isaac were both present, coats removed, billiard-sticks in hand.

"Good evening, Barnes," Isaac said, laying his stick down across the table. "You are just in time for some amusement. We are trying to determine a method by which a one-armed man can still play billiards. Thus far, we have been unsuccessful."

Jacob chuckled. "You were never great at billiards even with two arms."

His friend sighed and hung his head in a comical manner. "That is the truth of it." Then he brightened and adjusted his cravat. "What brings you here this evening?"

Nothing he could speak of in front of Mr. King. "I have come to take my leave of you for a short time."

"Ah, ordination. Congratulations. You will do a wonderful service for our parish." Isaac lifted his coat from where it hung on a chair. "Mr. King, will you forgive us a moment? I would like to have a word with my friend."

"Certainly." Mr. King made to put down his stick, but Isaac shook his head.

"No, old fellow. You stay here and practice playing one handed, so that you may give me instruction later." Then Isaac, with seemingly practiced ease, put his coat over his left shoulder, then reached behind himself to slide his right arm into the sleeve. The manner of putting on his own coat ought to have been inelegant, but Isaac acted as if it had always been natural. He pulled the front together and buttoned it closed.

Jacob bowed to Mr. King and followed his friend out of the room and down the passageway.

"You will come back to us a vicar and a week later give your first sermon," Isaac said as he pushed open the door to his library. "We have all gone down such interesting paths. Silas married my sister, I went off to war, you are taking orders, and the Everlys—"

"—are the reason I am here," Jacob said, shutting the door behind them. "I know you have been busy of late, but I must ask. Have you noticed anything strange about our friend?"

Isaac blinked. "Hope? Not precisely. I found it odd she did not defend Grace at dinner the other night, but perhaps she felt she could not, with her father there. I imagine it still hurts to know Grace is off on a grand adventure while Hope is stuck here with us." He settled into the couch before the fire as he spoke, adjusting a cushion for his comfort.

Not even Isaac had sensed what Jacob had immediately known. Dropping onto the couch next to his friend, he could not help but laugh, though the sound turned into something of a groan. "She has fooled everyone, and I thought she would be discovered in less than a day."

Lifting his eyebrow, Isaac tapped the arm of the couch with one finger. "Who has fooled everyone?"

"Grace." Jacob rubbed at his forehead with one hand and leaned back. "Grace and Hope switched places before the Carlburys left. Hope went with them, pretending to be Grace. Grace stayed here and has tricked the entire neighborhood into believing she is Hope."

For several seconds, Isaac simply stared at Jacob. "Confound it," he muttered at last. "I should have noticed."

Though privately agreeing, Jacob said nothing aloud. "She received word yesterday that Hope is gone from the country, so I imagine she will soon reveal herself. But as I leave in the morning, and I am the only one who knew, I thought I should tell you. In case Grace needs anything."

"Of course. Anything for either Everly." Isaac's eyes narrowed and he tilted his head back. "How did you know about the switch? I cannot imagine they involved you in the idea. You are far too honest."

Jacob sunk further into his seat. "I figured it out myself."

"Ah." Isaac tapped his fingers on the arm of the chair.

Had Jacob's friend nothing else to say on the matter? It did not satisfy the man about to turn vicar. "I cannot believe Grace would do such a thing. It is completely out of character for her to behave in such a devious manner. I might have believed it from Hope."

That made Isaac grin. "Is that really what you think? I daresay, they would have been discovered sooner had it been Hope's idea. She is more like me. We act without rehearsing or thinking through our plans. At least, I used to be that way. A captaincy in the army changed that aspect of my life somewhat." He raised his hand to rub the back of his neck. "The whole of it must have been Grace's idea. Grace is the strategist in our group, you know. She always has been."

Although Jacob opened his mouth to argue, he closed it almost directly. A dozen instances of Grace quietly offering her suggestions for their childhood exploits came to mind. Silas led them, but Grace had made sure everyone knew which direction to go.

"I would have given a great deal to have a mind like hers while we were in France." Isaac finally turned again to grin at Jacob, but the cheerful expression wilted. "You seem upset about this. Why?"

"How can you not be?" Jacob countered. "She came into your house, perpetuating a fraud. She tricked *everyone* for days. Disobeyed her parents by staying when she should have gone."

"You object to her actions from a moral standpoint. Yes, I suppose you must." Isaac shifted to better face Jacob, leaning into the corner of the couch. "She has not hurt anyone by her actions, surely?"

"Not that I am aware. But how will anyone trust her again?"

"Is that all you're worried about? Give it time. People will gossip about the situation now and again, but no one who knows Grace will truly doubt her honesty. Do *you* doubt it?" Isaac asked the question with his grin returning. "For myself, I plan to congratulate her."

The flippant response pushed Jacob's indignation further. He rose from his seat and paced before the fire. "Why? She has done nothing noble, nothing good, only acted selfishly." He expected so much more from Grace.

"And? We all behave selfishly now and again, do we not?" Isaac kept trying to find humor in the situation, but Jacob could not allow for that. He could not laugh at it. "Jacob, you must forgive her for hurting your sensibilities. I thought it the worst possible thing when I learned Grace was to be sent away. Anyone who knows her must recognize what a torture it would be to send Grace Everly into the wild places of the world. She is content here, in Aldersy."

Still pacing, Jacob threw up his hands. "That is not the point. The lies, the deception, those are what people will use to condemn her."

The next words from Isaac came out sharply. "And how her actions distanced you from Hope? Is that what bothers you most?"

That stopped Jacob mid-step. He folded his arms and turned on his heel to face the baronet. "You knew about that, too?"

"It's an arm I've lost, not my eyes," Isaac muttered. "Come off it, Jacob. As much as we all admire Hope's spirit, she was never meant for any of us. Not you, and not me."

Jacob's head snapped back in his surprise. "Not *you*? Are you saying that you — ?"

"Years ago." Isaac lifted both shoulders in a shrug, and his grin turned self-depreciating. "I actually said something to her about it once. Hinted that we might make a fine pair. Hope laughed and bid me never speak of such nonsense again. She was right. We are too alike, she and I. We would've driven each other mad. Hope needs someone who can love her nature and give her freedom. Neither of us are in the position for that." Isaac did not seem overly upset about it.

Really, Jacob wasn't either. He was more upset everyone seemingly noticed his feelings and never said a word about it to him before.

Perhaps he ought to trust Isaac with more of his concerns. If anyone could help Jacob set his mind and heart at ease, it would be one of his friends.

"At first, I was upset about Hope leaving." That much Jacob could admit. "But I have been confused of late over someone else entirely. You see, I think—it is entirely possible—that I have feelings for Grace." He dropped his hands limply to his sides. He had known Grace forever. How could his feelings change for her now?

Isaac gawked unabashedly at him. "That should be good news," he finally said. "Since she feels the same."

Jacob scoffed at that. "I doubt it. I meant to tell her yesterday when I saw her and ask if she might see me as more than a friend."

"What stopped you?" Isaac gaped at Jacob as though he were a lackwit.

Given that Isaac immediately knew the whole plan was Grace's, Jacob felt rather unintelligent admitting that the revelation had silenced him. He settled for giving only part of the explanation. "I am to be the vicar. People will look to me as an example and hold me to a higher standard than other men. When they learn about her deception, if I courted her, it might cause them to doubt me. A vicar and his wife must be above reproach."

"That is possibly the stupidest thing I have ever heard." Isaac leveraged himself off the couch and glared at Jacob. "You are the one about to be ordained, but it seems I need to remind you of some thing you will be preaching ere long. 'Judge not, lest ye be judged.' No man or woman is perfect, and we all have our faults and failings. 'Let he who is without sin cast the first stone.' You see? Perhaps I should have gone into the church instead of the army."

Jacob stared at his friend, taken aback and uncertain how to respond.

Isaac glared back, unflinching. "Grace is our friend. She did something you cannot like, but I believe she had excellent motivation. I know no one on this earth so good as Grace, excepting you."

The compliment chastened Jacob. His thoughts toward Hope, and then Grace, had not been charitable. They had been seasoned with anger and disappointment.

"If you are her friend, you will stand beside her," Isaac said when

Jacob remained quiet. "And if you harbor more for her in your heart, then you will forgive her." He put his hand on Jacob's shoulder. "You are my friend, too. Tomorrow you leave for your ordination. You will have time to think on all of this, and I will look after things in the meantime."

Thinking. Yes, Jacob had plenty of time for that.

CHAPTER 18

The two days in her room passed slowly. While sitting amongst familiar things gave Grace comfort, not knowing what happened outside her doors and windows drove her to distraction. Jacob would have left for his ordination, that she knew.

The servants had been informed of her true identity. Susan called Grace by name, reproachfully, while attending to her. Cook sent up trays of Grace's favorite foods, but the portions were unusually small, something Grace suspected Cook did on purpose. Grace was given enough to eat, but her favorite jam did not quite cover her toast, and her favorite roast lamb did not take up as much space on her plate as the boiled carrots.

If the servants knew, then the gossip had likely spread to everyone.

The morning of the third day, Grace's father sent for her to attend him in his study. As soon as Grace was dressed, in her favorite blue gown, she went to him.

Rain had fallen most of the morning, and the clouds remaining in the sky meant Papa's study was pale and gray even with the open curtains.

Papa sat in a chair this time, and he gestured for her to join him in the seat near his. "Grace," he said, his tone more weary than strict. "I trust you have taken the time these past two days to contemplate your actions?"

"Yes, Papa." She folded her hands in her lap, unwilling to tell him she did not regret her actions. Not unless he asked.

He sighed and removed his spectacles, tucking them into his coat. "I have given a great deal of thought to the situation as well. I have written a letter to Hope, and to the Carlburys. It will not reach them for weeks, perhaps months, but I felt it my duty to explain the situation to them. I also wrote to your mother, and I urge you to do the same. She should not be kept in ignorance of the situation, and I feel you ought to apologize for the disregard you have shown her in this matter."

"Yes, Papa. I will write her." Truthfully, she had started several letters to her mother only to give up after a few lines. She had cut the start of each letter off the paper until she had been left with a square too small to do any sort of explanation justice.

Papa sighed and rubbed his forehead, then dropped his hand onto the arm of the chair. "It is done, and there is little I can do to remedy the situation. Tomorrow is Sunday. I have asked Mr. Spratt if he will allow you a moment after services to speak to those assembled. It is an extraordinary request, but he agreed. I expect you to make a public apology and explanation for your actions. You may write it out if you wish, but it will be done."

The room went cold, and Grace shuddered. "Papa, in front of everyone—"

"Yes, in front of everyone. You pretended to be your sister for all the world to see, you can offer up your confession and the truth in a similar manner." His expression hardened and he leaned forward, his deep blue eyes a match for hers. "I am severely disappointed in you, Grace. You have never acted in such a manner that gave me cause to feel ashamed of you."

"There was no other way," she said, clenching her hands together. Her voice shook, her emotion spilling forth in a humiliating manner. "Papa, there was nothing else I could do to save myself. You would not listen to argument; you did not care what I wished or feared. I would rather have been locked in the attics than be sent so far. You *know* that, and you did not care."

Her father stared at her, posture stiffening, before abruptly looking away. He said nothing. Did he think to dismiss her with silence? Papa loved her. He must listen.

Getting control of herself, Grace lowered her tone. "I know you think I am small, and weak, and shy. But it is not so, Papa. My friends care for me, they respect me. I am important, my feelings are important. You would not force me to leave your house in order to wed a man I did not like. Why would you send me into the world in a manner that you know would sicken me? Your anger with Hope may have been deserved, but the punishment of keeping her away from what she wished had nothing to do with sentencing me to misery."

When he still said nothing, his hands flexing in his lap the only sign he had not turned into a wax figure, Grace stood. "I know you are upset with me, but I hope you can also understand my actions. I did not do anything in order to disrespect you, but to save myself from misery, as any creature with a heart would." Then she dared to step forward and kiss him upon his cheek. He smelled of strawberries and tobacco, comforting scents. He did not pull away or flinch. That gave her some comfort.

Grace withdrew from the room, her mind upon what she must say in the morning after Mr. Spratt's sermon. At least it was not his last. It would be a shame to mar the final Sunday he presided over their congregation with a mortifying public display.

Taking in a deep breath, Grace turned from the stairs and went out into the garden. She lifted a shawl from the hook on the way out but did not pause to do more. She had not been outside in days, and a walk through their little gardens would suit her nicely.

She went out the front door, intending to walk around the house to access the gardens, but she paused when she saw a horse and rider coming up the lane. The horse was not familiar to her, and the man upon its back did not look like one of her friends.

The rider saw her and increased his horse's speed with

purpose. It was Lord Neil, son of the Marquess. What business did he have at the Refuge? Although tempted to withdraw, her interview with her father had bolstered her spirits. She pulled the shawl tighter about herself and lifted her chin in the air, prepared to do battle.

Lord Neil pulled up short of her position. "Ah, Miss Grace, the very person I hoped to see." His broken arm was in a sling, keeping it still and tight against his chest. His free hand held the reins of the horse in a firm grip. "You will excuse me if I do not dismount. My errand is short, and it is dashedly difficult to mount with one arm and no groom."

"Perhaps you ought to ask Sir Isaac how he manages," Grace said tartly, then bit her tongue. Throwing her friend's injury out as some kind of challenge showed Isaac little compassion or respect. She lowered her eyes to the ground where the horse's hoof pawed at the gravel.

The nobleman surprised her with a chuckle. "I might do just that." Then he cleared his throat and she saw his riding boot twitch. "As I have said, it is you I have come to see. I have heard about what you and your sister did, trading identities."

Grace nodded, wondering if he expected an apology of some sort. They had thwarted the punishment given for causing his injury, after all.

"I wanted to tell you that I thought it was cleverly done, and I harbor no resentment toward either of you."

His words surprised her into looking up, a protest rising to her lips. He could not be serious. Lord Neil had ever been a rascal, after all, and often made things difficult for others. Yet Grace studied his face before speaking, taking in the bend of his eyebrows and the intensity of his stare.

"My lord, you have come to compliment me on my duplicity?" If ever there was an indication she had done something wrong, it would be Lord Neil's approval.

"It may be better to say I do not condemn them." He offered her a tight smile. "My sister went on something of a tirade when she heard of the matter, and I wanted to make certain you knew I did not feel the same. The whole situation might be viewed as something of a joke, you know."

What was she to make of such a pronouncement? "I thank you, my lord." She did not bother to hide her skepticism and he actually grinned at her.

"There is gossip, Miss Grace. Or Miss Everly, I suppose, with your sister gone away. People are speculating your reasons for such a thing. They are also saying it is a grave insult to my father, to Olivia, and to myself that your sister escaped punishment for my injury. I have done what I could to placate my sister, and I have assured anyone who has spoken to me that I feel no ill will toward you."

Still unable to believe him, Grace barely offered up the polite and expected words. "I thank you for that, my lord."

Lord Neil took up the reins and his horse stepped to the side in response. His lordship's face changed again, looking more serious. "I realize I am not often a pleasant person, Miss Everly. But I give you my word, today I speak sincerely. Good morning to you." He nodded deeply and when she returned the farewell he turned his horse about and left.

Watching him go down the lane, Grace narrowed her eyes in suspicion. "I suppose he could have made my life more difficult," she said aloud, still trying to puzzle him out. While Lord Neil had never done anything explicitly rude toward her, she knew he and her dear friend Silas had many fractious encounters. The most recent of which involved Lord Neil's flirtation with Silas's wife, Esther.

Whatever the man was about, she had no wish to know the particulars. Hoping he had been sincere to her was all she could do.

The sun peeked out from behind the gray swath of clouds, giving her a moment of brightness. Squaring her shoulders, Grace continued on her way, determined still to take her walk and enjoy the rain-freshened garden.

THE NEXT MORNING, Grace prepared for services with her usual care. She dressed modestly, in shades of cool green that reminded her of spring. Susan did her hair in intricate twists which would allow curls to escape from her bonnet in a fetching manner. When she came down the stairs, her father gave her an odd look before he led her outside to the gig.

The church was not far, and in previous years their family had walked because Papa insisted it wore the children out enough that they would sit still during the sermon.

Papa had hardly spoken to her at dinner the night before, but when he did speak he was polite. There was no frustration in his voice anymore. Though Grace may have imagined it, she thought he had even begun to look at her with something like understanding. One day, he might speak to her of her choices again, but she doubted another word would be said on the matter once she made her apology to the neighborhood.

Grace admired the church anew as they approached it. The old stone building had long ago been a Catholic chapel, built the year before King Henry VIII decreed himself independent of Rome and the Pope. Despite the church's age, it still served their parish well. The fine cut of the stone, the ancient stained glass, gave the smallish building distinction and beauty.

While she sat next to her father, listening to Mr. Spratt's reading of a sermon on forgiveness, she imagined what it would be like in a fortnight when Jacob stood to deliver his first scripture and sacraments. He would look well in his vestments, as distinguished as the church itself. His warm voice would wash over the room and reverberate against the stone walls most pleasantly.

Her heart throbbed, sore still from his parting words. Though she tried not to think on him, tried not to remember the way he had stared at her in the orchard as if he would kiss her, Jacob's smiles and frowns lived within her mind and heart. If only he had understood her, or at least made the attempt.

Their friendship had been damaged, she well knew. It would take a great deal of time to heal it again, if ever it was to be healed. Yet despite telling him the truth Grace had kept one thing back. Telling him of her feelings, her admiration and the love she felt for him, could have done no more damage than her actions already had.

Sir Isaac, seated near the front, turned slightly and beamed at her. Dear Isaac, always her friend no matter what. Did he know what she was about to do, in front of the whole congregation? She had noticed more than a few people turn her way only to next bend their heads to whisper to their neighbors. They were all judging her, speculating on what she had done and why.

The sermon drew to a close. A final hymn was sung after the prayer was said. Then Mr. Spratt looked to her father, his eyebrows raised behind his spectacles.

This was it. This was the moment Grace must speak. Every muscle in her body tensed as she prepared to stand.

To her surprise, her father silently shook his head, staring back at the vicar. Mr. Spratt nodded graciously at Grace, and then walked out of the building to stand in his customary place to bid everyone a good sabbath.

Grace stared after him, then turned to look up at her father. "Papa?"

"Grace." He heaved a sigh, as though he bore a great weight upon his chest. "My dear girl, let us go home. Our business is our own, what consequences that arise naturally from your actions will be enough."

She reached out and took his hand. "Thank you, Papa." He turned his palm over and squeezed her hand gently. "I love you."

"I love you, too." He offered her his arm. They left the church, greeted by a few friends, smiled upon by Mr. Spratt, and Grace held her head high all the way home.

CHAPTER 19

J acob sat with his eldest brother in a private parlor at their inn, the silence between them comfortable. The late afternoon sunlight cast a soft light into the room, and Jacob's thoughts lingered on the ordination he had undergone hours earlier. Matthew had accompanied Jacob to Norwich, to lend his support and companionship to the journey.

"You are a changed man, I take it?" Matthew asked, bringing an end to Jacob's contemplative state.

"I hope so." Jacob fought back a grin. "It would be a sorry thing if such an event had no impact upon my person. I have promised a great many things to God and to myself today. I hope I am ready for this responsibility."

Matthew leaned back in his chair, a gleam in his eye. "I do as well, for I must put a request to you. An official request to my priest. Would you officiate for a wedding ceremony between myself and Eliza Muir?"

Although the family expected, and hoped, for an announcement of the sort, Jacob's surprise delayed his response a moment. "I would be honored, Matthew. Why have you waited this long? Surely not for me."

"Of course for you," Matthew scoffed good-naturedly. "I can think of nothing finer than to have you perform the ceremony, and Eliza agreed. You ought to get your practice in with people who will not mind your novice recitation of the marriage sacrament."

Jacob laughed and raised his half-empty cup to his brother. "I salute you for finding a willing bride at last."

Lifting his cup, Matthew nodded in agreement. "And finally giving Mother grandchildren." They both tipped their dinner cups and drank.

"It is cheating to marry someone who already has children." Jacob had met Mrs. Muir's children on several occasions. They were young, a little girl and a boy barely out of leading strings, and as adorable as children that age could be. "You will be a fine father to them."

"That is my hope." Matthew stared into his cup, his eyebrows drawn down. "I have come to love them and their mother. I cannot imagine many more days without Eliza by my side and those children filling our old nursery with their joy."

Watching his brother over the past several months, Jacob had seen the change in Matthew, a change wrought by love. He was still himself, but a better version than he had previously been. Matthew was more thoughtful of others, and he laughed more, too.

"When do you think you will propose to the Everly girl?" Matthew asked.

Jacob laid an arm over the table and pushed his fork further onto his empty plate. "I do not think I can." Matthew scowled and opened his mouth to protest, so Jacob hastened to add, "Things have grown more complicated, Matthew. More than I am able to explain."

"You cannot get out of it that easily. I am your brother. Tell me and perhaps I might help." Matthew put his cup down and pushed slightly away from the table. "Did you at least take my advice from before?"

It took Jacob a moment to recall what that advice had been. "To determine if she would make me a good wife, not a good wife to a vicar. Yes. But since I am now a vicar, the point is one and the same."

"Not really." Matthew stood and went to the window, looking out into the inn's courtyard as he spoke. "You may be a vicar, but you are still you. The woman you marry needs to please Jacob Barnes, not whatever parish you shepherd. People will come and go, marry, die, leave. Your only constant in this life will be your family, the wife you choose for yourself, your children. So you must choose someone who pleases you, Jacob. Not someone who pleases the flock."

Jacob considered those words, measuring them against the vows he had that morning taken, promising to care for the souls in his parish and helping them seek their eternal salvation. He had promised to make himself, and his family, a wholesome example to his parish.

When he thought of Grace, despite all that had passed of late, he knew her to be a compassionate woman, kindhearted and good. Gentle and mindful of others.

"There is something else," Jacob said, lowering his voice. "A secret that I sincerely pray is no longer a secret."

"This sounds ominous." Matthew remained where he was, though he turned fully to give Jacob his attention. "What secret?"

Although reluctant to speak of it, Jacob could not keep it to himself any longer. Not in light of all that he had promised that day. It seemed everyone about him had given him advice about Hope, or Grace, and he had yet to settle his own mind and heart as firmly as he wished. After swearing his brother to secrecy, should Grace not have done the right thing by telling her father the truth, Jacob explained all that had happened since Hope had left for the West Indies, including their switch.

Matthew said little, though he listened attentively. His eyebrows shot high upon his forehead when Jacob admitted to almost kissing Grace in the orchard, and then Matthew covered his grin with his fist when Jacob described Grace pushed him away. When Jacob concluded the tale, he stood and went to one of the two chairs by the fire and collapsed into it. His mind and spirit were worn through, even if his body had been little taxed that day.

"It is rather like something out of a novel, or a play." Matthew came and took the other chair, staring into the fire. "There is too much confusion, with your heart near the center of it. Although I cannot say whether Grace's actions were right or wrong, it does sound as though this experience has proved difficult for her."

Jacob steepled his fingers before him. "I have tried not to think about it these past three days. Traveling, preparing for ordination. I had other things to occupy my thoughts. But Grace is still there. In my mind. Pleading with me to understand her."

"Do you worry about her character?" Matthew asked.

"No. Not at all." Jacob shifted in his chair and sighed. "I worry about mine." The truth had come to him as he had stood before the bishop and listened to the prayers and scriptures read. "How could I think myself in love with Hope and be so wrong? And how do I know that giving Grace my attention is any better? I was prepared to ask for a courtship when she told me the whole plan, the switch, had been her idea. It frightened me that I did not know enough about her, one of my oldest friends, to have guessed at it. Isaac knew right away who had planned it," he admitted, a trifle sourly.

The room had grown dark while they spoke, and a maid entered to light the candles above the mantle. Neither brother said a word while that was done, but when the door shut behind the servant, Matthew leaned forward, clasping his hands before him.

"It sounds as though you are afraid of making a mistake, and I understand that fear. Think on who you want by your side when you face illness, when you welcome a child into the world. Try to decide who you would have as your companion by the fire at night, who you trust to be by your side as you grow old." Matthew stood and gave Jacob a pat on the shoulder. "You have always been a steady man, Jacob. Patient and careful in what you do. I have faith you will make the right decision."

The kind words warmed his heart, even if they did not entirely bolster his confidence. Jacob nodded his thanks. "Are you for bed then?"

"I think it wise. We leave early in the morning. Mother will be anxious to have you home a few more days before you live at the vicarage."

"Good night, Matthew."

"Good night, Jacob. And good luck." Matthew left the room.

For some time, Jacob stayed where he was, considering the choices before him. He did not even know Grace's thoughts on the matter of a courtship. Or what she thought of him. She had always been a kind friend, and a tenderhearted woman. In the past weeks, Jacob had even imagined that she looked at him differently than she had before. Could Isaac have been right about her feelings?

Time. He needed more time before he spoke of his hopes for the future and before he made any plans.

CHAPTER 20

Grace settled at the pianoforte, her fingers trembling in her impatience. She had gone without her music while pretending to be Hope, and then abstained from playing in order to preserve peace for her father. That morning at breakfast, however, he had requested that she play. And he had spoken to her with such kindness that she knew he was well on his way to forgiving her.

First she played a piece by her favorite Austrian composer, Beethoven. *Für Elise*. She stumbled on the third measure, as the piece required a rapid pace her fingers were not quite limber enough to play. She did not stop, however. The joy of stumbling through the notes was nearly as perfect as if she had played flawlessly. Then she played one of her father's favorites, a sonata written by another Austrian musician.

She had moved on to another song when a knock on the open door startled her. Her fingers left the keys when she saw Jacob standing there, his expression uncertain.

"My mother has come to visit you." He shifted his weight from one foot to the other. "She insisted I come, too. Mr. Everly asked me to fetch you."

"Oh." She stared at him a second longer, then lowered her gaze to the instrument. "I will be there in a moment."

He did not immediately move, which tempted her into looking up at him again.

One corner of his mouth went upward. "You play beautifully, Grace."

"Thank you." Did he not want to get away from her quickly, as he had seemed to before? She gathered her music and stood. "I must congratulate you on your ordination," she said at last, the words polite rather than warm. "I know how much it means to you."

He ducked his head. "It is something I have wanted for a long time. Thank you."

Was this to be the new standard of their conversations? Polite phrases, impersonal words? Grace bit her lip as she returned the music to its shelves. Perhaps he was still angry with her.

"Grace," he said, his voice nearer. She turned to find him in the room, several steps inside it, though more still separated them. "Is everything all right? I heard that everyone knows, and there must have been some unpleasantness—"

She came forward, lifting her hands to stop his words. "No, nothing like that. A few people have looked at me strange, like Mrs. Parr and her daughter, and Miss Keyes may have said something less than pleasant, but—"

"But when does Miss Keyes really say anything else?" he interrupted, looking amused. "I am relieved to hear it. I worried for you."

"I thank you for your concern." She started to walk around him, but Jacob's hand gently caught her arm before she passed by.

"Grace." Lines creased his forehead, he stared down at her with an intensity she had rarely seen from him. "I'm glad you are you again."

She pursed her lips, slightly confused. "You always knew who I was."

He released her and ran a hand through his hair, mussing it without any concern. "I know. I still cannot understand why no one else realized what you were up to."

"I suppose no one else ever took the time to look too closely."

And he had looked because he expected Hope, wanted Hope, and found Grace instead.

She told herself to be brave. For her, that did not mean going on a voyage to a different world, as Hope had. For Grace, being brave meant something else entirely. Tucking her hands behind her so he wouldn't see her ball them into fists, she forced her thoughts into words.

"I have learned something from all of this."

"Oh?" Jacob's smile appeared, hesitantly at first.

"I have learned that speaking my mind can be beneficial. Especially when I told my father all my thoughts on the matter. I am not certain he has quite forgiven me yet, but he is much more understanding of my actions now." She took in a deep breath, aware of how forward she would seem. A lady should not speak to a gentleman as she was about to, but Jacob was her friend. "I have something I wish to say to you, too."

His lips stiffened, then he cleared his throat as though nervous. "Have you?"

"Yes." The truth had weighed upon her heart long enough. Perhaps her confession would offer a reprieve at last. "I love my sister, but in some ways it was a relief to have her gone. I know it sounds selfish, and I am happy for her to have her dream at last, but having your attention to myself made every moment of the ruse worthwhile." Grace ducked her head before seeing his reaction. She was not that brave. Not yet.

She hurried from the room, head low and heart thrumming. Telling him everything proved impossible. For a wild instant, she had considered revealing more of her feelings to him. Perhaps she ought to deliver only a portion at a time, so as not to shock him.

"Grace," his voice called in the passageway. She stopped but did not turn, near the stair. His footsteps caught up to her, slowing when he came up behind her.

When he spoke again, his voice was softer. "I am glad you did not go with the Carlburys." Then his hand touched her wrist again, barely brushing it, yet the contact sent electric tingles up her arm.

"Thank you. But I know you were disappointed that Hope did

not remain at home." The truth slipped from her like water down a rock.

He stepped around her, then offered his arm. Grace accepted it without seeing his expression, certain she would find pity in his eyes.

"At first I may have been. I had hoped to gain the courage to court her in earnest. But I can see now—and I have known for some time—that Hope and I would not suit one another."

The sincerity of his words comforted her. At least he no longer pined for her sister. Together, they went upstairs to the parlor, not saying another word to each other.

Mrs. Barnes stood when Grace entered, and after Grace's polite greeting, the woman crossed the room and enveloped her in a hug. Although momentarily surprised, Grace returned the embrace.

"Dear Grace." Mrs. Barnes parted from her, taking up Grace's hands. "I have been telling your father what I think of your actions, young lady."

Grace's cheeks pinked and she looked to where her father stood at his chair, Jacob coming to stand beside him wearing his curiosity quite openly.

"And what do you think of them?" Grace asked, looking up into Mrs. Barnes's kind face.

"I think you did the best you could in your situation, and I am not at all upset with you." Mrs. Barnes bestowed a kiss upon Grace's cheek before leading her to the couch. "I want to hear all about it. I imagine you had a difficult time, because no matter how alike you and your sister are in appearance, your characters are so divergent."

She wanted Grace to talk of what she had done? No one else had asked for that. Not even her mother, when she had written back after receiving Grace's letter of confession. In confusion, she looked to her father. "Papa?"

He settled back into his seat and released a put-upon sigh. "You might as well tell the story. In years to come, I imagine most will be more amused than troubled by it."

Grace looked to Jacob. He had been part of the story. As of yet, she had not revealed his place in it. His abhorrence of deception would make him reticent to admit to it.

"Tell your story, Grace," he encouraged gently. "I will let you know if you leave anything out."

Mrs. Barnes instantly turned to face her son. "How exactly would you be capable of that?"

"Someone recently told me I needed to be more courageous in my words and actions." He faced her father. "I knew of Grace's deception, from the very first day."

"You what?" Papa started to rise from his chair but seemed to think better of it and lowered himself back most abruptly. "Oh, I suppose that does not surprise me at all. You and the girls have always been thick as thieves."

Grace turned to Mrs. Barnes, ready to defend Jacob, but she stopped when she saw the way Mrs. Barnes was staring at her son. The woman regarded him with narrow-eyed amusement.

"I see. Well now. That does explain a few things." Mrs. Barnes tapped one finger against her lips in a speculative manner. "A great many of my son's conversations suddenly make sense."

Jacob blushed. "You wanted to hear the story, Mother."

"Indeed." Mrs. Barnes turned back to Grace, appearing vastly entertained. "Tell us all about it, Grace."

Gathering the threads of the story in her mind, Grace began her tale. To her immense relief, her father did not react to one detail in anger, and Mrs. Barnes laughed aloud more than once. Especially when Grace mentioned her efforts to put together the charity baskets under Cook's nose. Jacob said little, except when his mother appealed to him at points where he had been present to witness Grace's acting abilities.

When the story drew to a close, so did the visit. Grace and her father bid their guests farewell, walking all the way to the door with them.

"Will we see you at the ball held in Mr. Spratt's honor?" Mrs. Barnes asked, just before stepping into her gig.

Grace had not dared to ask her father if they might go. Though he had been in better humor with her, she had no desire to test the limits of his patience.

"We will attend, yes. Mrs. Everly will have returned by then; we will all go." Her father put his arm around her shoulder, giving her a quick wink. Her heart grew lighter.

Jacob handed his mother into the gig and then came back to the door. "Since you will be there, I must ask if you will honor me with a set."

Her cheeks warmed and she glanced at her father, who raised his eyebrows. She always danced with Jacob. Just as she always danced with Silas and Isaac when they were at home for such events. None of them had ever asked her, had ever bothered thinking they need ask her, before the evening of the event.

"Of course, Jacob," she said at last.

He bowed to them both and then went on his way, climbing up into the seat with his mother and taking up the reins.

"Perhaps," Papa said as they watched the horse and gig go down the lane, "we should have separated you and your sister a trifle earlier."

Grace blushed, but she made no reply. Jacob's gesture in asking was nothing more than giving her reassurance that he was no longer angry with her. That was all it was. A show of friendship. She would content herself with that.

❦

"WHEN YOU TOLD me your interests were redirected to another young lady, it was Grace you meant, wasn't it?" Jacob's mother asked as they left the Everlys' lane for the main road. She sounded quite smug about her discovery.

He saw her smirk from the corner of his eye and quickly focused on the horses. "What would give you cause to think that?" he asked, attempting to sound innocent.

"The way you have been staring at her, for one thing." Mother folded her hands in her lap. "You are trying to puzzle things out, I gather. One moment you appeared as if nothing brought you more delight than to hear her speak, the next you were confused. This is a most interesting development. I cannot wait to see how things play out."

Jacob winced. "Neither can I."

"Oh, come now. It cannot be all that difficult." His mother nudged him with her elbow. "She either likes you or she does not. Given how often she looked to you for approval during her story, I think your chances are better than not."

"I am not even certain that is what I want, Mother. We have been friends for so long."

"What better way to begin a courtship? And though it is premature of me to say it, what better thing to have in a wife than a friend? Your father was my very closest friend, before and after our marriage."

Jacob remembered well the way his parents had often looked at each other. Illness had stolen his father away five years previous, leaving their family shattered for a time. When Jacob thought back on those terrible days, he clearly remembered his friends making every effort to be near him. Silas and Isaac had distracted him, Hope and Grace had comforted him.

With all of them growing older, going down separate paths, Jacob had missed the companionship of those who knew him best. Spending as much time as he had with Grace when she began her masquerade had been a relief.

"What if I am confusing friendship for deeper feelings?" he asked, looking to his mother and hoping that she might have the answers he needed.

"Dear boy." Mother beamed fondly at him. "You must discover how much you care for Grace on your own. Given the behavior we have seen from her of late, I do not think she will keep you wondering about *her* feelings overly long." She chuckled and settled back into her seat, giving her attention to the scenery.

He had made a fool of himself regarding Hope. Thankfully, few people were aware of that. But with Grace, Jacob was prepared to do more. She had proven herself a woman capable of bold action, and she deserved nothing less than a man who acted the same.

If he meant to court Grace, he must do so in earnest, with an open mind and heart. And he must begin at once.

CHAPTER 21

Grace sat in the carriage across from her father and mother, the two of them holding hands and speaking softly to one another. Grace tried not to watch them too closely, keeping her eyes averted to the darkening sky out the window. She sneaked a glance a time or two, admiring her parents' obvious affection. They had missed each other during her mother's absence.

The ball held in honor of Mr. Spratt's departure was taking place in the Aldersy assembly hall. During larger community events, the upstairs rooms were all opened, creating one large area for dancing. The lower rooms would be spread with good food, tables, and chairs, allowing all members of the community to come and wish their retired vicar well while drinking to his good health.

The Everly family arrived at the hall in good cheer. Even Grace could not be nervous about her reception, given her anticipation for the entertainment of the evening.

No sooner did they step through the doors to the upper rooms than her parents were hailed by friends. She followed behind them, her eyes searching the crowds for Jacob. Or Isaac, she hastily reminded herself. Or any of her other friends.

Miss Parr found her first, stepping deftly between Grace and her parents to halt her following them.

"Miss Everly." The young woman smirked and waved. "Oh, it is so good you have come. My mother was convinced you would not."

"Was she?" Grace had no desire to enter into an exchange of insults. A deflection was in order. "How kind of you both to be concerned for my well-being. Mrs. Parr is certainly one of the most thoughtful women I know."

"Yes," Miss Parr said, stretching the one syllable out, her polite expression freezing a moment on her pretty face.

"Oh, and your gown this evening." Grace could admire the dress honestly enough. "That is a perfect shade for you, Miss Parr. The green sets off your eyes to perfection."

A blush rose in the young woman's cheeks and she lowered her eyes to her dress, smoothing the front of it self-consciously. "Thank you."

It was not the first time Grace had used kindness to thwart someone intent on speaking in a sly manner. Her quick tongue had spared Hope from exchanging petty insults in the past. "I do hope you are asked to dance a great deal this evening," Grace added, her tone still cheerful. "I am certain you will be."

The girl's color deepened, and Grace gave her a friendly smile before walking onward. Miss Parr was young yet, barely out in society, and merely acting as she had seen others act. Perhaps making a friend of her would be wise, lest she turn out more like —

"Oh, Miss Everly. Miss *Grace* Everly." Miss Keyes. It shouldn't surprise her that Miss Keyes found her next. Where some young ladies did not learn the dangerous games of flirtation and conquest until they had been out for a time, Merriweather Keyes had started learning the rules and all the ways to break them while still in the school room.

"Miss Keyes." Grace turned to the window where Miss Keyes stood, her fan languidly waving. "Good evening." Miss Ashworth, her brother, and one of the Kimball sons stood with her, all staring at Grace as though their conversation had stopped rather abruptly.

The Keyes had been more intimate with Isaac's family than her own, but in a country neighborhood, everyone knew each other quite well. What Grace knew of Miss Keyes made her ready herself for a different sort of verbal battle.

"I am so pleased you have joined the party," Miss Keyes said, her eyes narrowing. "I had heard rumors that you were being kept prisoner, or doing penance, for your daring actions. Do tell us, what inspired the deed?"

Grace took a step closer, joining the small group as though she meant to stay. "Oh, I could hardly deprive my dear sister of her chance to see the world. She is much more interested in travel than I have ever been."

"I certainly should not have liked a voyage," Miss Ashworth said swiftly, her fan moving rapidly as her eyes darted around the little group. She issued a nervous giggle when Miss Keyes cast her a baleful glance.

"Nevertheless, to deceive us all in such a manner. It must have taken a great deal of determination." Miss Keyes flicked her fan closed.

Grace considered her response. Anything she said would be met with vitriol. Miss Keyes either desired to cause a scene or find more ammunition for whatever gossip she wished to spread. At the moment, with her parents happy and the truth known at last, Grace had no intention of giving Miss Keyes the pleasure of taunting her.

"It took *substantial* determination." Grace looked about at the others, widening her eyes as much as she could. "You were all at my picnic. I thought I must certainly be found out when surrounded by so many friends. How did none of you guess? I must be a superb actress, indeed."

They laughed, and the tension Miss Keyes had created weakened.

"You certainly fooled me," Mr. Kimball said most cheerfully. "Almost makes me jealous I haven't a twin. It is the very sort of trick I should like to play. Had you ever done it before?"

"Switched places? Oh, long ago, when we were children intent on confusing our poor governess." As easily as that, Grace earned their interest. Mr. Kimball and Miss Ashworth pressed her for other stories, and she obliged most cheerfully.

Miss Keyes stuck her nose in the air and left, defeated for the moment. Though she held her ground, Grace's enthusiasm for the evening waned. If Miss Keyes had dared to bring up the issue to Grace, the gossip ran strongly about Grace's actions.

"Ah, Miss Everly." The new voice rasped with age. Mr. Spratt had found her. "Would you do me the honor of a walk about the room?" he asked, before glancing at the others. "If your friends would excuse you, that is."

"Of course, Mr. Spratt."

"It is a party in your honor, sir, your wishes must be granted."

He beamed at the young people, all of whom had grown up listening to his sermons. Grace would not be surprised if he had been the one to christen each of them.

"Thank you." He offered Grace his arm.

Although Mr. Spratt knew everything, indeed he had been ready to announce her public apology had her father required it, nothing in his manner indicated he thought any differently of her than he always had. "Miss Everly, thank you for humoring an old man."

"I enjoy your company, Mr. Spratt," she answered truthfully. "I always have. I must admit that I am sorry to see you go, though I do hope you are happy with your daughter and her family."

"I am certain I will be. There are grandchildren and great grand-children to distract me from any cares I may have." His wrinkles deepened with his delighted expression. "I have done what I love for most of my life, but it is time to give the parish into a younger man's hands. I am grateful to know that it is Mr. Barnes who will take my place. He is a very good man. A particular friend of yours, too, if I am not mistaken?"

"We have known each other for the whole of my life, yes." Grace lowered her eyes to the ground, thinking of Jacob's visit at her home, his request to dance with her. "I have confidence he will make a most excellent vicar."

"As do I. Though inexperienced as he is, he will make mistakes. We all do, from time to time." Mr. Spratt was about Grace's height, stooped as he now was with age. When he looked at her, it was squarely in the eyes. "My dear girl, you have been very good to this parish as well. Do you remember my late wife?"

Everyone remembered Mrs. Spratt. "I have never known anyone to show love more beautifully than she did," Grace said.

Mr. Spratt stopped their walk and turned to face Grace, taking both her hands in his. When he spoke, it was with almost the same reverence he used when speaking of matters holy. "Grace Everly, you remind me of her."

Her throat closed and she had to swallow to answer him, so taken was she by the sincerity of his words. "Thank you, Mr. Spratt. That is the highest compliment I have ever been paid." And it did not matter what anyone else in the room said, or thought, because she held no one in higher esteem than kindly, compassionate Mr. Spratt.

The old vicar bestowed a warm look upon her, and there was a twinkle in his eyes. He turned and nodded to someone just behind Grace. "Mr. Barnes, have you come looking for a partner?"

Grace started but did not move.

"Only if I may have yours, Mr. Spratt." Jacob's familiar voice, courteous as ever.

"You must appeal to the lady, dear boy." Mr. Spratt turned her about with no more than a gentle touch on her arm. "As I am old, and therefore permitted to speak my mind on occasion, I will tell you that if she agrees you will be the most fortunate man in the room."

A hot rush from her chest went directly into her cheeks. Grace lowered her eyes, touched and uncertain. There were others nearby. Had they heard?

"I am well aware of that, Mr. Spratt." The tenderness in Jacob's tone brought her attention back to him, to search his expression, certain she would see only the usual friendly look upon his face. "Would you do me the honor of dancing the next set with me, Miss Everly?" The smile was there, but it was different. There was a question in the tilt of his lips and in the depths of his eyes.

"Yes, Mr. Barnes." Grace took his offered arm, uncertain of her friend for the first time she could remember. In her flustered state, she nearly forgot to take her leave of Mr. Spratt. "Oh, Mr. Spratt—"

He waved his hand at her. "Go on, child. Do not stand on cere-mony with me." He tucked his hands behind his back and nodded deeply to them. "Good evening to you both."

Jacob swept her away, into the line forming for the next set. The dance was called: a lively reel. Nearly all the dances had been brisk and merry, the simplest of forms used so that all may participate regardless of station or grace.

Given that the way Jacob stared at her made Grace's heart beat at an abnormally fast tempo, she was grateful there would be no long, lingering moments to face him.

They were not able to converse easily. The room was loud, and the dance required fast hands and feet as partners exchanged clasps, twirls, and skips. Jacob did not try to speak to her, though from time to time his broad grin would change back to the inscrutable expression.

The next set was called, and Jacob spoke at last. "I have not enjoyed myself this much in ages."

"Neither have I," she admitted. When had she last felt as she did in that moment? Free and happy, content with her place in the world.

Probably not since the first time she caught Jacob staring at Hope, when she realized she had lost something precious. Her step faltered, but Jacob caught her hand anyway, as the dance forms required.

"Are you all right?" he asked, his voice low.

Grace tucked away the memory. "I am well." He cared for Grace as a friend, and nothing more. No matter how she wished she did not imagine the gentleness in his eyes as he gazed at her.

He raised his eyebrows skeptically but led her through the rest of the steps.

When the dance ended, Jacob escorted her back to her parents. She nearly laughed. This was no society event, so the gesture struck her as somewhat unnecessary. Any of their friends would have done. Perhaps his ordination had made him feel the need to maintain an air of reserve.

"Mr. Everly, Mrs. Everly," Jacob said, bowing to them both with

Grace's hand still tucked in his arm. "I wonder if I might ask your permission to call on Miss Everly tomorrow."

Instinctively, Grace tightened her hold on his arm. What was he doing? If someone heard, based on his wording, they would think Jacob meant to court her. That was taking the formalities too far, and she opened her mouth to say so when her father spoke.

"We would be delighted, Mr. Barnes."

Grace stared at her father in surprise. Did he know how this must sound? She spotted Mrs. Parr and Mrs. Kimball standing near enough to hear. But her father was staring at Jacob, with a far too approving look.

What had come over them both?

Jacob removed her hand, bowed slightly over it, and released her. That same mysterious smile on his face as before. He withdrew, looking for another dance partner most likely. Jacob loved dancing, and he made it a point to ask the young ladies most often overlooked. It was yet another thing she admired about him.

A rustle of fabric indicated her mother had stepped near. "I think you have an admirer, Grace."

Absolutely not. Grace shook her head, contradicting her mother immediately. "No. Not Jacob. He is acting strange, but I am only his friend."

Isaac and Mr. King appeared at the corner of her vision, and when she turned, she saw they were coming directly to her.

"I have convinced Mr. King that you are the best dancer in the room," Isaac said, without preamble or greeting. "You must prove me right at once."

This sort of thing Grace understood, and she relaxed. "If Mr. King wants to learn whether or not you exaggerate, he must ask for himself."

"As was my intention," Mr. King said. "But first, will you introduce me to your mother?"

After the proprieties were seen to, Grace allowed Mr. King to take her into the line of couples preparing to dance. Reflexively, she looked down the rows to find Jacob. He immediately met her eyes, as though he had sensed her look, and winked at her.

Winked. At her. In a public room full of people. There went her excusing his conduct due to stringent decorum.

Mr. King proved an apt partner in dance, but Isaac appeared to take the second half of the set. The usual gentlemen took their turns leading her about the room, too. Jacob did not seek her out again, though every time she glanced in his direction it seemed his eyes were upon her.

Tomorrow, she would ask him about his behavior. Tomorrow, she might even summon the courage to tell him something of her own heart.

CHAPTER 22

Mr. Spratt's belongings were loaded into a wagon, and his son-in-law had arrived in a coach to take him away. Jacob bid farewell to his predecessor and had not been surprised, not in the least, when Mr. Spratt took him aside for a moment.

"Grace Everly," the old man said, a glimmer in his eye. "You mean to wed her?"

Jacob could not help the laugh that escaped him. "I must be the most transparent of all men. Yes, Mr. Spratt. I do. If she will have me."

"Good. I worried you might be blind to her still." Mr. Spratt gave him a pat on the arm. "God go with you, Mr. Barnes."

"And with you, sir." Jacob had stayed at the house, walking through the rooms that were now his. It was a simple house, with simple furnishings. There were two levels, a cellar, and the smallest of attics. But it was his. He would bring his clothing to hang and stack in the wardrobe. His books would go on the shelves in his study. Someday, there would be children in the second largest bedroom, which might be easily turned into a nursery.

Looking out the window of the study, it afforded him an excellent view of the path that led from the road to his front door. He could also see the garden, not as well tended as it had been under Mrs. Spratt's care.

Would Grace like seeing to the garden?

The sudden thought made his heart trip and the tips of his ears go warm. He had promised himself to keep an open heart and open mind. Ever since that moment, Grace strayed often into his thoughts. He sensed her making inroads in his heart as well.

When Jacob walked through the small parlor, he noted that Mr. Spratt had left his wife's pianoforte behind. It was a small instrument, perfectly suited to its humble surroundings.

Humble. That was a good word for it, though the house was certainly comfortable. It was not as large as his brother's, or Isaac's, and the Earl of Inglewood's castle-like manor dwarfed the vicarage completely. Would the small house and modest income be enough for Grace?

There was only one way to find out.

Jacob went to the yard where he had tied up his horse, a handsome gelding gifted to him by Matthew. The horse had been raised to take a saddle and pull a gig. He was a handsome chestnut with black mane and tail. Though not a golden hunter, Jacob had immediately felt a kinship to the animal.

After mounting the animal, he made his way to Everly Refuge, all the while thinking on Grace and how best he could put the question of courtship to her. They knew each other so well. He did not have a closer friend than Grace.

Dancing with her the previous evening had reminded him of many other times he stood up with her. But it had been different, too. His eyes had never strayed from her lovely face, her enjoyment the deciding factor in his own. The way she smiled was familiar, and endearing, and beautiful. She had always looked like that. Why hadn't he taken notice of it before?

Birdsong filled the trees along the lane, lifting his spirits and his hopes. Clouds rolled in above him, promising a summer rain. The drizzle started when he came to the Everlys' property, light enough he felt no need to race up to their door.

As he drew closer to the house, he looked up at the windows. There, framed perfectly, stood Grace. Watching for him.

Jacob hurried the horse along. There was no sense in them getting too damp, after all. He went directly to the stables, allowing one of the grooms to see to the animal. He hurried to the house, going for a back door.

This call was different. Though he had visited the Refuge more times than he could count, this occasion must stand out from that day forth. The anticipation building inside him churned his thoughts, muddling the careful words he had planned until they were nearly forgotten.

One thing he knew for certain, based upon his reactions to even the thought of Grace: Jacob must apologize for ever thinking himself in love with anyone else.

❧

WHEN JACOB LOOKED up through the rain, seeing Grace in the window, she momentarily forgot how to breathe. Something was different, had been different the last two times she had seen him. Her mind recalled the moment in the orchard, when he had come so near she thought he might do something extraordinary.

She told herself that his mind was full of Hope, and Grace was a convenient substitute for her twin. Believing that had worked. It kept her safe.

Her lips parted, staring down at him, as though she might say something he would somehow hear. Then he looked away and nudged his horse into a canter, riding out of sight around the house.

"Mama?" Grace turned, brushing aside the curtains that half-concealed her from the room. "Jacob is here."

"Is he?" Mrs. Everly barely glanced up from her sewing, but she wore a neutral expression. "I always enjoy his visits."

At any moment, the door would open and Jacob would come in. He would sit down and chat about nothing in particular with her mother while Grace's insides twisted and spun. In front of her mother, she could say almost nothing to Jacob. Nothing that would calm her troubled mind.

"This visit is different," Grace said, voice almost a whisper.

Needle and thread paused in mid-air, Mama's whole body went still. Lowering her hand to her lap, she looked up at Grace with eyes full of understanding and sympathy. "I know. You must be calm, Grace."

A frightened laugh escaped from Grace. She hurried to cover her mouth.

"Oh. Grace." Her mother put her sewing down and came to Grace's side. "Dear girl, it is all right." She put her hands on Grace's cheeks, steadying her daughter. "This is Jacob. He is your dearest friend. Would it be a comfort to you if I told you how much I hoped for this to happen?"

Grace shook her head. "No. How could you want this? He is a vicar, and will be poor, and mothers want their daughters to marry lords and rich gentlemen." She bit her tongue, wondering where the nonsense came from.

"Mothers want their daughters to be happy." Mama stood on her toes to kiss Grace's forehead. They were both short in stature, so Grace bent enough to allow the token of her mother's love. "And Jacob has always made you happy."

They heard the steady rap of riding boots in the passage. Mrs. Everly gave Grace one last encouraging look before gathering up her sewing. Grace stayed near the window, watching the doorway. She would see it all when he entered. She would see that she was wrong. Nothing had changed. Jacob would bow in his usual way, take his customary seat, and speak of the inconsequential.

The door opened, Garrett bowing as he entered. "Mr. Jacob Barnes." Then Garrett's glance darted to hers, but she had no time to puzzle over the servant's knowing expression before Jacob strode into the room.

Jacob had never looked so happy as he did at that moment. An energy came into the room with him, setting her senses to buzzing.

"Good morning, Mrs. Everly." He bowed to her mother. "Good morning, Grace."

Had her name sounded different on his lips?

"Good morning, Jacob. Come in, sit down." Mama acted as though everything was completely ordinary, and the moment Jacob sat she asked after his family.

"I am reading the banns for Matthew and Mrs. Muir this Sunday," Jacob informed them, his eyes glittering with excitement. "You will all be there?" He looked at Grace, expectant.

"Yes, of course," she said, somehow maintaining an even tone of voice. "We would not miss it. It is your first sermon."

He stared at her, his expression falling somewhat. Had she said something wrong? How could she have? She answered a simple question.

"You two ought to go for a walk."

Grace blinked at the strange pronouncement, turning to stare at her mother. "In the rain?"

"Yes." Mama folded her hands in her lap, appearing most serene. "We have umbrellas, after all, and the fresh air is good for young people. Jacob, I charge you with making certain my daughter does not catch cold." Mama arched one eyebrow at Jacob in a manner Grace hoped she would one day learn.

Though a grown man, and now the vicar, Jacob hastened to obey the command. "Yes, Mrs. Everly." A grin stretched across his handsome face and he hurried to open the door.

Though she did not dare look at her mother again, guessing that Mama likely wore a most satisfied smirk, Grace hurried out the door and past Jacob. "I will get my spencer, and my bonnet."

"Grace," he called after her in the dim light of the passageway.

"I will meet you downstairs," she said over her shoulder. Grace was not going to have any sort of conversation with him in the house. It might be raining, but the relative privacy of standing outside was better than being in a corridor where anyone might come upon them.

She ran into her room and rushed to her wardrobe, hurrying to find a suitable spencer. Her hand landed upon a deep green shawl first, and she decided that would do well enough. Then she found a bonnet and fairly crushed it upon her head. Her hair had not been done in such a manner as to make a bonnet stay on easily. She found gloves in her bureau drawer and darted out with them still in her hand. Then she recalled her slippers and turned back to find her half-boots.

Why did one have to completely change one's costume just to take a turn in a garden? She grumbled to herself as she tugged the boots on and tied up the laces.

Finally, Grace made her way down the stairs to find Jacob. He was standing in the entry, with Garrett, hat on his head and gloves on his hands.

"I am sorry, Mr. Barnes," Garrett was saying. "But I could only find the one. The others must be lurking in the wrong closet somewhere."

When she took the last step, Jacob turned and she saw he held one umbrella. It was a large, black umbrella. The same one her mother would have two or three children use when they had need to walk in the rain from the carriage to the church.

Grace looked at Garrett, who appeared perfectly at ease with his lie. Interesting. She had seen the umbrellas in the downstairs closet near the door, where they always were, just the day before. Garrett pulled his shoulders further back and left, without even a backward glance.

Jacob cleared his throat, then went and opened the door. Garrett had forgotten that duty, it would seem.

With her head held high, Grace walked out in front of him. The rain was gentle; they hardly even required an umbrella. Jacob caught up to her and held it overhead with his left hand while he offered her his right arm.

Grace accepted his escort, her free hand balling into a fist at her side. The air smelled of rain, wet grass, and damp earth. She took in a deep breath, trying to anchor herself. On days like today, though they were three miles inland, she even fancied she could taste the salt in the air.

Several moments passed, the silence disturbed only by the smattering of raindrops thumping onto the umbrella.

They walked on the path around the house, in the direction of the orchards. Grace could hear the blood coursing through her ears, steadily beating in time with her heart. Her mouth had gone dry.

Had she not promised herself to be honest? And brave?

"Jacob," she said, keeping her eyes ahead of them. There was the hedge. They would turn around that and be nearly out of sight of the house until they were halfway to the orchard.

"Yes, Grace?" He sounded curious, not uncertain.

She stopped walking, pulling him to a halt as well. "I need to tell you something." She studied the buttons on his coat a moment, noting how evenly they were spaced, before she could look up into his eyes. They were so gentle, coaxing her to speak without him saying a word.

"You are my dearest friend." There was a flicker to his expression, but she pushed onward. "If I said something, or did something, to damage our friendship, I should regret it all my days. But there is something else I would regret if I left it unsaid. And I know this isn't proper—" She stopped, biting her lip as she tried to find the right words. She had thought of them days ago, repeated them over and over since realizing she must say something. Where had the words gone?

Jacob cocked his head to one side, his eyebrows lifted and his lips pressing together. She recognized the expression as the one he wore when he grew impatient but was too polite to interrupt. He would wait all day for her when he wore that look. Even if a thunderstorm burst overhead.

"It is not proper," she repeated firmly. "But I cannot continue our friendship unless I tell you how I really feel. About you."

His eyes darkened, and he took in a deep breath. "It just so happens that I came here to ask that very thing."

"Did you?" She had not dared even hope for his curiosity on the matter. "Then perhaps it is not improper." She glanced down, ready to gather her courage.

"Grace." Jacob released her arm. The soft leather of his glove touched her chin, guiding her to look up at him. "We have been friends all our lives."

She nodded as though unable to speak a word. The breeze picked up, ruffling her dress and throwing more rain down from the sky. They both ignored it.

"It is frightening to think of us as anything else," he added, his hand lingering at her jaw while he spoke.

"Terrifying," she amended, and his lips twitched upward briefly. "But I—"

A gust of wind hurtled around the hedge, blowing fiercely about them and taking Grace's bonnet with it. She gasped and turned to watch it fall, yards away. What had she expected? She had not taken the time to tie the ribbons properly.

"The umbrella," Jacob said, giving her the handle. When she took it, he bounded toward the bonnet—but the wind came back and sent the headpiece tumbling down the hill toward the orchard.

"Oh, bother the wind," she muttered, following after Jacob while he chased the horrid bonnet. "Jacob," she shouted after him.

He slipped on a patch of wet grass, nearly falling. Grace hurried after him, and he went for the bonnet again.

She hurried along, and he finally caught her hat. Jacob held it up triumphantly as Grace approached. Perhaps the weather itself was against her, interrupting as it had.

The bonnet was in no fit state to go back upon her head, and she did not care. When Jacob handed it to her, she clutched it by the ribbons with one hand and held the umbrella over him with the other.

Before anything else could happen, she made her confession. "I love you," she practically shouted, loud enough to be heard over the rumbling weather. The wind blew by them again at that moment, taking her words with it. Jacob grabbed her hand and pulled her the rest of the way to the orchard, nearly at a run.

When they stood beneath the trees, the wind stopped snatching at them. Jacob placed his hands on her arms and he bent closer to her. "Grace, did you say you love me?" His body was tense, he wore a serious frown.

There was no point in denying it, even if it displeased him. "Yes," she choked out. "I love you. I am sorry if that ruins things, but—"

Jacob leaned down, closing the distance between them, resting his forehead against hers. He closed his eyes, and Grace stood perfectly still.

He whispered her name as though it was a plea, a prayer, a wish. "My Grace. You are jumping ahead of me."

Though she did not expect him to return her affection right away, it still pained her to know he could not say those three words in return. But his endearment made it hurt less than she thought it would. She took in a shuddering breath, tears gathering in her eyes without her permission. They stood so close, and all the world around them had faded away to nothing. If only he loved her back. It would have been the perfect moment.

"I came today," he whispered, "to ask if I might court you."

Stepping back, Grace opened her eyes and stared at him. "Court me?"

His expression turned sheepish. "After what happened at the picnic, when you pushed me away, and then when we argued after Hope's letter came, I did not know if you could care for me. Or if you should."

Grace dropped her bonnet and lowered the umbrella, closing it as she did. She leaned the cumbersome thing against the trunk of the tree. "I pushed you away because I thought you wanted me to be Hope," she admitted.

Jacob shook his head. "I give you my word, I was only thinking of you. Admiring your determination, your beautiful eyes, and your mouth."

A warm, gentle swell began to gather in her chest. "My mouth? Not my sister's? I have been told we look a great deal alike, you see." She tried to laugh, but all that came out was a breathy squeak.

"Not to me," he said firmly. "I have always known which sister is which. And I have never been tempted to steal a kiss from Hope. From you, though? That is another matter." He closed the small distance she had put between them and tucked a loose curl back behind her ear. "May I kiss you, Grace?"

She did not need to consider her answer. "Yes."

The same hand that brushed aside the curl cradled the back of her head. She felt the warmth of his breath upon her cheek, and then his lips touched hers—gently, cautiously.

Lack of experience did not impede her in the slightest; Grace instinctively knew how to return Jacob's kiss. Her hands took hold of his forearms to steady herself, and she repaid his kiss as ardently as she could.

His arms wrapped around her, pulling her closer, and his lips parted from hers only to immediately fall upon them again. Grace smiled against the new barrage, her heart overflowing with joy.

Jacob gently pulled away, holding her still, he laid his cheek upon her head. Grace's head rested against the wool of his coat. His breaths were deep and slow, and soon hers matched his.

"I think I had better tell you everything, too," he said at last, the words sending a thrill through her. He stepped back, his expression earnest. "Grace, I love you."

"Yes," she said firmly.

He blinked. "Yes?"

"I will allow you to court me," she said, blushing deeply. "But not for long."

His eyebrows shot up. "Oh, no? Why not?"

"Because I have already made up my mind about you, and if you cannot decide what you want quickly—"

Jacob laughed and bent to kiss her again, silencing her well-meant threats. "My Grace. There is no need for a long courtship. After all, you are my dearest friend. I have discovered everything there is to know about you, now that I know how you feel. Forgive me for being blind to it before."

"Your attention was focused in a vastly different direction," she said without any hint of the sorrow it had caused her. That was in the past. She knew Jacob as well as he knew her. "And you must be certain, Jacob."

"I am. I love *you*, Grace. Determined, stubborn, compassionate, brave Grace."

His words settled in her heart, filling her whole soul. Their courtship would be proper, and public. Jacob was the new vicar, after all.

"I love you, too." Grace leaned into his shoulder; his arm tightened around her. Together they stood still for a time, listening to the rain against the orchard's leaves.

EPILOGUE

J acob took Grace about with him in his gig as often as he could, riding together through Aldersy, visiting his parishioners.

At first eyebrows raised, but Grace won back the good opinion of their neighbors easily. Jacob was not entirely sure how, until he listened to her chatting with several ladies after services one Sunday. Grace shared kindness with them, compassion, and a true interest in what each woman had to say. He had never thought of it before, but she personified her name quite beautifully. No one stayed upset long, especially given how enamored their new vicar was with her.

Isaac had practically crowed when they told him of their plans to wed. "I knew it. As soon as I saw you both together, when I came home, I knew it would work out this way."

His friend, Mr. King, was not all that enthusiastic in his good wishes. Jacob did not entirely blame him, either.

Mr. Spratt came out of retirement two months later, everything done properly, to join Jacob Barnes and Grace Everly in holy matrimony.

At their wedding, they were surrounded by friends and their

families. The only person missing on that day of days was Hope. Jacob had asked if Grace wished to wait the year until Hope returned.

"I have certainly waited long enough," Grace had said, a stubborn tilt to her chin. "And Hope, who is the most impatient person I know, will not object. We will make it up to her. She can be the godmother to our first child."

The night after their wedding, when they sat curled together on a couch before the fire, Grace snuggled against his side, Jacob considered himself the most fortunate of men.

"Are you happy, Jacob?" she asked, arm draped around his middle.

He pressed a kiss to her dark curls. "Happier than I have ever been in my life, with my dearest friend and beloved to share in it with me."

Grace raised her head, her beautiful face before him and her lips temptingly near. "What will we tell our children about all that happened? I imagine if we do not speak of it, others will." She bit her lip, regarding him with far too much seriousness.

Jacob kissed her temple. "We tell them the truth." Then he kissed the tip of her nose. "That their Aunt Hope caused a great deal of trouble." He kissed one cheek, then the other. "And that their clever mother found a way to save herself and her sister from pain, and in the process —" Jacob's lips hovered over his wife's, almost brushing them as he spoke. "In the process, the beautiful and compassionate woman helped their foolish father realize how much he loved her and needed her as his bride."

Grace closed the small distance between them, kissing him deeply as her lips curved upward, her heart content at last.

IF YOU ENJOYED THIS STORY, make certain you check out the next in the series, *Saving Miss Everly*. In that novel, readers will find out what happens to Hope Everly on her adventure to the Caribbean.

ALSO BY SALLY BRITTON

The Inglewood Series:

Book #1, *Rescuing Lord Inglewood*

Book #2, *Discovering Grace*

Book #3, *Saving Miss Everly*

The Branches of Love Series:

Prequel Novella, *Martha's Patience*

Book #1, *The Social Tutor*

Book #2, *The Gentleman Physician*

Book #3, *His Bluestocking Bride*

Book #4, *The Earl and His Lady*

Book #5, *Miss Devon's Choice*

Book #6, *Courting the Vicar's Daughter*

Forever After:

The Captain and Miss Winter

Timeless Romance:

An Evening at Almack's, Regency Collection 12

Entangled Inheritances:

His Unexpected Heiress

ACKNOWLEDGMENTS

Thank you, dearest readers, for choosing this book. I have wanted to tell Grace's story for quite some time. It's a relief to finally present it to you, though my words are often imperfect. You drive me to tell the stories that have long lived in my mind and heart.

Thank you to all my author friends, for the encouragement and late-night chats. Especially Joanna Barker, Arlem Hawks, Esther Hatch, Shaela Kay, Heidi Kimball, Mindy Strunk, and Megan Walker. We authors burn the midnight oil, and it would be a lonely watch if we did not have each other.

My editor, Jenny Proctor, really helped with this one. I had poor Jacob and Grace all befuddled midway through the book. Jenny showed me how to set things right. My proofreaders, who are also my sisters, Carri Flores and Molly Rice, you are both appreciated and loved. Thank you!

To Lucy, Tarver, Jane, and Teague, thank you for all your help with Mommy's book! Someday, I hope you read these words and know how much I treasure you. Being an author is wonderful, but being your mother is my absolute favorite.

ABOUT THE AUTHOR

Sally Britton lives in the desert with her husband, four children, and two rescue dogs. She started writing her first story on her mother's electric typewriter, when she was fourteen years old. Reading her way through Jane Austen, Louisa May Alcott, and Lucy Maud Montgomery, Sally decided to write about the elegant, complex world of centuries past.

Sally graduated from Brigham Young University in 2007 with a bachelor's in English, her emphasis on British literature. She met and married her husband not long after and they've been building their happily ever after since that day.

Vincent Van Gogh is attributed with the quote, "What is done in love is done well." Sally has taken that as her motto, for herself and her characters, writing stories where love is a choice.

All of Sally's published works are available on Amazon.com and you can connect with Sally on her website, AuthorSallyBritton.com.

facebook.com/SallyBWT

instagram.com/authorsallybritton

pinterest.com/sallybt

amazon.com/author/sallybritton

bookbub.com/profile/sally-britton

Made in the USA
Monee, IL
19 October 2020

45607243R00132